Murdering
Americans

To the memory of
Dr. Buss

Christmas 2007

AH

Also by Ruth Dudley Edwards

FICTION

Carnage on the Committee
The Anglo-Irish Murders
Publish and Be Murdered
Murder in a Cathedral
Ten Lords A-leaping
Matricide at St. Martha's
Clubbed to Death
The English School of Murder
The St. Valentine's Day Murders
Corridors of Death

NON-FICTION

Newspapermen: Hugh Cudlipp, Cecil Harmsworth
King and the Glory Days of Fleet Street
The Faithful Tribe: An Intimate Portrait of the Loyal Institutions
True Brits: Inside the Foreign Office
The Best of Bagehot
The Pursuit of Reason: The Economist 1843–1993
Victor Gollancz: A Biography
Harold MacMillan: A Life in Pictures
James Connolly
Patrick Pearse: The Triumph of Failure
An Atlas of Irish History

Murdering Americans

Ruth Dudley Edwards

Poisoned Pen Press

Poisoned Pen Press
6962 E. First Ave., Ste. 103
Scottsdale, AZ 85251
www.poisonedpenpress.com
info@poisonedpenpress.com

Printed in the United States of America

*To Máirín, who has been so horrified by what
she has learned from this book that she hates it
even more than she hates America;
to John for all the usual reasons;
and to all brave dissident students
on totalitarian campuses everywhere*

Acknowledgments

This has all been great fun, even if the central issue is terrifying. Thanks to the many people who have given me inspiration and support and answered questions, particularly Stephen and Deborah Cang, Amanda Carpenter, Nina Clarke, Beverley Cohen, Colin and Betsy Crabtree, Miles Donnelly, my brother Owen, Paul le Druillenec, Dick and Kathryn Kennison, Neasa MacErlean, James McGuire, Janet McIver, Ken Minogue, Séan O'Callaghan, Úna O'Donoghue, Henry Reid, Richard Reynolds, Robert Salisbury and Alec Swanson. Carol Scott, as ever, has coped in great good humour with the sheer mess I generate, Barbara Peters's suggestions were constructive editing at its best, and with her husband, my publisher, Rob Rosenwald, she has been a constant source of encouragement. So too has Jane Conway-Gordon, my agent, with whom I had a great time in Las Vegas.

I've been visiting America for work and pleasure since 1964, have had fascinating experiences from coast to coast, am fortunate to have good American friends and have always been deeply interested in its culture, its politics and its people. Over the past few years, with this book in mind, I've had a most enjoyable and instructive time reading innumerable critics and provocateurs in the American right-wing press, and am particularly grateful to Mike S. Adams, Tony Blankley, John Derbyshire, Victor Davis Hanson, David Horowitz, Roger Kimball, Bill Lind, John

O'Sullivan, Thomas Sowell, Mark Steyn and Walter Williams. I have also learned much from *South Park*.

Although several times a week—as I read of new lunacies from campuses throughout America—I have moaned 'Pity the poor satirist,' I should emphasise that Freeman State University and the town of New Paddington are products of my own fevered imagination.

We must indeed all hang together, or,
most assuredly, we shall all hang separately.
—Benjamin Franklin,
at the signing of the Declaration of Independence,
4 July 1776

It will never be known what acts of cowardice have been
motivated by the fear of looking insufficiently progressive.
—Charles Péguy, 1905

There is a thought that stops thought.
That is the only thought that ought to be stopped.
—G.K. Chesterton, 1908

Democratic civilization is the first in history to blame itself
because another power is trying to destroy it.
—Jean-François Revel, 1984

Prologue

'What in hell's going on here, Helen?' shouted Martin Freeman down the phone to the Provost. 'If any of the shit I've just read in the *New Paddington Sentinel* is true, the whole damn university should be closed down. And where's the blasted President when I need him?'

Having never known the Chairman of the Board of Trustees even to raise his voice, let alone swear, Helen Fortier-Pritchardson, Provost of Freeman State University, was unable to emit more than a series of little panic-stricken cries.

'Say something, will you, Goddammit? What is going on?'

As her shaking hand knocked over her cup and coffee spread over her toast, the Provost recollected that one of her unique selling propositions was that she was supposed to be calm in a crisis. 'I'm sorry, Martin. I don't know what you're talking about.'

Freeman took a couple of deep breaths. 'In that case, Madam Provost, you'd better find out fast. Get hold of the *Sentinel*, read its exposé, and call me. Oh, and set the wheels in motion for an emergency board meeting.' This normally considerate, polite man slammed down the phone without even saying goodbye.

The Provost, who had taken one look at the *Sentinel* when she first took up her job and had dismissed it as a pathetic little small-town rag, abandoned her coffee, ran from her house to her car, and drove wildly towards the nearest supermarket. When stopped for speeding, she burst into tears.

'They've got a group of students who've given them stuff anonymously,' she told President Dickinson, when she finally tracked him down in New York. 'They call themselves the VRC.'

'What's that?'

'No idea.'

'How bad is it?'

'Terrible. The headline is: VIOLENCE, SEX AND DUMBING DOWN: FREEMAN GOES TO POT. There's a lot on alcohol and drug abuse and sex orgies and violent hazing at the frat houses.'

'So fucking what!'

'And stuff on what the jocks do to cheerleaders that'll drive parents crazy.'

'Fuck 'em,' said Dickinson. 'There's nothing new here. Happens everywhere. We just deny everything and repeat our zero-tolerance of any kind of initiation involving bodily, mental, or emotional harm.'

'You don't understand, Henry. The students are alleging we're complete hypocrites who issue high-sounding statements of policy but ignore depravity because we think about nothing but money.'

'Shit,' said the President. 'That's more difficult.'

'And they're saying that mission statement about intellectual excellence is fraudulent, that we overlook plagiarism and collaborate with lazy, stupid students if they're rich or jocks…'

'Evidence?' asked Dickinson sharply.

'There's a story based on tapes of classes last semester in the sociology and education departments.'

There was a pause. 'That's serious,' said Dickinson.

'And they've got stuff on the row over transgendered bathrooms that makes us look ridiculous. And plenty about most of the faculty being intolerant left-wingers, and accusations of censorship of ideas and language in contravention of the First Amendment, and allegations about us persecuting dissidents.'

'We're no worse than most other campuses.'

The Provost said nothing.

'Well, not much worse. Depending on what they've got.'

'There's some stuff about how Brendan Martial and Lindy Dubois got tossed out.'

'Any details?' asked the President. He sounded edgy.

'No. But they say that intimidation is rampant and they were made an example of to terrify critics into silence.'

'Those pains in the butt had it coming. And they haven't sued.' He snorted. 'Is that it?'

'The editorial also reminds readers of the mysterious circumstances surrounding Provost Haringey's death.'

The President's voice was hard. 'It was judged accidental, Helen, and there'll never be any evidence to the contrary. We'll ride this shit out. I wonder what's got into the *Sentinel*.'

'Can't imagine. Maybe there's a new editor that has it in for us. I'll make enquiries. The editorial says this is only the first instalment. The VRC say their mission is to get rid of us. That's you and me and Ethan for starters.'

'We'll see about that,' said Dickinson grimly. 'Listen, Helen, we've got to buy time and find out who these little sneaks are. Get Gonzales on to it and tell him as well that I said he was to stop shit happening off-campus and that he's to be ruthless.'

'Ruthless? Ethan?' The Provost uttered a mirthless laugh. 'What do you want him to do this time? Thumbscrews?'

'Quit the crap, Helen. Tell Martin anything that'll calm him down for now, draft a statement reaffirming all our commitments to whatever is necessary and regretting that embittered and failing students should show such ingratitude to a great Indiana school that has made diversity and excellence a byword. Throw in all the bullshit. E-mail it to me for approval as soon as you're done. We'll talk then about how we search for and destroy the VRC crowd, if they exist at all. Could just be one little jerk with an agenda.'

'I don't know if I can hold Martin back.'

'You have to. There's a lot riding on this, Helen, as you very well know.'

4 Ruth Dudley Edwards

'But the timing is awful. The Distinguished Visiting Professors are on their way. What are they going to think?'

'Stop them seeing the *Sentinel* for one thing. Then start the process of getting them on our side. Hold your nerve, Helen. I have to go. I think this guy's ready to sign the cheque. Talk to you later.' He rang off.

The Provost took a deep breath, and dialled Martin Freeman's number.

Chapter One

'It was bad enough when my parents hijacked our wedding,' wailed Rachel, as Amiss closed the front door and came into the living-room. 'Now Jack wants to hijack our honeymoon.'

Amiss took off his coat and threw it towards an armchair, engulfing the cat he had overlooked. An enraged Plutarch sprang up with a yowl, and coat and cat fell to the floor in a heaving mass. It took a couple of fraught minutes for Amiss to disentangle them, staunch the blood from his new scratch, and embrace his distressed fiancée. 'I don't know what you're talking about, darling, but Jack can't hijack our honeymoon. It's ours. She's got a college to run and a nuisance to make of herself in the House of Lords, and besides, she wouldn't fit in our camper van.'

'For God's sake stop being facetious, Robert. This is serious.'

'Sorry, darling. But I'm right. Whatever this is about, it's nonsense. No one's going to hijack anything.'

Rachel began to pace distractedly. 'But that's exactly what we said about parents and weddings. Don't you remember how firm I was when Mum first mooted synagogue rather than registry office? "You must be crazy," I said. "Robert's a goy," I said. "What's more we're both atheists," I said, "so it would be absurd to have any kind of religious ceremony, let alone a Jewish one." I said all that and look where that got us. Landed with a big fat Jewish wedding, that's where.'

Through Amiss's mind went a whirlwind of random memories of angst-ridden debates about whose wedding it was anyway, screaming matches between Rachel and her mother, the moment when after a man-to-man conversation with Rachel's father—a proponent of the quiet life at all costs—he had (foolishly and cravenly, he realised too late) persuaded Rachel that it would be easier and kinder to give in, the compromise on having the ceremony at the parental home rather than the synagogue, the anguish of the daily reports of the frantic hunt for a rabbi who would accept intermarriage, the consequential arguments about how candid the happy couple should be with him about whether their children would be brought up Jewish, the painful conversations with Amiss's bewildered Yorkshire parents who could not grasp why their only child—whom they had tried (even less successfully than they realised) to set on a course of prudence, uncompromising truthfulness, and low-church Christianity—was involved in what to them seemed like an exercise in staggering hypocrisy, and the horrors of recent weeks, as Rachel's mother achieved complete dominance, the wedding plans became ever more elaborate and extravagant and Rachel ever more upset. At times, the rational, humorous woman he loved seemed to have metamorphosed into a touchy hysteric liable to throw a fit at the slightest provocation.

Still standing uncertainly in the middle of the room sucking his wound, Amiss shuddered at the memory of the rage and the tears that had followed Mrs. Simon's proud announcement that the embroidered velvet canopy she had selected for the ceremony would be the finest seen in north London in a month of Sabbaths. To Rachel's anguished protests that she was not a Jewish princess, that she had never been a Jewish princess, and that she was too old to become one now, her mother had reacted with alternating indifference, scorn, and noisy weeping about the pain of a daughter's ingratitude. Amiss thought, as he had thought a thousand times in recent weeks, of how weddings seemingly brought out not just the worst but the stereotype in everyone.

With a familiar pang of nostalgia for the carefree days before their impulsive decision to marry—a time when he had seen Hannah Simon as a warm-hearted, clever, and entertaining addition to his life rather than the nightmare Jewish mother to end all nightmare Jewish mothers who was driving her adored child crazy in the name of mother-love—he wrenched his mind back to the new crisis.

Plutarch had reoccupied the armchair, from which she glared at him balefully, so Amiss sat down on the sofa. 'OK, Rachel. Back to basics. What's this about Jack and the honeymoon?'

'Mary Lou says Jack wants us to spend several weeks with her in Indiana.'

'Indiana? Indiana in the U.S. of A.? What in hell has Indiana got to do with anything?'

Rachel stopped pacing, collapsed beside him and burst into tears. 'I'm sorry, Robert,' she sobbed, 'I know I'm being hopeless, but I had a conversation with Mum today about canapés that you wouldn't believe…'

'Oh, I would, I would,' said Amiss with feeling, as he put his arms around her. 'I'd believe it if you told me she was searching for a new rabbi because Miller's refused to have his nose hairs clipped.'

'And what Mary Lou told me just finished me off.'

'And that was?'

'What I said. That Jack's going to Indiana for three months and wants us to do a detour and visit her there for several weeks.'

'A detour from central Europe to Indiana,' said Amiss. 'That makes perfect sense. Any idea why she's going to Indiana?'

'Mary Lou said she was going to spend a semester there as a visiting professor of something or other and she thought she'd like company.'

'I don't understand any of this,' said Amiss. 'Why would she…?'

'It's no good asking me questions, Robert,' said Rachel, sitting up and mopping her eyes. 'What Mary Lou was saying was pretty garbled.'

The intellectual fog that was engulfing Amiss grew thicker. Garbled prose was not what he associated with his friend Mary Lou Denslow. 'What was wrong with Mary Lou? Why was she garbling?'

'Because she and Ellis are having a hell of a time with their wedding, of course. It's not just all that upheaval in Ellis's ancestral home…'

'His father training the peasants to tug their forelocks and shout "God bless the second son" and all that kind of thing, you mean?'

'Spare heir, surely?' offered Rachel, with a watery smile. 'Anyway, you know she's had all that family drama because they were pissed off that she's getting married in England instead of America and even though they've forgiven her none of her family's ever flown that far and they're apprehensive. And surely you remember her parents were upset anyway that she'd given up a safe and respectable academic job for the sinful world of television? And they're none too pleased she's marrying a white. And, what's more, being Baptists, they think the Church of England's too high-church and her mother is in a state about what they all should wear and where the aunties and cousins will stay, and now…'

'Enough already,' said Amiss. 'Thank God there isn't long to go or we'd all be sectioned before we ever reached our respective canopy and altar. I can't believe it's only three months since we told Ellis and Mary Lou we'd decided we too would get married and we indulged in that orgy of mutual congratulation about how we'd keep everything simple…'

'Have a joint wedding in a registry office…'

'No fuss…'

'Just immediate family and a few friends…'

'And a decent pleasantly boozy lunch in a jolly Italian restaurant before we went off on our happy and separate honeymoons.'

They sighed heavily as they contemplated what might have been. 'Anyway,' said Rachel, 'the Jack business just seemed too much on top of everything else, but I was so overwrought as a result of Mum's insistence that I help micro-manage the caterers that I didn't take much in. Give Mary Lou a ring and she will—if she's calmed down—be able to tell you the worst.'

Amiss patted her on the head and went over to the phone. 'You're having a tough time too, I gather,' he said when Mary Lou answered.

'You bet your ass I am,' said his uncharacteristically edgy-sounding friend. 'Yes, I know Ellis's dad means well—just like Rachel's mom does. And I see why he wants to show the local gentry that though his son has ended up a cop and I'm black, he's proud of us.'

'Just as my mother-in-law-to-be is trying to show she's not ashamed that Rachel has been involved in a scandal, has abandoned a glittering career, is currently unemployed and is marrying a wastrel with a chequered background and no fixed income.'

'You're rather industrious for a wastrel, Robert. But anyway, yes, Ellis's family have gone as over the top as Rachel's and it gets worse every day as my family get more and more jittery. Ellis has been working almost round-the-clock on a gangland shooting, I'm presenting a TV arts special tomorrow night that still needs a lot of homework, and there are floods of e-mails from Minnesota asking things like will there be hairdryers where they're staying and should they call Ellis's dad Your Lordship or Sir even though I've told them all to call him Reggie.'

'Not very egalitarian for Americans, are they?'

'You know better than that, Robert. Yanks are thundering snobs. Why else would we look up to rich dynasties like the Bushes and the Kennedys and the Rockefellers? It's because we love titles that Jack's being offered such a ridiculous deal to sit on her fanny for a few months at the University of Hicksville, Indiana.'

'Ah yes. Jack. What in hell is all this about?'

'Lust for one thing. I was at St. Martha's yesterday showing my face in case they forget I'm still a Fellow and helping the new Bursar make sense of things and when I was having a pre-prandial drink in Jack's room she took a call that made her go all croony. You know the scene.'

'She was either being told an enemy had bitten the dust or was being flattered shamelessly.'

'You got it. This time it was the latter, the ass-kisser being Helen Fortier-Pritchardson, Provost of Freeman University, New Paddington, Indiana, whom, it turned out, Jack had met a couple of days previously at some Cambridge shindig. Helen yakked and yakked seductively, told Jack how much she admired her achievements as a radical reformer and a feminist role model....'

'What! She called Jack a reformer and a feminist and lived?'

'Robert, Jack thinks Helen is hot. That's not the way she put it, of course. I think she said pulchritudinous. But the point is she fancied her chances with Helen enough to look favourably at her invitation, which seems to involve plenty of attention, very little work, and shitloads of money. So by the end of the call, she'd agreed in principle, subject to her being able to ensure St. Martha's doesn't fall apart in her absence. She's already been promised dedicated conference-call facilities, an unlimited supply of first-class plane tickets to fly her out for crucial meetings and fly others in, and excellent accommodation for her and any guests she wants at the main hotel where she'll be pitching camp. Oh, and she's making a big issue about taking Horace: Provost Pritchardson has been put in charge of investigating the rules about importing parrots.'

'But the mid-West, Mary Lou! What's she going to do at a provincial university in the mid-West? What's in Indiana, for heaven's sake?'

'Nothing, really. It's what you drive through on the way to or from New York and Chicago. But Jack's off in fantasy land, Robert. She's never been anywhere in the States except New York and she's gone tripping down memory lane to the cowboy movies of her youth and happy days when men were men and John Wayne was in his prime. She's probably hoping she'll meet someone just like him at Freeman. Helen told her Cole Porter had been born just up the road so she came off the phone in a romantic haze singing 'Night and Day' badly and noisily.'

Amiss winced in recognition.

'Of course I've told her the town will be deadly dull, the faculty full of knee-jerk lefties, the students mostly retards, independent thought and speech will be stiffed by political correctness and, even more seriously for her, the food will be hideous.'

'That should have given her pause.'

'Nope. She brushed it aside along with everything else, told me my trouble was I had rotted my brain reading innumerable crap novels for my course on modern American fiction, that I had forgotten how wonderful my country was and that I must stop exaggerating—and then began speculating lubriciously on what the cheerleaders might look like. I made the mistake of describing today's cheerleaders as sluts, and she said she liked sluts. And when I begged her at least to read Tom Wolfe's *I Am Charlotte Simmons* just to get the flavour of a modern American campus, she reminded me that she didn't voluntarily read books less than forty years old and that she was certainly in no mood to volunteer to do so now.'

'What's got into her? You've described Jack's idea of hell and she knows perfectly well that you tend to under- rather than over-state.'

'I guess now I've left St. Martha's and the four of us are embarking on something new, she's in need of an adventure herself. She hasn't had one since China. And this fell from the skies.'

'How will Myles feel about being deserted?'

'They don't have much time together at the best of times, Robert, and nothing fazes Myles. And he knows perfectly well that she has dalliances on the side. As he does, I guess. In any case, he's part of the problem, since he's abandoning her too as he's off for a few months to do something undercover in Iraq with some old SAS pals. And from what I've picked up, he did that unexpectedly and without qualms. I've a feeling Myles thinks Jack takes him for granted.'

'She takes everyone for granted.'

'As she would say, that's the way she is. Anyway, since St. Martha's runs itself these days and nothing is particularly engaging her in the Lords, in the absence of any other challenge, trying to get Provost Pritchardson into bed is about as good as it gets. Anyway, you will hardly have forgotten that once Jack has made up her mind, she's obstinate.'

'Obdurate.'

'Mulish.'

'Pig-headed.'

'So where does messing up Rachel's and my honeymoon come into it?'

'My fault, I'm afraid. After I repeated some of my scarier warnings over dinner, she took in enough to realise that the Indiana locals might pall, whereupon she hit on the idea of importing good company from the old country. Ellis and I are non-starters because of our jobs, but Rachel's still resting and you're freelance so you're fair game.'

'We are not going to Indiana. Read my lips. That is, metaphorically read my lips. We are not going to Indiana.'

'I told her you wouldn't, but you know Jack. She always thinks she'll get her own way.'

'I may sometimes be a pushover, Mary Lou. I admit that in the past I've succumbed to wheedling, bullying or blackmail from Jack and indeed Ellis to do absurd and dangerous things. I've even on occasion played Watson to Jack's Holmes, Hastings to her Poirot or Archie Goodwin to her Nero Wolfe, but I'm damned if, after all Rachel and I have been through, I'll contemplate for one minute messing up our leisurely perambulation around Europe to keep Jack Troutbeck company in the middle of a prairie. This time I'll be implacable.'

'And even if *you* crack, I certainly won't,' shouted Rachel from the sofa.

'And even if *I* crack, Rachel certainly won't,' added Amiss. 'Not that I will.'

'Sure, Robert,' said Mary Lou, in a tone of the utmost sincerity. 'You'll be implacable. Of course you will. I don't doubt it. Not one little bit.'

Chapter Two

From: Robert Amiss
To: Mary Lou Denslow
Sent: Tue 14/03/2006 11.14
Subject: Two Weddings and a near-funeral

Sholem-aleykhem and all that, Mary Lou. (I've been throwing myself into my forthcoming role as 'Jew for a Day' by learning a bit of Yiddish for schmoozing purposes.)

Well, now that all the hullabaloo has died down, I think I can justly report that your wedding can be classed as a knockout, in every sense of the word. If you've been foolish enough to answer your phones or pick up e-mails in Madrid, you've probably already heard about the spectacular dance sequence put on by Jack with your Uncle Lenny after you left. I hadn't realised the extent to which Jack fancies herself as a jiver, but what she has never known or else has forgotten in the technique department, she more than made up for in chutzpah and vigour. As indeed, did your Uncle Lenny. For a man of such generous proportions, he covered the ground with real speed. Jack described herself afterwards as having been tripping the light fantastic. "Like Margot Fonteyn?" I suggested. "More like Dumbo the elephant," she answered with commendable honesty, adding, however, that she liked to be the fastest elephant on the dance floor.

It was, perhaps, a trifle tactless of her to tell your uncle so loudly at the end that like all blacks he had a natural sense of rhythm, but at least you'd taught her not to say 'negro.' Or worse. Uncle Lenny seemed quite pleased, but I wasn't sure it went down too well with your brother. It was also a touch unfortunate that later in the evening—when they were both suffering from hubris—the *klutzes* crashed into Ellis's Great Aunt Lavender and her zimmer.

If you've seen the latest version of 'The Producers,' you'll remember the dance of the old ladies with their walking frames. From my vantage point, for several seconds it looked as if Great Aunt Lavender was auditioning for a part in it, but she was in fact vainly trying to stay upright. Unfortunately, when she fell down, she hit her head on the edge of the table and passed out—but fortunately not away, which might have put a bit of a damper on the rest of the evening. For your Master of Ceremonies it was what I can describe only as what we Yiddishers call an *oy vey*! moment, but I hope I rose to it competently.

Apart from that minor drama, Rachel and I thought everything went brilliantly. You looked gorgeous, Ellis spoke with unaccustomed wit and your dad spoke graciously. True, we were not the only people present to blench when in Jack's entertaining speech she described you as her favourite bit of black pudding, but your merry laughter dissolved the tension. Anyway, if you ask Jack Troutbeck to be your Matron of Honour, you have it coming. After the speech Rachel briefly lost her nerve and wondered if we could cancel her appearance in that capacity at our own matrimonials.

We thought the Pooley hospitality, as one might expect, was lavish without being vulgar and everyone seemed to enjoy themselves hugely. I bet we can look forward to a fine spread in *Country Life* which will make you Top

Totty, the Toast of the Shires, which will be a rare double in conjunction with being the newest holder of the TV title of Thinking Man's Crumpet.

That's enough racism and sexism for now.

Our agony continues, but now that there are only ten days or so to go Rachel has ceased *kvetching*. She's made a crucial psychological shift by deciding that she should see the wedding as her mother's big day rather than her own, so she's now thrown herself into trying to make it perfect for her and they haven't had a row for ages.

Jack and I didn't have much chance to talk at your wedding, but she's been in touch since, has told me a bit about Indiana, which she assures me Rachel and I would enjoy, but she hasn't brought out the heavy weaponry as yet, so a firm 'Forget it' has so far been all that was required. I did point out that it was her solemn duty to stay in Cambridge while we're away, since she'd undertaken to look after Plutarch and no one else in the whole world would take on the job, but she insists she's found a suitable carer, that anyway Plutarch is such an extinct volcano these days that St. Martha's won't know she's there and that if she's got any grievances, you'll be available as the London court of appeal. Hmmmmmn!

We hope you're both having a wonderful time and look forward very much to seeing you next week. I am afraid it'll have to be rather brief, since D-Day approaches and we will be in a frenzy of packing and parent-soothing.

Must schlep off now and get on with things.

Much love to you both from us both,

Shalom, Mazel Tov, and all that,

Robert

From: Mary Lou Denslow
To: Robert Amiss
Sent: Fri 17/03/2006 18.05
Subject: Two Weddings and a near funeral not to speak of Jack

Thanks for the news, Robert. Sorry to have been late getting back to you, but we've been very busy doing important things like looking at pictures and walking in the sun and having lunch and the Internet cafes usually heave with off-putting lines of backpackers.

Your speech was really funny and you were a fabulous MC and looked imperturbable, which is the main thing, which made us feel relaxed about disappearing relatively early and leaving our two families and their entourages to it. We've called our respective parents who seem very happy with everything and you'll be pleased to know that Ellis reports Great Aunt Lavender's injury as minor and her upper lip as stiff. Now if this had been a wedding back home, she'd have sued Jack, Uncle Lenny, Ellis's dad, and the band. Maybe even the manufacturers of the walker.

After a few days in London, which they thoroughly enjoyed, the entire Denslow contingent is now back in the old homestead. They still haven't got over the discovery that Ellis's ancestors have had that stately pile for more than three hundred years and, they are, of course, disappointed that we won't end up living there. But my family are good people, and though they think primogeniture is unfair, they would not want Piers to die for the crime of being the elder son, copping the family home and pretty well everything else and stopping me from being a Lady. They've developed a taste for titles, though, which they're beginning to think must be a dime a dozen. All they knew about Ellis for ages was that he was a cop—which to them seems normal and respectable—and then it was revealed that his father was a peer. Then Jack, whom they knew as my St. Martha's mentor, turned out to be a baroness. Aunt Eliza asked me seriously if I could earn a ladyship and I said that in England anything is possible, which amazed her—because, of course, like most Americans, she thinks she lives in the only land of opportunity ever invented in the history of the universe.

Oh, by the way, should Jack railroad you into going to Indiana—which of course she won't—you should know there are connotations to being 'Jew for a Day.' In the States some well-meaning sensitivity counsellors who want kids to understand discrimination put yellow stars on half the class on Holocaust Day and ban them from the water cooler. Apparently it always ends in tears. I hope it doesn't for you. The good news is it beats being 'Slave for a Day,' which has been known to include those designated as slaves being chased through the woods by bounty hunters. I love my country, but it can be very strange.

Apart from a long message on my mobile telling us which pictures to see at the Prado, which other museums to visit, which restaurants to eat at and what dishes to choose, we haven't heard from Jack. I bet you'll hear plenty. She won't abandon her campaign.

Best of luck with everything. We're both looking forward to seeing you. Ellis is polishing up his speech.

Adios and much love from us two to you two,
ML

From: Robert Amiss
To: Mary Lou Denslow
Sent: Tue 21/03/2006 13.19
Subject: Jack

She's ratcheting it up, Mary Lou. This Helen person is, apparently, prepared to provide bags of gold in order to please Jack by enticing us to Freeman University. Rachel can give some lectures about her time as a diplomat, while I can teach a writing class—which seems pretty ridiculous considering my first book won't be published for another few months. But I'm being implacable. And, even without Rachel, that's the way I'm determined to stay.

Love, Robert

'How long do you reckon before Robert caves in?' Mary Lou asked Pooley over dinner that night.

'I can't see him doing it this time. Usually when he's dragged into things by his friends it's because he's got nothing better to do. Travelling around Europe sounds a lot better than the alternative on offer.'

'So boredom won't be a motive. Nor will money. But there's still friendship.'

'If it's a question of pleasing Rachel or Jack, there won't be a contest.'

'True.' Mary Lou speared another prawn and ate it thoughtfully. 'Unless Jack gets into trouble, of course. In which case Rachel would want to rally round. She's become fond of Jack despite herself.'

'Why should she get into trouble?' asked Pooley absently, as he gazed at Mary Lou's sparkling eyes and thought how lucky he was.

'I can't believe you said that, Ellis. She's going to America, the citadel of political correctness—a universe in which a public official was sacked from his job for using the word "niggardly," which has as much to do with "nigger" as "patronising" has to do with "Pat."'

'Sounds like the Met,' sighed Pooley. 'The commissioner never shuts up about racism.'

'I know, I know, but America's much worse. Everyone's born touchy these days. What's more, Jack's heading for American academia, which is now in the iron grip of the thought police. Did you read or did I tell you about the Lawrence Summers affairs?'

'Don't think so.'

'Summers was President of Harvard. At a private conference convened to discuss how to attract more women to science, he made the gross error of trying to address the question from first principles. Were women in short supply, he asked, because a) they were discriminated against, b) they considered the commitment required for a scientific career incompatible with their family responsibilities, or c) there were innate differences between men and women which made science more a man thing?'

Pooley looked puzzled. 'So?'

'A female professor called Nancy something-or-other stormed out claiming to have been made feel physically ill by this outrageous sexism and all hell broke loose with the feminist ballbreakers, causing Summers—who had been imported into Harvard in the first place because he was a tough guy who would kick ass and face down pressure groups—to cave in, beg publicly for forgiveness and throw millions more down a drain called diversity instead of telling Nancy to lie down, sniff some smelling salts, and come to her senses. As that still wasn't enough to placate his enemies, in the end he resigned.'

'Oh, dear.'

'Well you may say "Oh, dear."' She took a generous sip of Rioja. 'What a wuss! And to think this is the guy who gave us all hope in the early days of his reign when he took on that bombastic poseur Cornel West…'

Pooley raised an enquiring eyebrow.

'Then Professor of Black Studies at Harvard, a mountebank, amateur rapper, and crowd-pleasing activist, who went off in a huff to Princeton because he thought Summers was showing insufficient respect by questioning his dodgy scholarship and his tendency to inflate his students' grades sky-high.'

'Black Studies is big at Harvard, is it? I'm surprised.'

'Big? It's mega. Just like Women's Studies. And now Queer Studies.' She snorted. 'Excuses to avoid anything rigorous.'

'You get more and more like Jack every day, Mary Lou. You'll have to curb your opinions a bit now you're a celeb.'

'I'm only a D list celeb, darling. And that probably won't last long. I'll try hard not to offend the tender PC sensibilities of the BBC, but we're alone and I can rant a bit. It's just that Jack going into the jaws of danger has stirred me up. I'm afraid she'll be lynched. From all I read and hear about American universities these days, you can prance around almost nude shaking your fanny at the athletes and screwing night and day under the bushes, you can accuse George Bush of being worse than Hitler or sneer at your country as the Great Satan and no one will even tut-tut, but cause quote offence unquote to the greatest asshole on the campus because of an innocent remark that could be construed as having racist or sexist overtones or reflect on someone's gender orientation, and you'll be fucked quicker than a frat-whore.'

She saw Pooley's perplexed expression. 'Sorry, Ellis. It's all those campus novels I've had to read: I'm falling into the vernacular. A frat-whore is a fraternity-house groupie.'

Pooley sighed. 'Things have moved on since my generation thought "Animal House" was cutting-edge, I suppose.'

'Compared to now, "Animal House" is "The Waltons."'

She pushed her plate away. 'I look at Jack and I see a lawsuit waiting to happen. And I can tell you that it'll be no defence that she's female, bisexual, or that one of her best friends is black. Or African-American as I'm striving to teach her to say. She's a walking dictionary of inappropriate words. And inappropriate words don't come cheap in my old country.'

'Mary Lou,' said Pooley, reaching across the table to take her hand, 'it's not that I'm not interested and it's not that I don't care about Jack, but we are on our honeymoon, it isn't long enough anyway, and I'd like to change the subject.'

She leaned across the table and kissed him enthusiastically. 'OK,' she promised, 'consider me back on your wavelength.'

◇◇◇

From: Commander Jim Milton
To: Detective-Inspector Ellis Pooley
Sent: Fri 24/03/2006 21.11
Subject: The usual

I expect you're back by now and hope Madrid lived up to expectations. Sorry I had to leave your wedding early, but another murder of a scum-bag by other scum-bags called me away. Things are hotting up seriously here and I'm short-staffed so can you call me at home on Sunday so I can let you know what's most urgent for Monday? Prepare to be at the Yard at sparrow-fart.

Love to Mary Lou. I did warn her not to marry a cop.

◇◇◇

From: Mary Lou Denslow
To: Robert Amiss
Sent: Tue 25/04/2006 11.15
Subject: Thank heaven it's all over

I hope now you're at peace and far out of reach of predatory baronesses. Your wedding was a triumph. Rachel was elegant, you were *soigné*, Hannah looked like a woman who had never in her whole life thrown a wobbly, the ceremony was moving, the food was great and not too ethnic, no one could have faulted the speeches and Jack was on her best behaviour. Her only lapse, I think, was enthusiastically hailing Hannah as Rachel's Yiddisher Momma. It's not quite how a Hampstead psychiatrist might be expected to visualise herself, though considering how Hannah's been behaving over the last few months, it serves her right.

I've been having anguished calls from Jack, who has had serious problems on the parrot front, owing to complications caused by airline precautions against avian flu. I shall definitely not fill you in on the detail, but she has bullied her way around officialdom and pulled strings shamefully, so I think Horace is being transported as diplomatic baggage. It's beginning to dawn on me that Horace is likely to run into trouble on the PC front too. 'Who's a pretty boy?' surely constitutes sexual harassment. And singing 'Onward Christian Soldiers' could cause offence to secular and religious alike.

She grumbled a bit about you two being in a rut and refusing to accept a challenge, so I assume you've remained unbending. Perhaps when she and Horace hit Hicksville, Provost Fortier-Pritchardson will live up to expectations and you will be surplus to requirements. But something tells me that this bird has an eye to the main chance and that Jack is no more to her than a titled trophy.

Still, I've decided to stop uttering warnings and giving advice as it's a complete waste of time and energy. Jack's in tunnel-vision mode and if she had a hearing aid, it would be switched off. I will confine myself to listening to complaints and delivering her and Horace to the airport next week.

Ellis is part of a team in hot pursuit of a very unpleasant gang of Albanian sex-traffickers. He remarked the other night that it's a poor look-out when you can't even say 'You're under arrest' without the help of an interpreter. He seems nostalgic for the days when the worst linguistic challenge for a copper was cockney rhyming slang and no one was expected to be culturally sensitive.

Aren't we all?

Since Ellis and I went back to work we've seen each other slightly but only slightly more than we used to when we lived in different cities, but at least we sleep in the same bed and we'll always have Madrid. You, on the other hand, you lucky people, will have the whole of Europe to store in your memories for the bad days when you are both proper wage-slaves again. Make the most of it and don't come back until you have to.

Much love from us both to you both, ML

Chapter Three

'Beverages!' cried the flight attendant.

'What a raucous voice,' said the baroness loudly to the tall, broad, white-haired man in the next seat, as she put the in-flight magazine back in the rack. 'She sounds just like my parrot. Though with a more limited vocabulary.' She leaned into the aisle. 'I wish she'd hurry up. What's taking her so long?'

'A few other thirsty customers to attend to, I expect, ma'am,' he said, in a soft Southern accent.

The baroness settled herself back in her seat with a grunt.

''Scuse me, ma'am, but does that box in the seat next to you contain your parrot?'

'It does indeed.'

'So that explains why you were talking to your baggage at the check-in.'

She beamed. 'You spotted me earlier, then.'

'You're hard to miss, ma'am. That was a very striking hat you were wearing.'

The baroness smirked. 'No point in hats unless they're striking.'

'So what kind is your parrot?'

'Horace is an African grey.'

'He must be a very special little bird if he gets a first-class seat.'

'I'm the special bird. He's along for the ride. And someone else is paying.'

'Does he talk?'

'Nineteen to the dozen, when he's on form, but I'm not encouraging him right now. He's here on sufferance so I've asked him to mimic a Trappist monk. I don't want the airline refusing to let him make the return journey. I've put that black cloth over the crate to make him think it's bedtime.' She snorted. 'Unbelievable palaver finding an airline that would take him, getting him certificated and training him to put up with a crate. I even had to prove he'd served his time in quarantine. You'd think parrots were in the habit of taking a couple of mates down to the pub on a Friday night.'

'So he won't be talking on board. That's a shame. I'd enjoy hearing what the little guy had to say.'

'He might talk later. I'll have to feed and water him at some stage. But I won't be encouraging him to get chatty.'

'Beverages!!'

'Yes,' called the baroness loudly. 'I want a beverage.'

The flight attendant, who was three rows away, looked down towards her and glared. 'You'll be served when it's your turn and not before. Beverages!'

'So why are you offering beverages at the top of your voice then?'

Her neighbour touched the baroness on the sleeve. 'If I were you, ma'am, I wouldn't get into an argument with Rosa. It'll do no good and she'll only take it out on you.'

'You mean she might deny me beverages?'

'Sure. Rosa knows how to bring us to heel.'

'Is she really called Rosa? Seems too nice a name for someone who looks and sounds like a bad-tempered serial killer.'

'Oh, it's not her real name. That's Joan, but I don't think anyone's keen to get on first name terms with her. Rosa's what some of us frequent flyers call her behind her back—after Rosa Kleb from the James Bond movie.'

'Well she's certainly old and ugly enough to have been in the KGB,' grumbled the baroness. 'Whatever happened to attractive young air hostesses? On Far East airlines they're as young and beautiful as cherry blossoms.'

'Anti-discrimination laws, ma'am.'

'Ridiculous! The whole point of air hostesses is supposed to be that they do the job for a few years until they find a rich husband. Means they're always agreeable as well as easy on the eye. What's the point of having someone who's so sick of her job it shows in her face.'

'Beverages!'

The trolley and Rosa arrived.

'I'll have a....'

'Not your turn,' said Rosa and directed her gaze left. 'Whaddayawant?'

'Please help this lady first.'

''Gainst the rules.'

'I'll have bourbon on the rocks then,' he said.

Crashing bottles and glasses, Rosa prepared his bourbon and handed it over. She stared with loathing at the baroness. 'Whaddayawant?'

'Dry martini. Straight up.'

'Can't.'

'What do you mean you can't? Martini is the American national drink. Has this airline no sense of national pride?'

Rosa said nothing.

'You have gin. You have vermouth. I'll make it.'

'No vermouth. Just gin.'

The baroness locked eyes with her. 'Vermouth is listed in the in-flight magazine.'

'Noneonthetrolley.'

'Then I suggest you search the galley.'

'Whaddaythinkthisis? A cocktail bar?'

'No,' said the baroness coldly. 'I think it's a first-class cabin for access to which your employers charge a stack of money. I want vermouth. And a martini glass.'

'No martini glasses,' said Rosa. As she stumped off the man gazed with interest at the baroness. 'Boy,' he said, 'you're something.'

By the time Rosa came pounding down the aisle with a bottle, the baroness had commandeered the trolley, filled a glass with ice, shaken it several times until she thought it acceptably chilled, emptied it and almost filled it with gin.

'Whatchadoin'?' shouted Rosa.

'Your job.' The baroness leaned forward, took the bottle from Rosa, added just a couple of drops of vermouth, handed the bottle back and sat down. 'Now I want a twist of lemon.'

'No twists. Only slices.'

'Then please cut some rind off a slice and bring it to me.'

There was another face-off, after which Rosa took a slice of lemon to the galley and returned with some rind, which she dropped haughtily into the baroness's glass. 'Beverages!' she shouted at the next row of passengers.

The baroness had her first sip of martini, smacked her lips approvingly, and turned to her companion. 'The seat's uncomfortable, the décor is shabby, and they don't know how to make a martini. If this is what it's like in first class, what's it like in economy?'

'I'm too rich to know, ma'am.' He held out his hand. 'Edgar S. Brooks of Jackson, Mississippi, at your service.'

She shook his hand vigorously. 'Jack I. Troutbeck, presently of Cambridge, at yours.'

'I'd better see to Horace,' said the baroness, two hours into the journey, extracting from her capacious handbag two small dishes, some pellets, and a bottle of water. Brooks watched with interest as she opened the crate and cooed at its occupant. After Horace had lost interest in the contents of his dishes, he emitted an ear-shattering sequence of wolf-whistles, which not only attracted the attention of everyone in the first-class compartment, but brought Rosa out of the kitchen. 'Who's making that noise?' she shouted.

The baroness stood up. 'It's my parrot.'

'Ohmigod,' said a large woman two seats behind. 'We'll all get bird flu.'

'Rubbish,' said the baroness. 'Even if my parrot had avian flu, you couldn't catch it unless he bit *you* or you *ate* him.'

'Who said you could bring a parrot on board?' asked Rosa threateningly.

'Your employers,' said the baroness icily. 'In exchange for a lot of money.'

'Pieces of eight, pieces of eight,' cried Horace.

'How do we know it hasn't got bird flu? And how do we know we won't catch it from breathing the same air,' cried the large woman.

'Don't be ridiculous,' said the baroness. 'Why would I travel with a diseased bird?'

'You might be a terrorist.'

'Oh, for God's sake, woman,' began the baroness, as Horace launched into 'God save the Queen.' Brooks tugged at her sleeve. 'Leave this to me, Jack.' She sat down; he squeezed past her and stood in the aisle. 'Ladies and gentlemen,' he said soothingly, 'y'all have nothing to worry about. This parrot hasn't met another bird in two years, he's been given the all-clear by his vet, and he's got less chance of having bird flu than I have. This lady I'm travelling with is an aristocrat and a member of the British parliament and is a fan of our great country, so let's all give her and her smart little parrot a warm American welcome.' There was a small ripple of applause which turned to laughter as from Horace's crate came a rasping cry of 'Beverages! Beverages! Beverages.'

'He's certainly talented,' said Brooks as he sat down. 'He's picked up an American accent in no time. Pity it's from the Bronx.'

◇◇◇

'And remember to tell them that chicken was rubber. When something's made of rubber, I want it to be natural rather than synthetic. Preferably, it should come from a plantation in Malaysia.' As Rosa shot her the dirtiest of dirty looks, the baroness nodded at her reprovingly and walked out of the plane.

'You never let up, Jack, do you?' said Edgar Brooks, half in admiration and half in weariness.

'Not knowingly,' she grunted. 'Anyway, that'll teach her to be sarcastic and ask me if I'd any more complaints. I could have made a much bigger fuss than I did. The pasta wasn't fit to be served to a horse and my favourite cat would have had harsh words about that excuse for fowl.'

'Your life must be a constant battlefield.'

'I enjoy battle.'

'I can see that.'

They walked along in companionable silence for a few minutes until Brooks stopped. 'This is goodbye, Jack. I'm going thataway to collect my bags and you'll be heading thataway to catch your connecting flight.' He handed her the crate he had insisted on carrying. 'That trip was a lot of fun.'

'Now remember what I told you. Get sassy with immigration or customs and you could be dead or on your way home in no time. And any problems at Freeman—just give me a call.'

They embraced and then began their separate marches down the long long corridors of the enormous Chicago airport.

'Whatyougotthere, lady?'

'My parrot.'

She thrust some documents at the customs official. 'You'll find these are in order.'

'Thasfurmetosay, lady. Open up the box.'

The baroness summoned up her failing reserves of patience. 'Do I really have to? He'll be distressed by the light and the noise.'

'Open.'

Grimly, the baroness undid the buckles, opened the lid slightly, said, 'There, there, Horrie, everything's fine,' and then half-opened the lid so the official could peer inside.

'He talk?'

'A bit.'

There was a whistle from inside the carrier and then Horace shouted at maximum volume, 'Pass the ammunition.'

The official froze. 'What?'

'Pass the ammunition,' repeated Horace obligingly.

'You come with me, lady. We're gonna visit with Homeland Security.'

'You cannot be serious, Officer. Are you suggesting my parrot is a terrorist? Where about his person do you think he would conceal explosives?'

'He ain't a terrorist. But he cuddabeen keeping company with some. He's certainly saying some funny things for a parrot.'

The baroness struggled to keep her temper. '"Pass the ammunition" is just part of an American phrase, Officer. I taught him to say "Praise the Lord and pass the ammunition," but he often forgets one bit or another.'

'So it's profane as well as threatening, is it?'

'It was said by a U.S. chaplain during the defence of Pearl Harbour.'

'Oh, yeah? Well, we'll see what Homeland Security thinks.'

'I'll miss my connecting flight.'

'That's your problem, lady. Mine is the defence of the good ol' U.S. of A. Follow me.'

Pushing a laden trolley, the baroness emerged exhausted out of Indianapolis airport more than three hours later. Her red velvet Tudor cap was slightly askew, so the pheasant tail-feathers stuck out at a strange angle. With a mixture of relief and disappointment, she spotted a large piece of cardboard reading LADY IDA TROUTBECK, behind which was a tiny blonde in micro-shorts and flip-flops with a t-shirt reading I ❤ FREEMAN U.

'Hi, Lady Ida. I'm Betsy. It's like really great to meet you. Wow, that's totally such a cool hat.'

'Thank you, Betsy. I'm glad you approve. Now where's the Provost? She said she'd meet me.'

'Hey, she was totally pissed she couldn't come, but she had like some crisis with her programme. She'll catch you at the hotel. I'm your roadie for the next few days so she asked me to pick you up. It's just as well, really, since you're so late. She'd have been like totally freaked waiting that long.'

'I'm totally freaked myself.'

Betsy's face fell. 'Hey, that's too bad. Wasn't the journey cool? I'll get you to the hotel quick as I can so you can chill. Can I push your cart?'

Although the baroness was not too tired to appreciate the physical attributes that Betsy had generously on show, she was in grumbling mode. 'I'm not Ida. I'm Jack. And not Lady Jack either, but Lady Troutbeck. I need to talk to the Provost. I've been travelling for 14 hours, I nearly missed my connection because of arguments about the parrot which your security people suspected of being a member of Al Qaeda, and the last 60 minutes were spent circling this airport in a toytown plane shaking in a violent hailstorm, which isn't my idea of cool.' Spotting that Betsy's pretty little face was registering increasing confusion and worry, the baroness added, 'I'm sorry. I'm tired and I'm cross. And thanks, you can look after my luggage.'

Betsy flashed her perfect teeth. 'Hey, way to go, Lady! You follow me and we'll be at the car in a minute. And the storm's over, which is really like cool.' She grabbed the trolley and set off at a brisk trot, with the baroness treading heavily behind her. As Betsy rounded a pillar, it clipped the edge of the crate, which fell to the ground on its side. Horace emitted a series of squawks followed by an eloquent, 'Oh, shit!'

'Well you may say, "Oh, shit," Horrie,' remarked the baroness, as she set about putting him the right way up. 'No, no,' she shouted at Betsy, who was dancing with anxiety and asking if she should call for help. 'Don't fuss, girl. He'll be fine. He just needs to find his bearings and have some light refreshment. Like me. We'll go to the bar for a few minutes and pull ourselves together.'

Betsy's little forehead wrinkled. 'It's like Sunday. There won't be like any bar open.'

'Oh, God.' The baroness failed to notice Betsy's look of distress. 'What? I thought this was supposed to be a civilised country.'

'Sunday's like serious in Indiana, Lady Troutbeck. It's very Christian here.'

The baroness gave a mighty yawn. 'All right, all right, Betsy. Let's get going. I'll sort Horace out in the car.' She looked at her watch. 'How far are we from the hotel?'

'About an hour. But, hey, that'll be great cos we can like get acquainted.'

'Cool,' said the baroness grimly.

She had been asleep for fifty minutes when they reached the Hotel New Paddington. A nervous Betsy shook her awake. ''Scuse me, Lady Troutbeck. We're here. I hope you're like feeling better. You've had a really good sleep.'

The baroness rubbed her eyes and groaned. 'What time is it?'

'Fifteen after five.'

'And you said the Provost will be here when…?'

'Six. She's taking you out to a really neat restaurant.'

'Can't think why she'd imagine I'd be interested in a neat restaurant. Decent would be more like it.' Unaware, as she climbed out of the car with Horace, of Betsy's bewilderment, she added, 'Fetch the bellhop,' and beamed proudly at her grasp of local argot. 'And tell him to be quick. I'll check in, settle Horace, and see you downstairs in fifteen minutes for a drink.'

The baroness shook the door of the bar fruitlessly, then marched across the ornate lobby to the reception desk. 'What's going on? The bar door seems to be locked.'

The tall, perky, pony-tailed redhead looked apologetic. 'Sorry, ma'am. It's a shame, but the bar's closed.'

'When will it open?'

The receptionist beamed. '6.00 tomorrow evening.'

The baroness deliberately took a deep breath and put on her most reasonable tone. 'Why is it not open now?'

The tone was as irritatingly chirpy as the news was bad. 'Indiana's a great place to be, ma'am, but the law says we can't open on Sunday.'

'And why are you not opening during the day tomorrow?'

'There's no demand, ma'am. Folks here don't drink in the daytime.' She beamed. 'But I'm sure you'll find a bar some place.' She paused. 'Well, maybe you will.'

The baroness sighed heavily, leaned forward, and read the name on the receptionist's lapel badge. 'Could we cut to the chase, Miss Barbara Lupoff? This is an hotel, so you can, presumably, serve a resident at any time?'

Barbara Lupoff was delighted to have a chance to be positive. 'Oh, sure, ma'am. We can serve residents all right.'

'Right, then. We'll sit in the lobby. What'll you have, Betsy? I'm having a gin and tonic. Will you have the same? Or perhaps a glass of wine?'

Barbara was downcast. 'She's not a resident, ma'am.'

'Hey, I'll just have a soda, Lady Troutbeck. I'm not like old enough to be allowed alcohol.'

'How old are you?'

'Nineteen.'

'Are you serious? This place is run by Roundheads.' She turned back to Barbara. 'However, at least this means we need not be troubled about her residential status. Get me the gin and tonic if you think I'm old enough to be allowed the gin.'

'Sorry, ma'am, I'm afraid we can't serve you. All the alcoholic beverages are in the bar and we haven't got the key.'

'And who has the key, Barbara?' asked the baroness, in her most controlled voice.

'The barman, ma'am.'

'And he is where?'

'Don't know, ma'am. He don't live in.'

The baroness took a deep breath. 'We can surmount that problem. I have in my bag a bottle of malt whisky I was intending to give to my hostess, but my need is greater. Just get me a glass.'

'I'm sorry, ma'am.'

'All the glasses are locked in the bar?'

'No. It's against the law to allow any alcohol to be drunk in a public part of the hotel unless it's provided by the hotel.'

The baroness exploded. 'Let me get this straight, Lupoff. I got up at 1.00 in the morning your time, flew across the Atlantic, met in Chicago the thickest customs official in the West, transferred in Chicago to a plane that in the subsequent storm behaved like a canoe in a tsunami, was driven for an hour across a prairie, am shortly going out to dinner and have to keep my eyes open, and you tell me the bar is locked and I can't even have a quick drink of my own whisky.'

Barbara smiled brightly. 'Unless you'd like to go up to your room, ma'am.'

The baroness growled. 'Dear God! Whatever happened to the land of the free?' She emitted a theatrical sigh. 'Very well, then. When in New Paddington one must, presumably, do like the New Paddingtonians. Send two glasses upstairs immediately along with the soda water.'

'Could I have like a Diet Coke, Lady Troutbeck?'

'You just said soda.'

'But Diet Coke is a soda.'

'No, it isn't. It's a revolting pop. But if you want it you shall have it.' She turned back to the receptionist. 'Two glasses and...' she shuddered theatrically, 'a Diet Coke. Now come upstairs, Betsy, and meet Horace...'

'I'm sorry, ma'am,' said the receptionist, 'but we've just been banned by Freeman U from allowing students in the bedrooms.'

'What?' The baroness's voice had once again risen by several decibels. 'Do, pray, explain.'

'It's a new rule, ma'am. Dr. Gonzales from the Provost's office called last week.'

'Rules are there to be broken. Can't you ignore her, whoever she is?'

Barbara shook her head and Betsy intervened. 'Dr. Gonzales is a man, Lady Troutbeck, and no one ignores him.'

'Who the hell is he?'

'He...he...works for the Provost,' said Betsy.

'And why do you look like a rabbit in the headlights at the mention of his name?'

'Please, Lady Troutbeck,' said Betsy, 'I don't need the Coke. And like I've got stuff to do so I'd better go now anyway. You just go upstairs and have a drink and I'll like see you in the morning.'

'Thanks to the mysterious Gonzales, the moment has passed,' said the baroness. Her face brightened. 'And, besides, here comes the Provost.'

Chapter Four

'I love that suit,' said Helen Fortier-Prichardson. 'Is it tweed?'

The baroness looked down at her skirt complacently. 'Yes,' she said. 'It's a light tweed and it's supposed to remind you of heather.'

'Who's the designer?'

'Holland and Holland. They're my gunsmiths.'

The Provost looked shocked. 'You shoot?'

'Sadly, not these days. I've been too busy. Perhaps I'll get a chance to do some hunting while I'm here? What's the local game?'

'I wouldn't know,' said the Provost stiffly. Then, remembering that she was supposed to be wooing the baroness for professional reasons, she softened her tone and said, 'I can find out for you and see if we can fix you up.'

'That would be excellent. I'd like to have a gun again.'

'But now you must be starving,' said the Provost. 'Server!'

A young man appeared beside the table, handed them both menus, and poured into their glasses water and ice from an enormous jug. 'I'll be your waiter this evening,' he said. 'I'm Randy.'

'You may very well be,' said the baroness, guffawing, 'but isn't it a bit early in our relationship to tell me that?'

'Randy is a given name here, Jack,' said the Provost, who seemed on edge.

'How odd,' said the baroness. 'Be careful if you ever go to England, Randy. You could get more offers than you'd like.' She took a healthy swig of water and spat it out again. 'Ugh! It's chlorinated. 'Orrible. Get me bottled water.'

'Sure, ma'am,' said Randy, and sped off before the baroness could demand an alcoholic drink. She and the Provost began reading the menu.

'The desserts here are to die for,' said the Provost. 'Make sure to keep room for the Banana Enchilada.'

The baroness cast a despairing look down the menu. Having ascertained that she was expected to feel tempted by a banana deep-fried in a tortilla with lashings of cream, ice cream, and toffee fudge sauce, she returned to reading incredulously the descriptions of the appetisers.

The Provost looked at her sympathetically. 'Still not decided, Jack? I know it's tough. Everything's so good. I've had a hard time choosing, but I'm going for the Mozza Melts.'

'This Mozzarella will not be authentic artisan, Helen,' said the baroness.

'How do you mean "authentic artisan"?'

The baroness looked at her gravely. 'Proper Mozzarella is made with milk from buffalos that have grazed in the malarial swamps south of Rome. It must be made—not in creameries or factories—but by the hands of the buffalo farmer himself.' She paused. 'Or, of course, his wife.'

The Provost pursed her lips in irritation. 'I guess this won't be authentic then,' she said, 'but Mozza Melts are just delicious.'

'I can't myself see that a dodgy cheese is improved by being fried in beer batter, whatever that is.' The baroness put down the menu. 'I'll just have a rare steak.'

'Aren't you hungry?'

'I seem to have lost my appetite.'

'Of course it wasn't rare,' grumbled the baroness later that evening to Mary Lou, whom she had pursued by phone from office to home. 'And it hadn't been properly hung. And would you believe the madwoman wanted me to order it with something called battered prawns? Why would I want to put prawns on my steak? And they had no green vegetables. And the portions were so enormous the food was falling off the giant plates. And when I finally got a drink, the tonic was sweet and I had to send it back and get whisky and water instead and the glass was crammed with ice and the water was chlorine-ridden so I had to send it back as well and get neat whisky and bottled water. And all the wine on their list was so young, drinking it was infanticide. And I asked for the cheeseboard, and it consisted of a huge piece of sweaty, processed, orange, alleged cheddar.'

'I warned you about American food.'

'Not enough. Anyway, that wasn't the worst of it. Once she finished exclaiming over the menu, the bloody Provost got down to telling me about campus life, and apart from the obscenity of talking about students as customers and dons as service providers, I couldn't understand anything she was saying because of the vocabulary she uses—resource-allocation models and leading-edge paradigms and recalibrating and recontextualising interfaces and cutting-edge programmes.'

'They learn it at Provost school, I guess.'

'Well this half-wit seemed to think it would all make sense to me as I was the head of St. Martha's. The bloody woman is a crashing bore. I don't even fancy her any more. I wouldn't dream of sleeping with someone who thinks battery chicken covered....No, let me get that right...battery chicken *slathered* with melted cheese is the food of the gods.'

'So lust has fled?'

'It most certainly has.'

'You must wonder why you're in New Paddington in that case.'

'There are other possibilities,' said the baroness coyly.

'Really? Already? Who?'

'Never you mind.'

'Sometimes I'd like to slap you, Jack, but there's not much I can do about that at this distance. Didn't you find out anything at all from her about the university, or is that another secret?'

'I learned that she has two interests: getting ever more bums on classroom seats and making sure that their owners think the right—that is, the left—way. She confided she'd had problems with a couple of right-wingers. Silly bitch. What does she think I am? And that her first year here was blighted by a humanities dean called Godber who was so "last century" that he was resistant to her profit-maximization schedules, which I presume meant he wouldn't dumb down to pull in more punters. Worse still, he was apparently unsound on diversity, whatever that means here.'

'What happened to him?'

'She got him replaced as dean by someone called Diane who apparently is "now-centred."'

'So you'll be seeking Godber out as soon as possible, I guess.'

'I certainly will. There are also, I gather, though she was vague about this, some troublesome students, but she says she'll tell me more about that later. Additionally, she said if all went well there was an even more distinguished visiting professorship paying mega mega bucks that might be on the cards next year. If I didn't know there was no reason to bribe me, I'd think that was what she was doing.

'However, I'm knackered and I'm off to bed for a vigorous sleep. I'm going to need all my strength to take on this place.'

'Reception. Can I help you?'

'This is Jack Troutbeck. What the hell is going on? I keep being woken by what I presume is a train shrieking "Whoo! Whoo! Wah! Wah!" I thought the entire hotel was taking off for Chicago. Is this going to go on all night?'

''Fraid so, Mr. Troutbeck. Would you like to move to another room?'

'At 4.00 a.m.?' With a muffled sob the baroness slammed down the phone.

'Did you enjoy your breakfast, ma'am?' asked the head waiter.

The baroness took a deep breath. 'No, I most certainly did not enjoy my breakfast. In fact I sent everything back except the salt, and even that was sub-standard because it wasn't sea salt. The toast was sweet and under-done, the butter frothy, the orange juice iced, the fruit salad freezing and unripe, the coffee was filth, the bacon fatter than a sumo wrestler, and the tasteless eggs appeared to have been fried in baby oil.'

'I don't know what to say…' he began.

'Try sorry,' she barked, as she stalked out of the dining room.

◇◇◇

'Hi, Lady Troutbeck,' said Betsy. 'So how are you this beautiful morning?'

'Exhausted, starving, cross, and in an uncustomary mood of self-pity.'

'Oh, gee, I'm really sorry. Is something like wrong?'

'Apart from being unable to sleep because the Chattanooga Choo-Choo went through my bedroom all night and being unable to eat because everything is unfit for human consumption, all is fine.' She paused. 'Mind you, it's also unfit for animal consumption, come to think of it.'

Betsy's little brow furrowed. 'What's the Chattanooga Choo-Choo?'

'What's the Chattanooga Choo-Choo? Dear God, I thought you were an American.' She burst into loud and tuneless song: 'Pardon me boy, is that the Chattanooga Choo-Choo? Track 29, boy, would you give me a shine?'

Betsy looked around nervously and blushed when she saw they were being regarded with interest by two receptionists, the porter, and three guests. 'You're talking like about the train, I guess.'

'Exactly.'

'So are they like giving you a quieter room?'

'They most certainly are, and it's better than the one I had last night, but it's still not satisfactory and will have to be improved on when the hotel manager is back on duty tomorrow. I've been supervising the move for the last hour.'

'So you've got better accommodation because of the train. That's cool.'

'I suppose it is.'

'And like the food? You've like issues with the food?'

'It's disgusting.'

Betsy frowned again. 'Is food fixed different in Europe from like the way it is here?'

'It sure is, Betsy. At least where I come from.'

Betsy's face brightened. 'Hey, it's just that you're not like used to it. You'll see. Our food is great. You'll get to love it.'

'Your optimism does you credit. Now, let's get going.'

'Sure, Lady Troutbeck. I'm parked just outside.'

Betsy had swapped the enormous station wagon of the previous evening for something more modest, though it also was decorated with a large logo of black, brown, and yellowish-white hands reaching towards each other, accompanied by the message: FREEMAN UNIVERSITY: TOGETHER IN DIVERSITY.

The baroness gazed at it with distaste. 'I was hoping for something more on the lines of a beat-up Chevrolet.'

'I'm afraid we don't have anything like beat-up, Lady Troutbeck. I don't even think the carpool has like any Chevrolets.'

'Romance is dead,' said the baroness, climbing into the passenger seat. 'Now what instructions have you been given?'

'The programme is to show you the campus, then we grab lunch, and then I take you to the Provost's office.'

'Before you do that, I'd like you to drive me round New Paddington till I get the lie of the land.'

'Sure thing, Lady Troutbeck. It won't like take long.'

Ten minutes later, they were back outside the hotel.

The baroness gaped at her. 'You mean that's it?'

'Yep.'

'But I didn't see any shops, any restaurants, even any bars. Not even one of those diners I was looking forward to. Just run-down garages and decaying buildings and torn posters on rickety bill boards. And almost no people.'

'That's like the way New Paddington is, Lady Troutbeck. They say that like in olden days it was busy, but then like they built the shopping malls outside town and everyone like moved to the suburbs. There's like lots of American towns like that.'

'Not the way I remember them from the movies.'

'Do you like go to the movies much?'

The baroness ruminated. 'I suppose I haven't been to half-a-dozen since the 1960s. That possibly explains it. Still, where are the students? Why aren't they roaming the streets?'

'We like stay on campus pretty well all the time, Lady Troutbeck, and, of course, lots of people like go home at the weekends.'

The baroness snorted. 'Clearly, this joint is not jumpin'. Drive on, Betsy.'

'I suppose it's utilitarian.'

'What's that, Lady Troutbeck?'

'Useful, Betsy. This campus is what our politicians back home would now, God help us, describe as "fit for purpose," i.e., it undoubtedly provides students with the necessary facilities—places to sleep and work and be taught and lounge about in. But it has no soul, Betsy. No soul at all.'

'But we can't like all be students in Cambridge, Lady Troutbeck. I looked it up on the net when I heard I was like looking after you, and of course it's like awesome. But we're only like ordinary American students. We don't expect like historic buildings, just places that'll help us get the degrees we like need.'

The baroness looked at Betsy with more interest than before. 'I accept your rebuke. Now let's go and find some lunch. A beer and a sandwich will do fine.'

'There's no like alcohol in the food courts, Lady Troutbeck. They're just a collection of fast-food outlets. And even if we could like find a bar in town, I couldn't go in, because Dr. Gonzales has students banned unless they're like over 21.'

'And if we go to the hotel, the bar will still be closed and....'

They looked at each other and laughed.

'What I can't understand, Betsy,' said the baroness, picking up and discarding pieces of blue cheese from a salad from which she had already removed an enormous slab of alleged turkey and a big slice of sweating cheddar, 'is how there are so many fat people in America when the food is too horrible to eat. Just look at this....' She gesticulated towards the body of the room.

'Food court.'

'Food court. Wall-to-wall junk food. What's a responsible university doing encouraging the young to eat ersatz pizza, breaded processed fowl...' she read from the menu, 'mile-high meatloaf sandwich on egg bread, topped with mashed potatoes, fries, and a side order of pink and white marshmallow? Marshmallow! Marshmallow! Not to speak of paving-stone-sized slabs of cheesecake with artificial cream.'

'There's like the Health Zone low-carb section where you got your salad,' pointed out Betsy.

'A section full of little cards listing ingredients, calories, fat and sodium content for everything, I note, thus making it all feel like a penance.' She ate a piece of lettuce and winced at the dressing. 'Is there no demand here for natural ingredients properly cooked?'

Betsy took a sip of her strawberry milk shake and said nothing.

'What exactly is that you're eating?' asked the baroness.

'It's a Surf 'n' Turf.'

'A what?'

'You put the meat from a Big 'n' Tasty hamburger together with the fish from a Filet-O-Fish. I don't eat the buns.'

The baroness put her head in her hands. 'Is mixing fish with meat an American thing? The Provost was trying to make me do something similar last night.'

'We like it, Lady Troutbeck.'

The baroness took a bite of tomato and spat it out. 'Tastes of nothing. It's all horrible.'

'Maybe it's horrible to you, Lady Troutbeck, but it isn't like horrible to us. We think our food's like cool.'

Two enormous students lumbered past and began slavering over the ice-cream bar. The baroness gestured towards them. 'Look at them. They should be grazing in the lettuce section.'

'Doesn't anyone get like fat in Europe?'

'Some do. And I certainly am no sylph, as you can see...' She sighed when she saw Betsy's face. 'A sylph is a mythological being of the air, but we won't go into that. The term is used to mean slender, which, as you can see, I am not, though the way things are going, I soon will be.' She pushed her still-laden plate aside. 'But we don't do fat like Americans do fat. Americans do fat on a grand, grand Rocky Mountains scale. As a people you seem to be puritanical about alcohol and tobacco, while actively encouraging gluttony. And incidentally, our food is vastly superior. It actually tastes of something.'

'You mean you don't have like McDonald's and pizza chains and Krispy Kremes? Poor you.'

'Well, we do have...' The baroness's face contorted. '...fast food.'

'Hey, I think maybe you like don't live like ordinary people?' said Betsy, and gave the baroness a broad grin.

'You mean I live in an ivory tower?'

'What's that?'

'It's figurative, Betsy, but I have a hazy idea it derives from a stand-offish Old Testament king who lived in an ivory house and didn't know what his people were up to and came to a sticky end. It's used of academics to suggest, rightly, that with a very few exceptions they have no grasp of what goes on in the real world.'

Betsy was frowning with concentration. 'Does figurative mean like a picture in your mind that like helps you get an idea?'

'You've got it. A metaphor.'

Betsy looked blank again.

'Betsy, didn't you tell me earlier that you were studying English?'

'You don't really do like much English as English here, Lady Troutbeck. You've got to see it through different kinds of specialist studies and this year most of my programme is Women's Studies.'

'I take it you learn no grammar, no figures of speech, nothing like that.'

'Our professor says things like that are like repressive and patriarchal.' Betsy laughed. 'Hey, maybe she like lives in an ivory tower and isn't normal like me.'

'So tell me something about you normal people. You're a student. Why are you squiring me about? Why aren't you in the library?'

'My parents don't have much money, so I work as well as study. Mostly I drive visitors around and right now I'm helping look after VIPs. It's really exciting. I get to meet such interesting people.'

'Like whom?'

'Well, like you. You're my second, but I met a lord from England last week. And I've never met a lord before.'

'Who was this English lord?'

'Lord Cunningham. He's another DVP.'

'DVP?'

'Distinguished Visiting Professor.'

'Cunningham? Not Rowley Cunningham? Squat little chap with glasses.'

'He's short and has glasses. He's here like to do a programme at the Peace Centre.'

The baroness snorted. 'Hell and damnation! What a creature to meet up with here. Never could stand the little prat. Talk about giving peace a bad name....'

'He was a bit cross,' said Betsy. 'So were you, but you said sorry.'

'So how was he interesting?'

Betsy giggled. 'I just like said that to be like positive. I thought he was a bit mean really. He shouted at me for being late, but like it wasn't my fault cos he caught an earlier airplane than he said. And then on the way he asked me was I ashamed of living in like the most hated country in the world.'

'Sounds like the little bastard. What did you say?'

'I said I was totally proud to be an American and then he was totally rude about the President being like a war-monger. I don't think it's cool to go to a foreign country and start insulting it the minute you like land.'

'Like I have,' grinned the baroness.

'You've only been rude about silly stuff.'

'I wouldn't call food and drink silly stuff.' The baroness grimaced as she nibbled on a piece of garlic bread. 'Rotten bread. Still, essentially you're right. He had no right to say what he did to a stranger. You did well to stand up to him. America has its faults, but it's a great and generous country and you can usually guarantee that the people who hate it are ignorant or envious shits. Or both.' She pushed away her bread plate and returned miserably to the salad. 'So what were you doing before you went on VIP duty?'

'I was a cheerleader.'

The baroness sat up. 'Really. But wasn't that a hobby, not a job?'

'Oh, no. I got a scholarship for cheerleading and I had to spend 25 hours a week on it.'

'So what happened?'

Betsy looked at her plate. 'I like flunked out.'

'Not good enough?'

'Sort of. But I'm really glad I'm doing this instead.'

'You're a real little Pollyanna, aren't you, Betsy?'

Betsy was confused. 'Pollyanna?'

'Dear God, don't they teach you anything? Pollyanna is a fictional character who was—if my memory serves me—hoping for a dolly from the bran tub.'

'The bran tub?'

'It was, I thought, an American custom to hide prizes in a bran tub and have a lucky dip.'

'Oh.'

'I see we have a generational as well as a cultural chasm, here, Betsy. But we will plough on. Since Pollyanna's father was the clergyman in charge of the bran tub, she was the last to choose, and there was no dolly. Only a crutch.'

Betsy's face crumpled. The baroness feared she saw a tear in her eye and went on hastily, "Yes, indeed. It was very sad, but Pollyanna said that she was glad glad glad that she didn't need the crutch. This was the approach she adopted to all setbacks even when orphaned. In fiction, it made her universally loved. In real life, it can grate. In any case, you remind me of her.'

This time Betsy's eyes were definitely glistening. 'You mean I get on your nerves?'

'No, no. Well, only a very little and not as much as I expect I get on yours. I like you. And though Pollyannas can be annoying, they are much preferable to Eeyores.'

'Eeyores?'

'We'll cover that another time. Now what's next?'

Betsy looked at her watch and jumped up in alarm. 'We must run. It's time to visit with the Provost.'

'Meet my personal assistant, Dr. Ethan Gonzales, Jack.'

The baroness looked with interest at the enormous black man and proffered her hand. 'Delighted to meet you, Dr. Gonzales.' His grip was deliberately firm to the point of being painful, so she strengthened hers and heroically exhibited no sign of discomfort. Looking disappointed, he eventually let her hand go and she sat down opposite the Provost without being asked.

'Any progress with fixing me up for hunting, Helen?'

The Provost tried to hide her distaste. 'I've made some enquiries. There is deer-hunting, but it's only in the autumn and just for two weeks. Someone suggested squirrel-hunting, but there are problems about you having a gun since you're not a citizen. I don't think you'll get a permit.'

'Oh, come now. You're the Provost. I'm sure you can use your influence with the local police-chief. Isn't this supposed to be a gun-toting society?' She swivelled around and gazed at Gonzales, who was glaring at her from the doorway. 'Surely you tote a gun, Dr. Gonzales?'

'Certainly not,' he snapped.

'How disappointing. I'd have expected better from a macho chap like yourself.'

'Less of that stereotyping shit, lady,' said Gonzales.

The Provost cut in. 'Ethan is a pacifist and Freeman U isn't gun-toting, Jack. It's anti-militaristic. No one's allowed guns on campus and we don't allow the military to recruit. But I'll look into whether you can join some kind of hunt and maybe rent a gun. Maybe you could see to that, Ethan?'

'When I have time,' snarled Gonzales, and left the room.

'What a charming man, Helen. I'm sure he'll sort things out for me. I really feel like bagging myself a few stags. But if they're out of season I suppose I'll have to fall back on rodents.'

'Now can we talk about what you'll be doing here? I'm a bit concerned that from something you said last night, you're not in favour of Affirmative Action.'

'You're quite right. I'm a meritocrat. I don't believe in patronising people by lowering standards for them. I'm sure you didn't do that with the enchanting Dr. Gonzales.'

'You're at Freeman U now, Jack, and I hope you'll honour our rules.' She picked a piece of paper from her filing tray and read out:

'Freeman University is an Equal Opportunity/Affirmative Action employer and educational institution and does not discriminate on the basis of age, race, colour, religion, sex, sexual orientation, size, disability, national origin, or Vietnam era or other veteran status, in the admission to, or participation in, any educational program or activity which it conducts, or in any employment policy or practice.'

'Yes, yes, yes, Helen. You don't have to read to me. I'm literate. I don't need Affirmative Action.'

'I just want to be sure we're on the same page, Jack. Of course we want you to think outside the box, but we don't want any disconnects. Frictionless team-playing is our goal at Freeman.'

The baroness scrutinised the document from which the Provost had been reading. 'You've left a category off that list,' she observed.

'What? Where?'

'Species. Should you really be allowing for discrimination on the basis of species? Is my parrot to be denied his equal opportunities?'

The Provost looked at her coldly. 'At Freeman we don't like inappropriate humour, Jack. We are envisioners and empowerers. Not comedians.'

'Oh, I don't know,' said the baroness. 'You shouldn't discriminate against comedians either.

'They've got lawyers too.'

The baroness took a nap after Betsy delivered her back to the hotel. Invigorated, she decided on a stroll before dinner. Within a few minutes she was in a wide and virtually empty street lined by dilapidated Victorian houses, few of which offered much evidence of even partial occupancy. Searching hopefully for a bar, she found signs only for a notary, an accountant, and a realtor before coming to a large area of waste ground full of tin cans and bits of cars. There was no bar on the other side, but a young man in a belted raincoat and a fedora jammed low over his forehead was leaning against a lamppost, smoking. On the front door to his left was an old-fashioned neon sign which read 'M and V Private Investigators. No case too small.'

The baroness nodded at him. 'Do you mean that about too small? Do you do misplaced spectacles and cats up trees?'

He touched his hat in salutation. 'Beats killing time, lady.'

'I don't think it would if it was the cat in my life,' she said with a guffaw. 'Maybe I'll be back to you about the spectacles.'

'So it wasn't a bad day, considering how appallingly it began,' she told Mary Lou that evening. 'I'm having fun winding up the prissy Provost and the unpleasant heavy she calls her PA by pretending I'm dying to go massacring animals, I have a fine office where Horace can be accommodated during the day, a share of an efficient-seeming secretary, an attractive gopher who's a lot brighter than she first seemed, an enemy in the shape of Rowley Cunningham to keep my hand in, and, tomorrow night, I hope I will, inter alia, be meeting the renegade ex-dean at a dinner for faculty and distinguished visitors.'

'You're certainly whining less than last night. Did you find some real food?'

'I invaded the hotel kitchen, bribed the chef, and stood over him until I got a rare steak and hot chips. I also procured a plain green salad with a simple dressing by making it myself and refusing all offers of extraneous ingredients. Various people kept wittering about me breaching safety rules and regulations by even being there, but I ignored them and they retreated.'

'Wise people.'

'Oh, and the bar was open and I found a bottle of wine that was not an insult. Tonight, Horace and I are on the train-free side of the hotel, and tomorrow I intend to get a serious grip on matters culinary. Indeed I plan to carry all before me.'

'Of course you do, Jack.'

'Any word from Robert and Rachel? I rang his mobile phone, but it seems to be out-of-order.'

'As I explained before, Jack, it's switched off. They're set on avoiding avoid any post-wedding hysteria from Rachel's family or demands from you, so they respond only to text messages and emails.'

'I don't have a mobile here so I can't send a text message, even if I knew how. And obviously I can't do emails.'

'If you choose to handicap yourself through intellectual laziness and stubbornness, Jack,' said Mary Lou icily, 'don't expect any sympathy from me.'

There was a silence.

'You're very sharp today.'

'You're very provoking.'

'Well, so be it. I am what I am. You didn't answer my question.'

'I had a brief email from Italy. They're happy.'

'Remind them America awaits them.'

'Sure, Jack. But it's quite clear *they* are not awaiting *it*.'

From: Mary Lou Denslow
To: Robert Amiss
Sent: Mon 15/05/2006 22.15
Subject: Be afraid. Be very afraid

She's bored. She's frustrated. For her to ring two nights in a row—ostensibly to ask about Plutarch, which is improbable enough—but really to moan about her troubles, is unprecedented. She's had a horrid time on the food-and-drink front and the object of her lust has proved to be unworthy, but though she's now showing off about her success in kicking ass rather than simply wailing and fulminating, I detect a whiff of bravado. What's more, she must realise that going on and on about culinary deficiencies is going to win her no friends in her new town.

She's missing us and she's missing Myles and she knows she's been a complete idiot to go where she's gone, but of course she won't admit it. She went so far as to ask about you—not, of course, in the sense of "Are they having a good time? Where are they going next?"—but so she could yet again pass on the info that you would be welcome in Indiana.

Of course you must feel free to sacrifice Austria for New Paddington, but I have faith that you'll resist the temptation. I'm hoping this Indiana experience might teach Jack to value the people in her life more than she does now. I'm an American. I believe in redemption. But suffering has to come first.

Love,

ML

Chapter Five

The baroness was in a much sunnier mood the following morning after a ten-hour sleep and an edible breakfast consisting of a fresh orange (which on her insistence had been kept at room temperature), two boiled eggs (disparaged for blandness, but eaten), and rye bread. The hotel manager, just back from his long weekend, was summoned to her room, where she was cleaning out Horace's cage and trying to teach him to sing 'Pardon me, boy, is that the Chattanooga Choo-Choo?' As she answered the door, Horace had got bored listening and was complaining that he was only a bird in a gilded cage. To the baroness's horror, he followed that up with an ear-splitting 'Whoo! Whoo! Wah! Wah!'

'He thinks he's a freight-train,' she explained to the thirty-something with dark curly hair and a tentative smile, who came into her room and bowed. 'I am Stefano Ricciano, Lady Troutbeck. At your service.'

'You mean you're Italian? That augurs well.'

'American-Italian. But still Italian.' He beamed. 'You like Italians?'

'Well, you may not be people to go into the jungle with, but you are…'—she cleared her throat dramatically to herald that she was attempting to speak in a foreign language—'…sym*pati*co. In general you certainly add to the gaiety of nations. And from what I've seen so far, this is one nation that needs all the gaiety it can get.'

'Beverages!' roared Horace. 'Beverages! Beverages!'

Ricciano jumped. 'So your little bird talks as well as whistles.'

'All sounds are grist to his mill, if you follow that convoluted metaphor.' She went over to the cage, where Horace was swinging himself on the door, and picked him up. 'Come and meet Mr. Ricciano, Horrie. Mr. Ricciano, this is Horace.' Ricciano stretched out his finger and she grabbed it. 'No, no. Don't touch him. He bites pretty well everyone, I'm sorry to say. But otherwise he's gregarious. Perhaps you might teach him a little Italian. He already knows "Bravo!"'.

'Perhaps another time, Signora. You had some problems you wanted to tell me about?'

'Call for some Prosecco, Mr. Ricciano, and we'll discuss it.'

'Alas, Signora, we have no Prosecco, but if you have finished tending to the little bird, please come downstairs and we will find what the bar has to offer.'

An hour later, they approached the end of room inspections and complex negotiations.

'It is not as good as the bridal suite, Signora, but I am glad you are satisfied.'

'Well, if the price of getting the bridal suite is to get married, it's too high a price for me.'

'What a pity, Signora. You are a loss to matrimony.'

'It's hard to flatter me too much, Mr. Ricciano, but you've almost reached that point. I can't imagine any of my friends visualising me as a blushing bride.'

'I remain to be convinced.'

'What I want to be convinced of is that the fridge will be installed by the time I get back with the groceries.'

'That was confirmed in that last phone call I took. It will be in your room by midday.'

'Excellent.'

'And all your possessions will have been transferred by then too. Do you wish to look after Horace yourself, Signora? Or shall I move him?'

'I'll install him in the non-bridal suite before I leave the hotel. Now, you won't forget to tell the chef that he is to cook what I provide him with in the manner in which I instruct him?'

'Of course not, Signora. I'll do that right away.'

'And you are sure that I can rely on the parrot being looked after in emergencies? However long they last?'

'I come of Sicilian stock, Signora. You have my word and my cell-phone number. Ring me any time in an emergency.' He paused. 'You do know what I mean by an emergency?'

'Yes, yes,' she said impatiently. 'When I need something.'

'No, Signora. I have a job. I have a family. When you need something that is truly important and there is no one else to call, that is an emergency.'

She looked at him with mingled irritation and respect. 'Dying parrot but not overdone steak, you mean?'

He took her hand and kissed it. 'I think we will do well, Signora.'

'It's no good, Betsy. Any more of this and I'll explode.' She extracted her diary from her handbag, opened it and handed it over. 'Ring this number and then pass me the phone.'

'It's an emergency, Mr. Ricciano. And I mean an emergency. I'm in a supermarket the size of the Colosseum and I can't find anything I want. Even the simplest products are mucked up. There are fifty kinds of milk. When it isn't described as "lite" it's full of additives. There are a hundred kinds of flavoured coffee, mostly decaffeinated. Who in hell's name wants blasted flavoured coffee? And there are miles and miles of plastic bread, and what they call 'flavoursome fruit' look like the product of some plastic factory and…'

'Whoa, whoa, Signora. Calm down. Calm down. You should have consulted me.'

'I would have, had I realised you can't get food in American supermarkets. Now what do I do?'

'Pass the phone to your little Betsy and I will tell her how to find the delicatessen my wife and I shop in.'

'What do you eat at home?'

'My wife's cooking. It is beautiful. She cooks just like her mamma. And mine.'

'You mean real food?' asked the baroness suspiciously.

'Yes, yes, Signora. Real food. Ragouts and pastas and saltimbocca and it is all bellissimo. You should come home with me for dinner sometime.'

'I'll come tonight if that's all right, Mr. Ricciano. Now, before I pass you to Betsy, just one question. If you like real food, why do you serve garbage in the hotel?'

'We serve what the customers like, Signora. And most of them like it.'

'I find that hard to believe,' she grunted, and returned the phone to Betsy.

◇◇◇

'We'll have a picnic in my suite, Betsy,' said the baroness, as they staggered towards the car.

'Sorry, Lady Troutbeck....'

'Oh, God. Of course. You're banned. Any idea why?'

'I think there was like some trouble,' said Betsy hesitantly.

'This is ridiculous,' said the baroness. 'I wish to feed you, not corrupt you.' She dumped the bags beside the car. 'Get me the Provost.'

The Provost caved without a fight.

'I'm glad you've seen sense, Helen. Now I want you to ring the hotel manager immediately and tell him I can entertain any Freeman student anywhere I want—bedroom, bar, anywhere. And the same applies to the bars in town, if there are any.... What?...Only two....Don't be so sure I wouldn't like them. It's already clear our tastes are dissimilar. Give me a letter of authorisation tonight saying that the rules barring students are waived if they are accompanied by Lady Troutbeck. Is that understood?…Good. And by the way, has what's his name?…yes, yes, Gonzales, sorted out my hunting needs yet?…No?…Tell him to get a move on.'

Betsy, who had been industriously packing the groceries into the car boot, gazed at the baroness in awe. 'Did you meet Dr. Gonzales when you visited with the Provost, Lady Troutbeck?'

'Indeed I did. Ugly piece of work in more ways than one. And uncouth. Which is a criticism I rarely level at anyone, for obvious reasons.'

'So you're not scared of him?'

The baroness snorted. 'You have to show two-bit bullies like that who's boss.'

'Hey, you really know like how to kick butt, don't you?'

'Comes easily to Troutbecks. Does it come easily to…what's your surname?'

'Brown.'

'Does it come easily to Browns?'

'To some, but not others,' said Betsy quietly.

'You're not one of the butt-kicking Browns, I surmise. Who is?'

'Mom….Hold on, you're getting in on the driver's side.'

'It's very annoying this business of you Americans driving on the wrong side,' grumbled the baroness as she walked around to the passenger door.

'Don't you drive on the right in Europe?'

'No. Well, that is, we don't in the United Kingdom. They do in the rest of Europe.'

'So why don't you change?'

'Change is bad,' said the baroness. 'Unless it's change I approve of, that is. And I don't approve of driving on the right. Now get going. I can't wait to eat some of that mortadella.'

Replete, the baroness sat back and looked about her happily. Horace was nibbling contentedly on a fig, and Betsy was finishing a large plateful of antipasti with relish. 'There now,' said the baroness, 'there's more to eat in New Paddington than muck. Now if only I could persuade you to drink wine rather than Diet Coke....'

'Oh, I do, Lady Troutbeck. I drink lots of things. But I can't be seen doing it in public. And I wouldn't like risk it when I'm driving a Freeman U automobile.'

'So the rules are ignored?'

'They totally are.'

'But you told me no one disobeyed Gonzales's rules.'

Betsy looked at her warily. 'There are some rules Dr. Gonzales minds about. And others he doesn't seem to much. We party a lot here. Half the campus is wasted every night.'

'Is it really? I thought it was completely dominated by prigs like the Provost. Perhaps Gonzales is a cavalier at heart.'

'What's a cavalier?'

'I'll spare you the historical background for now, Betsy. Essentially it's someone who likes to enjoy himself.'

'Or herself. I guess you're a cavalier, Lady Troutbeck.'

'You guess correctly. That's why I often wear feathers in my hats. Now tell me, do cheerleaders participate in this Bacchanalia?' She saw Betsy's expression. 'I mean do cheerleaders drink?'

'Do cheerleaders drink? I can't believe you asked that, Lady Troutbeck. You gotta be like totally kidding. Haven't you read the paper?'

'What paper?'

Betsy looked shifty. 'Sorry, nothing. Just papers like go on about students sometimes. Anyway, you bet students drink.'

'Well, well. Who'd have thought it of such Barbie dolls.' The baroness caught sight of Betsy's expression. 'Oh, sorry, Betsy, I didn't mean you. That is, you may look like a Barbie doll, but you don't talk like one. Except for your strange turns of phrase, of course.'

Betsy laughed. 'You're just so like totally tactless, aren't you?'

'So people tell me. Can't see it myself. Anyway, back to the cheerleading. So these Barbies drink. Are they looking for Dutch courage?'

Betsy's brow furrowed. 'Dutch courage? What's that?'

'Courage sought through alcohol. I'm amazed you don't know that.'

'Oh, yeah. I remember now. It's on the banned list of racist terms.'

'Oh, God. Well, anyway, do Barbies resort to it?' Absently, she refilled her glass with Sancerre.

Betsy chuckled. 'Hey, you couldn't drink before a game. You could kill yourself. Or someone else.'

'Running around cheering?'

'I guess you've never seen cheerleaders in action?'

'No. We don't do it in England as far as I know.'

'It's totally a sport here. I trained for like fifteen years.'

'What! Trained at doing what?'

'Gymnastics, mainly. Jumping and tumbling and twisting and lifting and so on and then you've got to learn to do everything in like close formation and develop squad stunts. Here at Freeman U we end our routine with a pyramid twenty feet high.'

'How extraordinary.'

Betsy jumped up, ran to the door, took aim and managed three backflips before she hit the opposite wall. 'That's like baby stuff, but you get the idea? And, of course, you have to be able to chant too.'

The baroness was agog. 'Chant? Chant? The only kind of chant I know about is Gregorian, but I expect what you do is different. Give me a sample.'

'You have to have pom poms to do it properly.' Betsy picked two small cushions off the sofa, jumped her legs wide apart, and leaped up and down as she moved the cushions in circles to the right and circles to the left and chanted:

Buckle down,
Buckle down,
Do it, do it, do it!

Buckle down,
Buckle down,
Do it, do it, do it!

'Or,' she added, 'there's "Go! Go! Go, Fight, Win, Freeman U!", which we might chant a dozen times. Or—now you gotta imagine one of these poms poms is crimson and the other is blue, cos you shake them according to which colour you're chanting about—we'd do:

How about,
How about,
How about,
How about a colour shout?
Crimson, crimson,
Blue, blue, blue, blue, blue, blue, blue,
Crimson, crimson,
Blue, blue, blue, blue, blue, blue, blue!

She threw the cushions back on the sofa.

'Thank you, Betsy,' said the baroness, who had been watching transfixed. 'I don't think I'll be taking it up. Why did you stop? Did you say you were fired?'

'It's complicated,' said Betsy. 'I'll tell you sometime. Now, aren't we supposed to be like going to your office?'

'Good Lord, is that the time? Come on, Horace. Back in the cage. We'd better rush. I had a date to sort a few things out with Marjorie. Just drop me off there and don't wait. I'll walk back.'

'Walk?' said Betsy. 'Nobody walks.'

'I walk, Betsy. Otherwise I'd be as fat as an American.'

'Are you going to dinner dressed like that, Lady Troutbeck?'

'I hadn't given it any thought, Marjorie. I don't have to be there for another couple of hours.'

'It's a quarter after five now.'

'So?'

'Drinks begin at 6.00, you'll be sittin' by 6.30, when the speeches begin.'

'Oh, hell.'

'Would you mind not blaspheming, Lady Troutbeck? I'm a Christian. We don't take the name of the Lord in vain.'

'*Il ne manquait que ça,*'* muttered the baroness, falling back for comfort on one of the few French phrases she knew. ('It took me all my self-control,' she told Mary Lou later, 'but the biggest rule of survival in the academic jungle is to keep secretaries sweet.') 'I'll try, Marjorie,' she said, with as much humility as she could muster. 'But if I fail, you will, I hope, forgive me. I come from a secular culture and I have a loose tongue.'

Tall, elegant, stern Marjorie Heath Maloy visibly unbent. 'Gotya, Lady Troutbeck. You'll be pleased to know that even religious people say rude words in Texas. It just cussin' we don't like.'

'I'm a bit fogged about the distinction, Marjorie, but it sounds like good news. Now why is this dinner so early?'

'It's the normal time. Do you eat later in England?'

'Blimey!' The baroness looked nervously at Marjorie, to whom fortunately the blasphemous origins of the word seemed unknown. 'We certainly do. Now what'll I do?'

'I'll take you back to the hotel and wait while you change into your glad rags.'

'Thank you,' said the baroness, as she headed for the door. 'What's suitable? Top hat? White tie? Tails?'

'You needn't put on the Ritz, Lady Troutbeck,' said Marjorie with a smile. 'A nice frock will be just dandy.'

'Who's going to be there, Marjorie?' asked the baroness, now resplendent in an intricately knitted Missoni dress of red, mauve, and purple. Since purchasing an entire job-lot of designer garments that had been donated to a Cambridge Oxfam shop

---

*'It needed only that.'

by a woman of her own generous proportions, the baroness was beginning to develop a reputation as a bit of a fashionista.

'Didn't the Provost give you the list?'

'She gave me a ton of paper, but I ignored it. She'd been reading me some stuff I thought was guff, so I assumed all this was guff as well and anyway today I had pressing matters to attend to.'

'In that case you'd better bring all that paper along to the office tomorrow and I'll show you what's important. You need to know your schedule. As for tonight, there will be you and the other three DVPs as well as the President, several deans, a half-dozen or so senior professors, and Martin Freeman, who's the Chairman of the Board of Trustees and whose family bankrolled the university. Some wives will be there as well.'

'Will Professor Godber be there?'

'Why do you ask?'

'Just something I heard about him made me interested in meeting him.'

Marjorie looked at her curiously. 'I don't know. Warren Godber doesn't socialise much. And I don't know that he'd be invited anyway. It'll be mostly people…' she chose her words carefully, 'closer to the administration.'

'Will we have speeches inflicted on us?'

Marjorie gave a slight smile. 'You sure will. After all, you'll be making one yourself.'

'I will? Shit! What about?'

'Didn't the Provost tell you?'

'Maybe she did, but what with all the travel and jet-lag and general fuss, I'm afraid I didn't take it in. What do I have to do?'

'Just five minutes or so on why you've come here and what you hope to do should be fine.'

'I wish I'd given that some thought, Marjorie. However, no doubt something will occur to me.'

'President Dickinson, may I present Lady Troutbeck?'

Dickinson—expensively coiffed, orange-tanned, and smooth-faced—wrung the baroness's hand firmly and gazed into her eyes with an expression of deep sincerity. 'May I bid you a hearty welcome to Freeman University, Lady Troutbeck? We are honoured to have a person of such distinction visiting with us.'

'Greetings from the United Kingdom, President. It's an honour to be invited to be part of such a fine institution, even for such a short time.'

Dickinson introduced her cursorily to his more darkly tanned wife, an anxious bottle-blonde with enormous lips who looked half his age, and then began a welcome speech to Rowland Cunningham.

'Can I get you a cocktail, Lady Troutbeck?' asked Traci Dickinson.

'You certainly can. Gin and tonic…no, no, on second thoughts, I'll have whisky. Large, bottled water, no ice.'

Her drink arrived quickly. As she took it from Traci, she was impressed by her nails, which were painted fuchsia, elaborately etched with a yellow that matched her dress, and were so long they seemed almost to encircle the glass. Within a few minutes, the chore of listening to Cunningham, who was oozing unctuousness, caused the baroness to request another whisky. The discovery that she also knew and despised the other two Distinguished Visiting Professors caused her to ask for a second refill. The third she took to the dinner table, for she had seen with alarm that there was, as yet, no sign of any wine. Just ubiquitous jugs of chlorinated iced water.

She was placed between Dickinson and the pleasant, rubicund Martin Freeman, who seemed anxious to tell her about Indiana's history. 'I'm a Hoosier through and through,' he explained, 'and proud of it.' As she was about to request an explanation for this perplexing statement, the President asked the gathering to bow their heads and said grace. 'Now,' he added, 'before we tuck into a hearty meal, we are fortunate that our four distinguished visiting professors have kindly consented to share with us their mission statements.

'Before I call on our speakers, can I just welcome all of you this evening, particularly our DVPs, who we know will add lustre to our campus. To them I say that here at Freeman U we have three goals we pursue passionately: the welfare of our students, the embracing of diversity, and the lighting of beacons of excellence that lead all our young people to high educational achievement. Our DVPs are four such beacons and we know they will inspire our students to strain every sinew to bring academic and sporting credit to their beloved school.

'As I always remind my colleagues, we can never stand still at Freeman U: innovation will always be at the forefront of our strategy, along with the challenge of change. There will always be enemies who will seek to undermine our great mission, but we will take them on and we will win.'

He paused for sycophantic applause, which was forthcoming.

'Now, I call on Lady Ida Troutbeck. All our DVPs are remarkable people, but even by their standards, Lady Ida is exceptional. Not only does she head up the University of Cambridge, but she's a senior member of the British parliament and an aristocrat. We are more grateful than we can say that she has taken time out of her busy schedule to be with us for a half-semester. Lady Ida.'

'It wasn't an absolute catastrophe,' she explained later to Mary Lou. 'But it was close. I had expected to speak after dinner, not before, and probably last because of alphabetical order, and my mind was reeling with the discovery that in addition to the appalling Rowley Cunningham, the other members of the job-lot of DVPs—as we are known—that Helen Fortier-Prichardson acquired on her trip to England were that ghastly New Labour stick-insect Constance Darlington....'

'Oh, that's funny. What was it she said about you during that debate about House of Lords reform? I seem to remember you two had a particular face-off.'

'Don't remember. The usual stuff about dinosaurs and the Stone Age, I expect. I remember denouncing her as a constitutional and cultural illiterate and vandal, which of course she is, but she took it rather badly. The cow has no discernible sense of humour, naturally. Like all lefties.'

'What about Woody Allen?'

'He doesn't count.'

'Oh, get on with it, Jack.'

'There's worse.'

'Worse than what?'

'Worse than Constance Darlington.'

'Who could that be? Jack the Ripper?'

'Jimmy Rawlings.'

'You've made my day, Jack. Mind you, I should have guessed she'd want someone ethnic.'

'That ethnic? Burn-out-whitey ethnic? Allah-the-merciless-who-will-root-out-the-infidel ethnic?'

'That's religious rather than ethnic. Anyway, your Provost was probably as ignorant about him as she is about you. Perhaps he'll liven things up.'

'He may do so. How he got into the country is beyond me when you think Horace was almost clapped in chains. Anyway, as you can imagine, I was somewhat preoccupied between wondering what a Hoosier was....'

'You can't have done two seconds reading on Indiana if you didn't know that's what the natives call themselves.'

'I haven't. So be it. Stop interrupting. Do you want to hear about my speech or not?'

'Oh, I do. I do.'

'I hadn't thought of anything to say—and since I hadn't even looked at my time-table I hadn't a clue what I was expected to be doing while I'm here or even what faculty I'm assigned to, and I had to start by correcting the President's mad claims about me. By the time I'd managed that—without, I hope, making the idiot feel as silly as he deserved and me seem disappointingly unimportant—I burbled about the common cultural values of Britain and the United States and then explained that my mission was to learn more about their wonderful country.

'I thought a bit of light relief wouldn't be a bad thing, so, since it's much on my mind, I explained I'd been having cultural difficulties with their cuisine. "There was a stage earlier today," I told them at one point, "when I thought New Paddington was a culinary desert and that I would end my stay as skinny as Lady Darlington. I couldn't even get an egg that tasted of anything." Then, to make them laugh, I added that I'd even toyed with the idea of driving out into the prairie to scratch around for a Red Indian who had free-range chickens. I thought I detected bafflement, so I pointed out that if you couldn't find an Indian in Indiana, where would you find one.'

'Oh, God. You didn't. I'm surprised you haven't been deported.'

'Well, a combination of a boo from Jimmy Rawlings and a general sharp and noisy intake of breath made me realise something was wrong, so I muttered something about having found a wonderful delicatessen that had solved all my problems, added that everyone was warm and welcoming and that I was sure I would be very happy in New Paddington, and sat down to what was only just a light patter of applause. The smarmy president then explained that Lady Troutbeck would in time come to love the unparalleled and diverse cuisine of Indiana and that I needed to know that at Freeman U, Indians were called First Citizens, since these were the people from whom the country had been stolen. Then Rowley Cunningham made a leftie speech about world peace and the evils of neo-imperialism that went down well with everyone except Martin Freeman, who turns out to be a Republican. Constance droned on mind-numbingly about human rights and Jimmy Rawlings said his mission was to eradicate inequality and discrimination from the face of the universe or something like that and to stand up for victims everywhere.'

'How did the rest of the evening go?'

'Great mounds of horrendous food and a very little horrible wine. Still, I made myself a modest feast of salami and cheese when I got back here and the California merlot I've acquired is really rather good.'

'I wasn't asking about food.'

'Why ever not?'

'Get on with it, Jack.'

'Oh, all right. Freeman was OK. He's the fourth generation of Freemans, who've been the main funders of this university for decades. The family firm continues to make a fortune out of spare parts for cars and Freeman is a big time philanthropist. I hope I may in due course be able to charm a couple of million out of him for St. Martha's. Freeman likes England and was pleasantly surprised that we were on much the same side in politics since he thought all academics were left-wing. I made quite a speech to him about my respect for American self-reliance and can-do, which went down well.'

'Did you get any gossip about the university from him?'

'Not really. He talked mainly about the history of New Paddington. Apparently it was once a steel town. When the mills died, New Paddington died. Any questions I asked about the university were batted away. He seemed uneasy talking about it at all.'

'And the President?'

'Regurgitates platitudes rather than conversing, ex-Wall Street, lives for fund-raising and has no discernible interest in anything of the mind. However he got lively once. When the first lot of plates were removed, revealed in front of each of us was a circular piece of paper with a picture of a sword in a rather elaborate silver scabbard, on which was written "TRUTH" in gold and, on the hilt, an acronym—"VCR" or something.'

'This was an ad for video cassette recorders?'

'No, no, no. It certainly wasn't an ad. Judging by Dickinson's barely contained fury, it was more like a threat. Wait a minute and I'll get my copy—which I held on to despite Dickinson's best efforts.' She was back in a moment. 'It's VRC, not VCR. And no, I've no idea what it stands for except that it made the President and the Provost cross, Gonzales was breathing fire, and Martin Freeman looked thoughtful. I asked Dickinson what it meant, and he said something curt about student pranks and told me to throw it away. So obviously I immediately hand-bagged it.'

'VRC? VRC? We had a Video Resource Centre in my university.'

'What's that got to do with anything? It might as well be Vassar Rowing Club. However, no doubt all will be clear in time. It was, in any case, a welcome episode, though soon I was back to chit-chat with the president about his dreary goals. I'd have fallen asleep at the table had it not been that the whole event mercifully ended at 9.15. I gather that they all get up at about 4.00, so I may have to become less nocturnal.'

'Then you should go to bed now, Jack.'

'I intend to. Any word from Robert?'

'They've reached the Czech Republic. They seem to like it. Then on to Slovenia or Slovakia or one of those places.'

'Did he say anything about Indiana?'

'Just that it sounded like the last place on earth he wanted to visit.'

The baroness bit her bottom lip. 'Pity,' she said. 'Tell him that things are hotting up and he and Rachel still have time to change their minds.'

Chapter Six

Within two days, the baroness and Marjorie had reached an understanding. Having swiftly accepted that her secretary was intelligent, sane, and ultra-competent, the baroness had surrendered herself into her power where all practical matters were concerned. For her part, Marjorie appreciated having her worth recognised: while the baroness deferred to her, the other three DVPs treated her like a flunkey. And once Marjorie had cross-questioned the baroness about how she ran St. Martha's and they had established that maintaining academic standards was a joint passion, they became partners in bile. 'I wouldn't pee on the Provost if she was on fire,' was a sentiment Marjorie produced on the third day with which the baroness heartily concurred. Dr. Ethan Gonzales—who, it emerged, liked to be known as The Enforcer—she referred to as the Goon.

'Are Provost and Goon an item?'

'They deny it. They've worked together for years and they call themselves a team. I don't know if they screw. But that would break the rules so they wouldn't admit that anyway.'

'Is he as much of a plug-ugly as he looks?'

Marjorie cast her eyes to heaven. 'Is Bill Clinton a skirt-chaser?'

'I may have led a sheltered life, Marjorie, but though I've met many academics, I've never come across one who acts like an understudy for Mike Tyson in a bad mood.'

'Academic? The Goon's dumber than a box full of hammers, Ph.D. or no Ph.D. Just because you put a boot in the oven don't mean it's a biscuit. He's just a jumped-up minder, but he's good at bein' frightenin'.'

'And is that essentially his job?'

'Yep.'

'This campus takes some getting used to. Even Horace is a bit subdued.'

'Wouldn't it be simpler to have a permanent cage for him here, Jack? That way you could transport him in his carrier rather than hoistin' that cage over and back.'

'But where would I get a cage? It's been difficult enough to get bird seed.'

'You leave that to me. And don't you worry about payin' for it. I have enough money in the DVP expenses budget to burn a wet dog, as my granny used to say. And the others are already dippin' in there good.'

'For what?'

'Rawlings spends a lot taking people out to eat. I don't know where he finds so many people.'

'He's probably financing the local Islamist terrorist cell.'

'And limo hire for the three of them. They wanted a proper chauffeur, not a student.'

The baroness frowned. 'Does that reduce Betsy's income?'

'I guess so.'

'In that case I want her given as many hours as she needs working as my research assistant.'

'I'll organise that.'

'And will the budget run to buying me decent food?'

'Don't see why not. You need your nourishment. Give me some idea of what's involved and I'll organise an allowance for your special dietary requirements.'

'Thank you very much, Marjorie. You've cheered me up and God knows...sorry, Marjorie...dear knows, I need cheering up. The President's trophy wife has asked me and Constance

Darlington to dinner tonight to keep her company while her husband's in Chicago. Goodness knows why.'

'Because Traci Troutpout….'

'Her surname is Troutpout? Extraordinary. I wonder if they're related to the Troutbecks. I hope not.'

'It's a nickname for what your lips look like if you overdo the collagen implants.'

'Ah, that's why they're so huge. I thought she'd maybe had some Negro ancestry. Ooops, no, I'm not allowed to say that, am I? I should be saying "African-American." Really, Marjorie, normal conversation is very difficult in this country.'

Marjorie smiled indulgently. 'Don't let it worry you. It's not as if you're looking for tenure. Anyway, it's nothing to do with Traci's ancestry. Just her busy cosmetic surgeon. And the reason she's invited you two, I guess, is that she can't stick her husband bein' the centre of attention, and she wants to show you two that with the rooster away, she's the queen-of-the-walk in the henhouse.'

'How will she do that?'

'Showin' off. She's that dumb she thinks she'll impress you with her acquisitions. She shits and flies, that woman.'

'You've lost me, Marjorie.'

'Granny again,' said Marjorie, smiling. 'It means new money showin' off. You'll find out tonight.'

'Hey, Lady Troutbeck. You're looking good today.'

'You too, Betsy. Are you well?'

'I'm good, thanks. And thanks for inviting me to lunch.'

'You need building up. Right, I'm finished here. 'Bye, Marjorie. See you later.'

'Before you go, Jack, here's your cell phone.'

The baroness peered at it suspiciously. 'I don't know how to use it. It's different from my mobile back home. Looks very complicated.'

'Why don't you stop grumblin' and go get lunch? I'll teach you later.'

'All right. Come on, Betsy, we'll walk to the hotel.'

'Like walk?'

'Like walk.'

'That's totally cool.'

The baroness saw and learned a lot during the walk that depressed her. 'Why do students eat all the time?'

'Do they?'

'Look. That one's eating crisps. And the one with her is scoffing a bar of something. And half of them are glugging something out of a bottle.' She stopped. 'Look at that crowd beside that building. They're all eating hamburgers.'

'That's because they're like going to have to fast in a minute. Look at the banner.'

The baroness squinted into the sunlight. 'PLAY POVERTY. What's that?'

'It's like a sociology programme. You get a credit for like spending lunchtime role-playing being poor, so you don't get much to eat.'

'You're having me on.'

Betsy shook her head. The baroness was so appalled she didn't speak for two minutes. Then she burst out, 'Why do they all dress so horribly?'

Betsy was puzzled. 'Horribly?'

'Look at that group.' They stopped and surveyed it. 'Those girls in long, skin-tight rubber knickers, whatever they're called?'

'They really are, like, called knickers. They're for sports. You know, cycling and that.'

'Where are the bicycles?'

'They probably don't do like sports. People wear them cos they like them.'

'My God, how can they like them?' cried the baroness. 'Look, the thin girls can just about get away with them, awful as they are, but look at that fat one. She's bulging out all over.'

Betsy shrugged. 'People wear what they want.'

'This place is turning me into a body fascist.' The baroness jabbed her finger towards the group. 'Look at those boys with those hideous long, baggy shorts.' She shook her head. 'Yecchh! And those grotesque multi-coloured ones?'

'Oh, they're board shorts. Everyone thinks they're like really cool.'

'Why are they called that?'

'I think it's to do with them having been like invented for surf boarding.'

'If you're surfing, at least the waves cover you. What possible excuse is there to wear them to class?'

Betsy shrugged again. The baroness looked at her in despair. 'Are you telling me you could see one of these as a sex object?'

Betsy shot her a startled look. 'You mean would I like date one?'

'Look at that fellow there. He's got a Hawaiian shirt. And that one. His stomach's flopping over his waistband. And like all the other clones, he's wearing a stupid baseball hat backwards. Whey do they even need hats? I'm not suggesting they dress like Cary Grant....'

'Like who?'

'He's an elegant dead film star, Betsy, whom, being a realist, I'm not suggesting they emulate, but why do they have to dress so repellently? Or am I just so old-fashioned I don't realise they look divine.'

Betsy laughed. 'I'm not too keen on the look either. I think guys look cuter in like jeans and sweatshirts and showing their hair.'

'So what's the reason for the fashion?'

'Fashion's fashion. Why are my shorts frayed? Because it's fashion. It's the way it is.'

'But you look good in them. Mind you, you'd look good in anything.' Another group of students passed in front of them. The baroness shook her head. 'That's another thing—though I admit this is not peculiar to the U.S. Why do so many people pay good money to wear advertising slogans? Isn't that the wrong way round? Shouldn't you get the advertisers to pay you?'

'I never thought of that.'

The baroness lost interest in her own rant. 'What's that building?'

'The undergrads' library.'

'And what's that flag flying from the top? It's not the Stars and Stripes. Is it a university flag?'

'No.'

'Well, what is it?'

'I don't know.'

'Can you make out the lettering? It's too small for me.'

'Sorry, Lady Troutbeck, I can't make it out either.'

'How good is the library?'

'They say it's got hundreds of thousands of books, but they're like going to get rid of most of them because there isn't much demand.'

The baroness stopped dead and gazed at her in horror. 'How can students do without books?'

'We don't get assigned them much. We get handouts of the bits we need or we like do research on the web. The Provost told the student newspaper that undergrads don't need books. They need…what did she call it?…software suites.'

'Which are?'

'Computer centres, I guess. The Provost said like students needed to acquire skills that suited their career path. And they came from like computers, not books.'

'The woman's a barbarian. That's not what I think a university education is about.'

'In Freeman it is,' said Betsy quietly. 'Nowadays people think you're like a freak if you read. That's why I'm hoping to make it to Honour College. I've heard it's different there. They still have reading circles and all. Though I heard the Dean's cracking down on what they can read. A lot of books have like been banned as inappropriate.'

The reason Betsy had failed to get into Honour College as a freshman, she explained, had to do with so much of her time at high school being given over to cheerleading.

'Why didn't your parents insist you spend more time on study?'

'My mom insisted I spend more time on cheerleading,' said Betsy bleakly. 'You ever heard of soccer moms?'

'Mothers who get over-enthusiastic about how their sons do at soccer?'

'Something like that. Well Mom was the cheerleading equivalent. She took me to cheerleading gyms, to cheer camp, we watched cheer competition tapes. She never like let up. Not for a minute.'

'Did you enjoy it?'

'Not really. I wasn't that good so I was always anxious. But Mom said I just had to try harder so I did and I got like the scholarship so I could go to college.'

'But did you want to get to college to cheerlead?'

'I had to get to college. If you don't get to college you've no future. No one will like hire you except to fill shelves at Wal-Mart.'

'Ridiculous.'

'Isn't it like that in England?'

The baroness grunted. 'The bloody government is trying hard to make it like that. But it's all wrong. Universities are for people who genuinely want to learn. Not for people who want a piece of paper.'

'I'd like to learn. But being a cheerleader doesn't like leave much time for study. It was as much as I could do to complete basic assignments. It's not just the practising and the performing. It's like the socialising. You can't like get out of it if you want to be popular and if you're not popular, you won't be picked for the team. "You work hard. You play hard. You get on the team." That's what Coach was always saying.'

'But you were fired.'

'Yep.'

'Because you weren't popular?'

'Something like that,' said Betsy, opening the hotel door for the baroness. 'Anyway, I'm glad really cos this job takes less time and you don't have to worry about like breaking your leg.'

When she was satisfied that Betsy had had enough to eat, the baroness said, 'I'm curious. People have said things to me about low standards on campus. What's your experience?'

Betsy looked at her nervously. 'I work for the Provost's office, Lady Troutbeck.'

'I'm not going to tell the Provost—or anyone else—anything you say.'

'But there's been like hassle about this and Dr. Gonzales said if I said anything to anyone I'd be in trouble.' She shuddered.

'Are you talking about the stories in the *Sentinel?*'

Betsy relaxed. 'So you've seen it. I thought all the copies had been like removed from campus. And the hotel.'

'They may have been. But some enterprising person brought in some more last night and I happened to pick up a copy.'

'So that's why you invited me to lunch?'

'It's why I invited you to lunch today. I'd have invited you soon in any case. I like you.'

'Even if I'm Pollyanna.'

'Maybe it's because you're Pollyanna. There's not that much going on that I find it easy to be glad glad glad about. However, I'd be pleased if you wouldn't look on the bright side when you're telling me about campus standards. I'd like the dirt.'

'If I promise to tell you, will you order me up some cheesecake from downstairs?'

The baroness groaned. 'You exact a high price, Betsy.'

'It's a Faustian pact.'

Betsy swallowed her last forkful of cheesecake. 'What's that?'

'Faust was a chap who sold his soul to the devil in exchange for knowledge and power. In this case, your teachers—though that's clearly the wrong term—sell their souls to the students in exchange for a job.'

'It's like tough for them, Lady Troutbeck. They're on contract and they won't get renewed unless they get like the numbers and the positive student assessments. And they won't get the numbers and the positive assessments unless the students like them. And the students won't like them if they make them work and don't give them like good grades.'

'Unless the students want to learn and the teachers are inspirational?'

'Sure. But if you're going to college because you have to go to college, if you like just want your degree or you have to pay your own way or you just like want to drink and screw around all the time, what kind of teacher are you going to want? Most kids totally want the one that gives you the handouts that mean you don't like even have to go to the library, that tells you the questions before the test, that doesn't care if you like copy stuff off the net, that lets you have a half hour to do a test that's supposed to be done in five minutes, that tells you bad spelling and punctuation don't matter, and that rounds the marks up.'

'Is that what you want, Betsy?'

'No. I want to come out of college like knowing something, not having to ask you what you're talking about all the time because I'm like totally ignorant. I didn't have time to learn anything much at high school. But it doesn't seem to me as if the college cares about anything except like getting my money and shutting me up. No one ever says we should like think. They say we shouldn't.'

'Do many students feel like you?'

'A few.' Betsy looked at the baroness and grinned. 'I guess some of them have been talking with the *Sentinel*.'

'Ah, yes. The VRC. That was their flag on the library, wasn't it, Betsy? I could see what looked like a sword and the letter V?'

She nodded.

'So why didn't you say? Are you one of them, Betsy?'

Betsy looked at her in terror. 'No, no. Don't even go there. Do you know what would happen if they thought I was?'

'Who's they?'

'The Provost and her office.'

'They'd fire you.'

'That'd be only the start.'

'Are you really scared?'

'Everyone's scared of the Provost and Dr. Gonzales.'

'I'm not.'

'You're not scared of anyone though. But then you're not us.'

'I can't fault that analysis, Betsy. Now back to the VRC. You're not one of them, but do you know anything about them? What VRC stands for, for instance?'

'I've no idea. None. And if you'll excuse me, Lady Troutbeck, I've got to go now. I've got a class.'

On her way back to her office, the baroness took a detour along a familiar street, unaware that she was being followed at a distance of about fifty yards by a thin, spotty youth. The young man was there again, smoking, though this time he was leaning against the bonnet of an old, blue car.

As she walked towards him, he took a final drag of his cigarette and flipped the butt into the gutter. She stopped, and her follower dodged into a nearby porch.

'Still killing time?' she asked.

'Let's say if you ain't found those specs yet, lady, I'll take on the case.'

'We could discuss it. What's that car, by the way?'

'A 1953 Chevy.'

The baroness was enchanted. 'My God, you've actually got a beat-up Chevrolet.'

'You want a ride?'

'Do I just,' she said. With one hand, he opened the passenger door and with the other, he swept off his hat in a courtly gesture. 'Get inside, lady.'

'Is this an heirloom?' she asked, as he drove past her hotel.

'Nope. Bought it a couple of months back from a dealer. It'd been living unused for decades in a local farmer's barn.'

'It's in great condition.'

'I smartened it up some.'

They toured around the town in contented silence and after ten minutes arrived back outside his office.

'Why, thank you, sir,' said the baroness, after he had helped her onto the pavement. 'You have brightened my day considerably.'

'And you mine, lady.'

'Now we need a word about those specs.'

He grinned. 'Come right in,' he said, and headed towards the door. The baroness followed him in. The thin boy still lurking in the porch waited for a couple of minutes and then retired to the waste ground and made a phone call.

Inside the office, the baroness watched with interest as the man tossed his hat toward the hat stand: it fell to the ground. His coat, which he had aimed at the back of the armchair, disappeared out of sight. 'Shit,' he said. 'I keep trying to improve my aim.'

The baroness retrieved his hat, retreated to the door, and took aim. 'Shit,' she said, as it missed its target. 'Dishonours are even.'

The man grinned. 'Cool,' he said, and held out his hand. 'The moniker is Mike Robinson, ma'am.'

The baroness shook his hand. 'The moniker is Jack Troutbeck, Mr. Robinson.'

He swept a pile of papers off the seat of the armchair and beckoned to her to sit. As he walked round his messy and shabby desk to a swivel chair that had seen better days, the baroness looked around the small office. The carpet was threadbare and the furnishings generally redolent of a thrift shop, but it was all surprisingly clean.

'Does that neat desk in the corner suggest you don't work alone?'

Robinson lounged back and put his feet on the desk. 'Yeah. That's Velda's. She's my partner. Now on an assignment chasing a jerk who's two-timing his broad. Should be back any time. You'd like her. She's a babe. A babe to make a bishop kick a hole in a stained glass window.'

'That's a familiar line. Raymond Chandler?'

'Got it in one.' He pulled something out of his pocket. 'Want a Lucky? We'll be living dangerously if the cops come, but hell, what's life without the risk of having the cuffs slapped on?'

The baroness was charmed. 'What a good idea,' she said and leaned forward and tugged a cigarette out of the packet. 'I'm a pipe or cigar woman myself, but in the circumstances, a Lucky would be just fine. I'm in revolt against the health police, so on principle I'll accept most things that are illegal and bad for me even if I don't much like them.'

Robinson shoved a small manual typewriter aside to make a space, opened a desk drawer and produced a bottle and a couple of plastic cups. 'Nuts to the health police. What do you say to a finger of rye?'

'I say yes, Goddammit.'

He grinned. 'I think we're going to get on just fine, lady.'

Aware that she had to be at Traci's at six and had things to do, the baroness prudently stuck to one drink, and after half an hour got up to leave. 'You're clear about what you're doing, Mike.'

'Yeah, sure thing, Jack. You want stuff on that Gonzales asshole and you want it fast.'

'That seems a fair summary. I'm sorry to have missed Velda.'

'You should be. She's one gorgeous dame.'

'Sadly, I have to postpone this pleasure. Another dame—albeit less gorgeous—awaits me.'

'Hey, I love your darling European accents,' said Traci.

'Thank you,' said Constance.

'What do you mean "European"?' asked the baroness, but she said it sotto voce because she didn't really want to hear the answer.

'I guessed you must be homesick,' said Traci, 'so I thought I'd get right in there and show you a proper American welcome.' She tossed her hair and gave a dazzling smile, her teeth so gleaming that the baroness thought for a wild moment she could see her reflection in them.

'How very kind,' said Constance.

'It's nothing. I'm such a feeling person, I just had to show you I'm here for you. I'm Traci Hunter Dickinson and I'm right here for you. Here. Let's hug.'

She threw herself on the baroness, who flinched, and then on Constance, who patted her on the back in an embarrassed way.

'What I think is just because you're high-powered gals don't mean you don't need to have fun. When you're with all those egg-heads all day, a girlie-night can be just the thing. So, hey! Relax and enjoy yourselves.'

Constance smiled wanly. The baroness said nothing. Having endured half an hour of Traci's aggressive vacuity, she would have walked out had she not been so enjoying watching Constance squirm and had she not had recourse to plenty of champagne, which, judging by her exaggerated vivacity, Traci had been indulging in for some time before their arrival. 'Kristal, of course,' said Traci. 'I wouldn't drink anything but the best. And, of course,' she added, with a metallic laugh, 'I wouldn't serve it in anything but the best crystal.'

Constance managed a weak smile; the baroness remained stony-faced. She refused to accompany them outside to view Traci's newest car. 'But you gotta see it. It was my birthday present. It's a BMW and I made Henry get it resprayed in fuchsia.' She waved her nails at them. 'To match these.'

'Sorry, Traci. It would be wasted on me. Cars bore me. I think they exist to get us from A to B with the minimum fuss.'

'You gotta see it. You gotta.' Traci began to cry. As the sobs grew louder and louder, Constance looked pleadingly at the baroness, who grumbled, 'Oh, all right, if you insist.' Traci calmed down, but the examination of the car was perfunctory, since she had little to say about it except to invite them to exclaim at the quality of the upholstery and to tell them it was worth every penny of the $150,000 Henry had spent on it. 'Now we'll go back inside, unless you want to see the SUV.'

The baroness said nothing, but walked back through the French windows. 'Right, ladies,' said Traci, 'now it's time for the house-tour. Just gimme me a minute. I have to go to the bathroom.'

She was back soon, in even better form. 'OK, off we go. We'll take our glasses with us. You can't have too much Kristal when you're having fun.' Constance refused more champagne. The baroness did not.

They began with the kitchen, which was big enough and sufficiently elaborately equipped to service a modest but expensive hotel. Two Mexican maids—whom Traci ignored—were working at two of the four sinks. 'I don't come here much,' explained Traci. 'Why keep a maid and work yourself, is what I always say. Over here now to the elevator and we'll go to the top.'

They emerged into an enormous room dominated by a pseudo-French, gold-embossed, white four-poster bed, piled high with perhaps twenty pink silk cushions and a huge teddy bear. 'It's an Antoinette canopy bed,' said Traci. 'I just love the loops at the top and the real stylish carvings. Henry didn't want it, he said it was fussy, but men have no taste. And he complained it was expensive—like he's always complaining—but I tell him I'm worth it.'

The baroness averted her eyes as Traci pointed out other pieces of furniture not appreciated by her husband, and followed sullenly as they were led into an enormous room with about sixty feet of fitted wardrobes. 'Henry has his stuff in the bedroom,' explained Traci. 'All this here is mine. Look, here are my shoes.'

'Your collection is of positively Imelda Marcos proportions,' said the baroness.

'I don't know who she is,' said Traci, truculently, 'but I bet she don't have anything like as many Manolos as I've got. Or Jimmy Choos.' She closed the doors and flung open some more. 'Look, these are my Donna Karans and here are the gowns from Oscar de la Renta, and....' After about two minutes of this, the baroness walked off and went downstairs to the living room, averting her eyes from the elaborately draped gold satin curtains. She poured herself more champagne, pushed aside a mound of gold satin scatter cushions, made herself comfortable on the larger of the shiny purple leather sofas and—for lack of anything else to read—settled down with a coffee-table book on Indiana artifacts. Bored with the Paleoindian period, she had skipped forward to a contemplation of banners of the civil war when her phone rang. 'It's Mike.'

'Have you news?'

'Enough to think this asshole's really some asshole. Can you talk?'

The door crashed open. 'Not now. Later.'

'So this is where you got to,' said a truculent Traci. 'You haven't even seen the bathrooms.'

'I'm not interested in bathrooms,' grunted the baroness. 'They're for washing in.'

'Not just for that,' said Constance to her in a low voice, as Traci tossed her hair around and shouted for a maid to open another bottle of champagne. 'I spotted some suspicious-looking white powder.'

The champagne was forthcoming, but it was another half-hour—during which Traci paid another visit to a bathroom—before dinner was announced, by which time Traci had told them where she'd bought everything from her overstuffed chairs to the gold bath taps and the baroness had finished her book. Holding out her glass for a refill, the baroness noticed with interest that Constance was glassy-eyed—though probably with boredom rather than drink—and that Traci's voice was becoming more and more high-pitched. 'I buy what I like,' she shrilled, as she led them to the dining room, 'and I don't say sorry to no one.

I'm my own person. I have a beautiful soul in a beautiful body, and if people don't like me, they can fuck off.' She looked at them threateningly. 'Gimme a hug.'

United in wishing to avoid more tears, the baroness and Constance reluctantly obliged and after a minute, they were allowed to sit down. The baroness found solace in the Mexican appetizers. 'The soufflé's good,' she said. 'A bit heavy on the cheese, but there's a satisfactory amount of chilies.' Traci paid no attention, being focussed on describing her exercise and beauty routine, which apart from regular visits to her colonic irrigator and sports masseur, appeared to involve a minimum of three hours a day in a gym and beauty parlour and on her sun bed. The care of her decorated nails alone, she explained, spreading them out for inspection, required a visit twice a week to a specialist salon in Indianapolis.

It was while they were eating the lobster salad that they got on to plastic surgery. 'So how old do you think my husband is?' asked Traci.

'Sixty-five,' said the baroness.

'Fifty,' said Constance.

'Sixty-eight,' said Traci triumphantly. 'That face-lift and the hair graft have made all the difference.'

'I thought his face barely moved,' grunted the baroness, but the remark was lost on her hostess.

Traci giggled. 'And that's not all he got done, but I'm not going to tell you. 'Cept it proved that size matters.'

The baroness and Constance caught each other's eye and cringed.

Traci was now in high good humour. 'And how old do you think I am?'

'Thirty,' said Constance cautiously.

'What a politician you are, Constance,' said the baroness. 'Tell the truth. Traci must be closer to forty.'

Traci was enraged. She threw down a lobster claw with such force that it bounced off her plate onto the floor. The maid glided over and picked it up. Traci began to cry. 'How can you say that? You must be blind. I'm only thirty-five and everyone thinks I look ten years younger.'

Constance gave her an awkward hug which dried up the torrent. The baroness shrugged.

'Have you any idea what work and money and pain I've put into looking as good as I do?'

'I think we're getting the idea,' said the baroness. 'And your lips and expressionless face tell their own story.'

Constance looked at her in horror, but Traci was so caught up in an earlier grievance that she hadn't been listening. Rage had now triumphed over distress. 'Who do you two snobs think you are telling me I look old?' Ignoring Constance's protestations, Traci's voice rose higher. 'If anyone needs cosmetic surgery it's you. Ana, more champagne.'

She turned on Constance. 'Look at you. You've got lines on your forehead, your eyelids droop, your lips are thin, your neck's wrinkled, your teeth need bleaching, your ass is saggy and you've boobs the size of walnuts.' Snorting triumphantly, she thrust her décolletage forward. 'These are great boobs. They cost a fortune, but that doesn't matter now money's no object. Twenty thousand bucks. What do you think of that? And worth every cent,' she added with emphasis. She gazed down complacently. 'Not that they weren't good to begin with, but they're awesome now.'

'They look rather like half-melons to me,' observed the baroness, casting a side-glance at Ana and winking. She received a tiny twitch in recognition. Constance looked at her plate and Traci, her face as contorted with anger as her surgery would allow, rounded on the baroness. 'As for you, you need an extreme makeover.'

'Really?' said the baroness, invigorated by the prospect that the conversation would now be about her. 'How interesting. What would you suggest?'

'I'd start with those teeth. You won't come out under $40,000. They're a disgrace. I don't know how you can appear in public with uneven teeth. One of them's even crooked. You'll have to have recontouring and implants and veneers....'

'I quite like crooked teeth,' said the baroness. 'I find American teeth very boring. They all look the same so everyone looks the same. When did individuality go out of fashion? You'll be cloning yourselves next.'

'You're sick, you are,' said Traci. 'Only trailer-trash have crooked teeth.'

'You speak of what you know, I expect,' said the baroness. Traci looked at her uncertainly, wondering vaguely if she'd been insulted, and then returned to her main theme. 'You need liposuction to get rid of that stomach. If you get any fatter, the only people who'll fancy you will be blacks....'

'Sidney Poitier? Condoleezza Rice? Yum yum!' said the baroness.

'...and of course rhinoplasty on that nose, a full face-lift, and then....'

'And then I wouldn't look like me.'

'So what's wrong with that? Why would anyone want to look like you?'

'I don't suppose they would,' said the baroness mildly. 'But I do. And I daresay Constance is happy enough to look like her. We're British.'

'Soon we'll be in the minority in Britain too,' said Constance gloomily. 'Everyone's thinking of doing it. Half the women I know are using Botox.'

'And what holds you back?' enquired the baroness.

Constance managed the closest approximation to a grin that the baroness had ever seen her produce. 'I'm at the end of my career and I just don't care enough any more to get on that treadmill. Once you start you can't ever stop without people thinking you've got a terminal disease.'

'You'll be like freaks soon if you don't do something,' said Traci. She stared at the baroness. 'You've even got some grey hairs.' With a complacent smile, she pulled at her own ample locks. 'Hair extensions. Cost a fortune. I'll only have European. I always go for quality.' She twisted round in search of the maid. 'Ana, more champagne. And then get the dessert.'

She turned back to the baroness. 'As for your voice, it's too deep to be feminine. You need surgery on your vocal cords. I'll tell you about that when I've had a comfort break.'

'It's Jack, Mike. So what's the news?'

'I talked to a snitch I know on campus and what he told me says you're dead on about this Gonzales being a dangerous asshole. I need to dig up stuff on his background. Is it OK if I go to Ohio tomorrow to follow up a lead I've got?'

'What's the lead?'

'It's a hunch, Jack. I'd rather not say. But I'm not bullshitting.'

The baroness shrugged. 'OK. Go for it. But don't spend more than your retainer without coming back to me.'

Robinson laughed. 'Don't worry about that. Your retainer's all I have.'

Chapter Seven

'Is that typical of an evening with Traci Dickinson, Marjorie? She's not exactly my kind of gal, though I like the fact that she doesn't worry about causing offence. Unlike Constance, who was shocked to the bottom of her priggish soul, I found it overall quite entertaining.'

It was the following evening and they were in the baroness's sitting room having a drink preparatory to the arrival of a dinner she had carefully planned with Stefano Ricciano. Cole Porter was playing softly in the background. Occasionally the baroness sang along for a bar or two.

'However, she does seem completely bonkers. There was all this extraordinary hugging and crying.'

'The kids are like that. They're always gettin' choked up and then huggin' each other.'

'Sometimes I really do feel like a dinosaur.'

Marjorie began to laugh. 'When I first typed Troutbeck, my spell check didn't like it and suggested "throwback" instead.'

'Whatever a spell check is, it is clearly prescient. Anyhow, back to Traci. When she wasn't crying and snorting, she never ever shut up.'

'An empty bucket makes the most racket, as my granny always said. I've never seen Traci at home. I'm not faculty or society and she wouldn't entertain anyone she thought was her inferior. All I do know is she spends so much money it makes me think President Dickinson must be as crooked as a dog's hind leg.'

'How long have they been married?'

'Only a few years. She's his second wife.'

'Where did he find her?'

'She says she was a receptionist.'

'I'd have said tart.'

'My money's on pole-dancing. But whatever she did, she sure isn't cut out for what she's doing now. I guess she's bored. This place must be hell after New York. She's already had nearly five years of it, he's away a lot and the faculty despise her. It was no surprise once she got money she took to throwin' it about. Some folks are all right till they get two pairs of britches.'

The baroness fished the bottle out of the ice-bucket. 'Have some more wine. This Mondavi fumé blanc is really pretty agreeable, don't you think?'

'I sure do.' Marjorie looked around the room. 'You've certainly made yourself comfortable here, Jack. I doubt if any of the other DVPs have private dining facilities like you have.'

The baroness smirked. 'I like being comfortable. And Stefano has been extremely helpful in providing necessities.'

'Step down,' roared Horace, who was swinging on the door of his cage. 'Step down.'

The baroness sighed but got up and carried him back to sit on her lap, singing, 'But now, God knows, anything goes' along with the music as she sat down. 'Oh, sorry, Marjorie, but it's Cole Porter taking the name of God in vain, not me.'

Marjorie laughed. 'It's OK, Jack. I appreciate you takin' my feelings into account.'

'You're not the only one. I asked Betsy if she'd mind trying to stop saying "like" every third word and she said she'd try if I stopped saying God. She's a Christian too.'

'She's tougher than she looks, then.'

'I'm working on toughening her up more.' She placed Horace on her shoulder. 'Are there a lot of Christians on campus?'

'Not many admit to it. The Provost doesn't approve of Christianity. Can't use the word "Christian" without sneering and adding "redneck fundamentalist." Of course by redneck she means anyone who believes in God, who votes Republican, and salutes the flag. That woman's meaner than a junkyard dog.

'People like Betsy and me may be fundamentalist in that we believe in God and the Bible. But we're not fanatics. We don't expect non-Christians to convert. On this campus it's the secularists who are fanatical fundamentalists. They hate God. Though of course they'd never say anything rude about the minority religions. If Dubya turned Muslim it'd be different.'

'Step down, step down,' said Horace, and the baroness moved him to her lap.

'You must have a great time with Horace,' said Marjorie.

'Yes and no. I bought him on an impulse, probably foolishly. Now I don't have the St. Martha's support system to provide a great deal of bird care, I find him very demanding.'

'Don't you enjoy having him to look after?'

To his evident pleasure, the baroness stroked Horace's head. 'I'm extremely selfish and I don't want to look after anyone or anything. Even a parrot. However, I have a sense of duty. He has bonded with me so I must lump it.'

'Isn't he company for you in the evenings?'

'He's diverting. But I don't really need company.' She waved at the pile of books on the desk. 'I've plenty to occupy me if the occasion arises. So far, solitude is not exactly one of my problems.'

'Are you reading up on America?'

'Yes. But not yet contemporary America. At the moment I'm in 1830s America with Alexis de Tocqueville to remind me why I have a romantic attachment to American ruggedness and individuality and many other qualities I prize which seem to be in short supply here. I defend America at home, but exposure to people like Helen and Traci make me wonder why I do. Next I'm going to read Aristotle and Cardinal Newman to remind me what education is supposed to be about so I can tell Helen. Which reminds me, is it really true she's having the books removed from the undergraduates' library?'

'Sure is. Mind you, that's happening on a lot of campuses. Kids can't understand books any more. There was a survey the other day saying only 31 percent of college graduates could read and understand a grown-up book.'

'It certainly takes vision to decide that the solution to that is to banish books completely.'

There was a knock. 'That'll be dinner.' The baroness got up, put Horace back on her shoulder and opened the door to two men and a serving trolley. 'Stefano. Emilio. Welcome. Come on, Horace. Back to your perch.'

Ricciano and Marjorie both knew the baroness well enough by now to effect introductions themselves rather than wait vainly for her to think of doing so. Emilio began laying the table.

'Our dinner,' explained the baroness, 'is being cooked downstairs by Stefano's wife….'

'…Paola,' said Ricciano.

'Paola. Stefano took me home for dinner the other night and the food was….' She smacked her lips. '…*Bella, bella*. Paola even has her own kitchen garden. So we came to an arrangement for her to fulfil….'

'…Some of your special dietary requirements.'

'Exactly.'

'All is ready, ladies,' said Ricciano, and with great ceremony he escorted them to the table and laid their napkins on their laps. He removed the lid from the serving dish and displayed the contents.

'It's casarecce with sardines and wild fennel, Marjorie. I hope that's all right.'

'What's casarecce?'

'Pasta.'

'Fine.'

'You can serve it, Stefano. I hope Paola's put in plenty of anchovies.'

'She certainly has, Jack. You did remind her several times.'

'Most satisfactory, don't you think?' said the baroness, as she cleared her plate.

Marjorie downed her last forkful. 'It's not the sort of food I'm used to, but it's very good.'

The baroness dialled Ricciano's number. 'We're finished.... Right.'

She sat down again. 'Now, I'd like to have stuck to Sicilian cooking this evening, but there was a problem with ingredients. Fresh swordfish is in short supply in the mid-West. So we're reverting to Roman and having Saltimbocca. Stefano was able to get hold of free-range veal. Is that all right with you?'

'It's all the same to me, Jack. You do the fussin'. I'll do the eatin'.'

Much later, Marjorie asked, 'How did you get on with Warren Godber this afternoon?'

'Pretty well. It wasn't a long conversation, but he cut to the chase. He said he'd spent decades building up a history department that was first class—mainly by hiring gifted people who were swimming against the trend of fashion and imposing such high standards that only motivated students took the course. As dean, he did the same, he said, on a larger scale.'

'He certainly did. The Department of Humanities was respected by anyone who knew anything, until it got sunk by the Axis of Evil.'

'The President and the Provost?'

'And the Goon and the Dean they put in place of Warren.'

'Who is?'

'Diane Pappas-Lott.'

'Not another woman with three names. Why do you all do it? It overloads the memory.'

'It's kind of hedgin' bets for some when they get married. For others like me we just like to hang on to our family name. And for others like Helen it's feminism and they make the husband do the same.'

'Is there an unfortunate Mr. Provost?'

'I think there once was but he's never mentioned.'

'What interests me is what happens when a girl called Mary Cook-Scrimgeour gets married to Horace Swanson-Scappaticci? Does their daughter end up being called Josephine Cook-Scrimgeour-Swanson-Scappaticci? And what happens in turn to her daughter?'

'Ours are just called by my husband's name. A lot of feminists have the kids take theirs.'

The baroness snorted. 'Why does everything have to be so complicated? If you ask me, it's just another example of conspicuous American consumption. A sort of surf 'n' turf variation of nomenclature.'

'I was telling you about Dean Diane Pappas-Lott.'

'Another philistine, presumably.'

'Oh, boy, is she a philistine. And a fundamentalist. And a zealot. She's worse than the Provost in some ways because she's stupid and she can never see when she's gone too far. She's an ignorant sociologist who understands nothin' but believes in diversity like Osama believes in Allah. I don't say she'd kill for diversity but I wouldn't be surprised if she did.'

'Is she black?'

'White, but pretending to have the credentials. Pappas is a Greek name, so she describes herself as a 'woman of colour.' And she alleges she's bi-sexual, but who knows?' She snorted. 'I'd rather have Horace as dean than her.'

Hearing his name, Horace, who had just finished a piece of cheese, said 'To be or not to be….Rubbish.'

'To be or not to be, that is the question,' shouted the baroness. 'To be or not to be, that is the question.'

Horace ruminated, shouted 'Rubbish' a couple of times, followed it up with an ear-splitting 'Whoo! Whoo!' and adjourned to amuse himself on his swing.

'Standards are dropping everywhere,' said the baroness. 'To get back to Godber, he said that since almost everything he'd spent his life building up had been comprehensively destroyed, he'd given up and was in negotiation to take early retirement. He didn't have the energy to fight any more, and has decided he'd be better off cultivating his garden.

'I asked him for details, and he told me a bit about how the Provost and the Dean between them had introduced the new courses for imbeciles and idlers, how the honours and pass grades had been compulsorily halved, how there was irresistible pressure on young staff to over-grade coursework, and how the Provost's revamped kangaroo court as run by the Goon had been used to get rid of some of his best staff through manufactured complaints from intimidated students. It was getting really interesting, but then he had a phone call and said he had to go.'

She refilled their glasses. 'Before he went, I asked him about the VRC group. He said he'd heard of it because of the *Sentinel* reports, but he was out of things these days. I asked him who'd know and he said you'd be a good source. To be precise, he said something along the lines of "Marjorie always knew what was going on. And even though they exiled her to Siberia, I'll bet she still keeps her ears open."'

'Did he say that?' Marjorie seemed pleased. 'I hardly ever see Warren Godber these days, though we were hand in glove when I was Provost Haringey's secretary.' She smiled ruefully. 'But we've no call to run across each other these days.'

'Who is Provost Haringey?'

'Was. Jim Haringey was Helen Fortier-Pritchardson's predecessor. He died suddenly more than four years ago and I'm still all choked up about it.' She paused and looked squarely at the baroness. 'The inquest said it was an accident. Maybe. Some said it was suicide. If it was, then hogs fly sideways. But Warren and I thought it was probably murder.'

'What happened?'

'He was killed by a peanut.'

'You mean he choked? The way Dubya nearly choked on a pretzel?'

'No. It was an allergy. It was a funny thing. He never used to be allergic to peanuts, and he didn't often eat them, but apparently allergies can build up, and one day several years back he had a peanut butter sandwich and went into anaphylactic shock. His throat was all swelled up and he couldn't hardly breathe by the time the ambulance got to him, but they saved him. This time, he wasn't so lucky.'

She brooded for a moment. 'There were two funny things about what happened. How did the peanut get in his sandwich? And why didn't he have his EpiPen?' She saw the baroness was looking puzzled. 'An EpiPen's a kind of syringe with the antidote—adrenaline. Warren carried one everywhere. But it wasn't on him when he took bad and it was never found.'

'How did he come to eat the peanut?'

'It was in the ham salad sandwich that he'd brought to work that morning. If Jim wasn't going out to lunch—which he hardly ever did—he'd always buy a ham sandwich on his way to work and put it in the office fridge. He didn't like the food in the cafeteria.'

'Sound man,' grunted the baroness.

'That day, like most days, I made him coffee round midday and went out to grab a quick lunch. When I got back, he was lying on the floor just about breathin' and his lips and throat were badly swollen. He couldn't talk and he seemed nearly out of it.

'I called the emergency services and then tried to help him. I knew because of how he looked that it was probably an allergic response. We'd discussed it a couple of times and I'd read stories in the press about anaphylactic shock.

'I could see Jim had been trying to find his EpiPen. He'd turned his pockets inside out while he was lying on the floor. He couldn't stand up to reach the phone. I searched and searched, but the EpiPen wasn't there.' She shook her head. 'I couldn't get my head round that. Jim was really careful about it. He knew traces of peanut could come up in food quite unexpectedly and that next time, he could die within a minute or two. So he'd always have an EpiPen in his jacket pocket, a spare in the car, and another at home.

'I grabbed his keys, rang 911 again to tell them what he needed and what I was doing, and then ran to the parking lot. But by the time I got there and back, he wasn't breathin'. I injected him with the EpiPen, but when the ambulance men arrived a couple of minutes later, they said he was dead.'

'Sounds fishy to me, Marjorie. Very very fishy.'

'It *is* fishy, damn it, Mary Lou.'

'It's four years ago, Jack. There's nothing you can do about it.'

'On the contrary. There is something I can do about it. I have my methods.'

'Which methods are you talking about?'

The baroness ground out her cigar into the ashtray as if it were a pestle. 'I've already got myself a gumshoe,' she announced, her voice redolent with triumph.

'You've what?'

'You heard.'

'Why?'

'I thought it was the done thing to do if intending to spend any appreciable time in the States.'

'Are you going to stop being ridiculous?'

'Probably not.'

'Jack!!!!!!!!!!!!'

'I wanted to know a bit more about the Provost's hitman and—serendipitously—I happened to walk down a mean street and find a hero.'

'The Provost's what?'

'I told you before.'

'All you told me was that she had an unpleasant bit of work as her PA.'

'She has the sinister Dr. Gonzales. I think he roughs up students so I'm having him investigated.'

Mary Lou paused to take this in. 'Who or what have you hired?'

'A rather delightful chap called Mike of M and V Private Investigators. I took to him immediately. Exactly what I hoped for in an American private eye.'

'Trench-coat, fedora, and Colt 45, no doubt?'

'I don't know about the Colt 45, but Mike's certainly got the trench-coat and fedora.'

'Has he a partner called Velda with a figure a man would kill for?'

'He certainly has a Velda, but sadly I haven't yet had the chance to check out her figure. How do you know about her, anyway?'

'Oh, for God's sake, Jack, have you never heard of Mike Hammer?'

'Sort of,' said the baroness. 'But Mickey Spillane was a bit unsubtle I seem to remember. I was more of a Chandler man myself.'

'Unsubtle isn't quite the word. Hammer was given to blowing people's guts out with his trusty rod even when only slightly piqued.'

'This guy seems more even-tempered. Besides, he's Mike Robinson. Perhaps he's just a Spillane fan.'

'Is he around ninety?'

'More like twenty.'

'Sounds like a weirdo. And a child to boot.'

'Whatever or whoever he is,' said the baroness, with as much dignity as she could muster, 'I've hired him. If he's no good, I'll fire him. But if he delivers on Gonzales, I'll get him on to checking out the prime suspect for Provost Haringey's murder.'

'Who's that?'

'President Dickinson, of course. He was in his office just down the corridor, and Marjorie said he had means, motive, and opportunity.'

'Means?'

'How hard is it to buy peanuts? Or how onerous to carry round a small packet awaiting your opportunity.'

'Which was?'

'Haringey was at a meeting in Dickinson's office that morning where everyone took their jackets off. When everyone else had gone, Dickinson and Haringey stayed behind to try to resolve a major difference of opinion about grade inflation and failed, and in a rage, Haringey marched off without his jacket. Marjorie said she'd never seen him so angry. The jacket was delivered a few minutes later by the President's secretary. So all the Pres had to do was to remove the EpiPen and then await an opportunity to insert the peanut in the sandwich in a fridge used by half a dozen people. Then fingers crossed that Marjorie wouldn't be around when he ate it.'

'Motive?'

'The Provost was blocking him from turning the university into a factory. Apparently they absolutely hated each other.'

'Couldn't he just have fired him?'

'Not that easy. Apparently Haringey was one tough cookie. But once he was dead, Dickinson was able to get the benighted Helen Fortier-Pritchardson in to do his dirty work. And she moved Marjorie out the day after she took over.'

'Presumably the cops investigated all this.'

'Only cursorily, apparently, and not at all after the inquest said it was an accident. The autopsy indicated that Haringey's last mouthful of sandwich contained a peanut, but that didn't prove it had been there when it left the shop. His wife tried to find out what had happened by following the time-honoured American custom of suing the sandwich shop for $100 million, but though her lawyers got a private eye on to it, they found nothing. They used peanuts in the shop and the sandwich-maker could theoretically have accidentally dropped one into the salad, but, as the sandwich shop pointed out, they went to great pains to avoid such a thing happening and someone could have put it in his sandwich deliberately when it was in the fridge or he could have done it himself.'

'I love the idea of committing suicide with a peanut, Jack, but I'm too busy to get involved with an engaging mystery that happened four years ago and four thousand miles away.'

'Pity. Traci said something intriguing last night that I must follow up on.'

'Which was?'

'Never you mind. You said you weren't interested.'

'Sulk then if you want to.'

'I shall. Where's Robert?'

'Still dawdling around the Czech Republic.'

'Getting bored?'

'Not one bit, Jack. Forget about Robert and Rachel. You'll be home before they are. Now apart from the matter of Haringey, the deceased, what are you up to?'

'Pedagogy. I have an event tomorrow.'

'What?'

'The Distinguished Visiting Professors will speak to the final year humanities students and answer questions. The Dean of Humanities, the Greek woman of so-called colour, will be in the chair.'

'How many do you expect?'

'Hundreds and hundreds, apparently. It'll be a full house, since….' She wrinkled her nose with distaste. 'They get something called a credit for just turning up. And as well it's part of what they call the outreach programme, so the public can come if they like.'

'I'd buy a ringside ticket to see you four together.'

'Might be very tame. Constance and I no longer hate each other with the ferocity of yore and Rowley is just so boring I doubt if he's likely to get me roused.'

'Jimmy Rawlings?'

'Ah, yes,' said the baroness. 'Jimmy Rawlings is a different matter entirely.'

The following morning, the baroness stopped by Mike Robinson's office. The curly-haired brunette in T-shirt and jeans tapping at her laptop was pretty, though not spectacularly so.

'Are you Velda?' asked the baroness.

'Oh, he's been giving you that bullshit, has he?' said the woman fondly. She laughed. 'The silly fantasising son-of-a-bitch. No, I'm Vera and I refuse to be called Velda. And he's not Mike, he's really Maurice. But he just can't bear either of our real names, so he calls us after Mike Hammer and his girlfriend. I don't mind. It's a bit of fun. Our pet names for each other are Maurice-Mike and Vera-Velda.'

If this example of the American propensity to tell complete strangers their innermost secrets disconcerted the baroness, she didn't show it. 'I can't really complain about the name business,' she said, as she sat down in the armchair. 'I don't use my Christian name either. But should I distrust anything else he tells me?'

'No, no. Mike's a good P.I. Just gets a bit carried away with the retro stuff sometimes. Never interferes with the job, though. Are you his new client?'

'Jack Troutbeck.'

'I guessed you were. Mike described you accurately.'

'As what?'

'A no-nonsense broad.'

'That's me. Now I haven't heard anything from your silly fantasising son-of-a-bitch since the night before last, though I've tried him a few times. Do you know how he's getting on or has he run off with my five hundred dollar advance?'

Vera giggled. 'Times are a bit hard, but Mike wouldn't skip town with five hundred dollars. Or even five thousand. He's not like that. It's just that he sees himself so much as the guy who works alone that he hates providing information along the way. Prefers to get back with the full story.'

'I understand that.'

'If he calls in, what'll I tell him?'

'That I want to see him asap. Preferably with you. There's more afoot. I think I'll be needing you both.'

'Diversity is not something you can be half-hearted about,' said Dean Pappas-Lott, a large woman with what looked suspiciously like a fake tan and hair so frizzy it looked as if she had suffered a severe electric shock. She was sitting behind a long table. To her left were Constance Darlington and Rowland Cunningham and to her right, the baroness and Jimmy Rawlings. All five had a large white card in front of them bearing their names. The white paper table-cloth bearing the trade-mark VRC message had been grabbed by the quivering Dean and dumped in a waste bin as soon as she arrived.

Having seen that they were variously described as Lady Connie, Lord Rowland, and Lady Ida, the three peers had requested a black marker and had written on the other side of their cards the more conventional version of their names. Not to be outdone, Jimmy Rawlings had changed his to Mujaahid, which he explained to them he used when meeting people who didn't know him in his old incarnation as a boxer.

The baroness's midnight-blue suit, made of fine wool, was severely tailored, and the blue-and-white polka dot blouse had a floppy bow. That it was a sartorial tribute to Margaret Thatcher was not lost on Constance.

Reading from a script, after a good deal of general welcoming waffle, Dean Pappas-Lott had embarked on what was clearly a familiar theme. 'As you all know, here at Freeman U we're passionate about embracing diversity. Embracing diversity is what makes a school a great school. Embracing diversity is what makes a society a great society. And embracing diversity is what will make this world a place where everyone can realise her or his potential.

'Our goal, here at Freeman U, and we pursue it 24/7, is to give minorities the chance that the majority has shamefully denied them throughout human history. As Martin Luther King said, "Almost always, the creative dedicated minority has made the world better." As Toni Morrison has said, "The range of emotions and perceptions I have had access to as a black person and as a female person are greater than those of people who are neither."

'At Freeman U, we reject the dominant cultural narrative that has indoctrinated society with the idea that white is better than black, that male is better than female and that abled is better than differently abled. And as a wise, deaf parent said to me recently, "How dare anyone say I was wrong to want my child born deaf. Or that I should want her deafness fixed. It's not an affliction. It's an identity."

'And how dare too anyone suggest that being American is better than anything else. Here at Freeman U, we are learning that—as Emma Goldman said—"Patriotism is a superstition artificially created and maintained through a network of lies and falsehoods."'

She looked slowly around the audience from the left to the right and the front—where the academics were sitting—to the back, and returned to her rather laboured reading. 'When we have truly abandoned patriotism for the superstition it is, we will learn the truth of what Muriel Lester, the Mother of World Peace, said many years ago: that "war is as outmoded as cannibalism, chattel slavery, blood-feuds, and duelling…an insult to humanity." It is our minorities who will teach us that.

'There's much more that I long to say to you, but I must stop now and introduce our Distinguished Visiting Professors from England, radicals all. Do you know what Angela Davis said about radicals? She said that radical simply means "grasping things at the root." We are privileged to welcome to New Paddington four people who in their own country are a byword for radicalism. They are the kind of people that change the world. People you can learn from.

'I'm going to ask them to tell you who they are and why they care and then I'm going to open proceedings to questions from the floor.'

She turned to her left. 'Lady Darlington. Tell us about yourself.'

◇◇◇

The true facts about Constance Darlington were that she had been head girl of one of the best girls' grammar schools in England, had read law at Oxford, where—under the influence of a mesmeric lecturer—she had become a Trotskyite, had spent many weekends protesting noisily against the Vietnam war, had gone after graduation to work for the civil liberties lobby, and had been a fervently left-wing member of the Labour Party.

In her thirties, married to a prosperous barrister and with two children and a nanny, Constance was elected to the local council, where she became a shrill voice for levelling down. She opposed the sale of council houses to tenants, as chairwoman of the education committee she fought against any selection for and in schools, and she made much headway in ensuring that non-English speaking children could be taught and take exams in their own languages—at serious detriment to their futures and vast expense to the taxpayer. Her own house being in a prosperous, middle-class area with excellent state schools (the only immigrants in the neighbourhood were doctors), her children were unaffected by her reforms. They did well at school, and with the help of private tutors, were sufficiently academically successful to win places respectively at Oxford and Cambridge, institutions which their mother campaigned to have closed to all but the products of state schools.

Constance saw racists under every bed and insisted on the introduction of politically correct language to all council communications. It was she who caused much merriment in the media when reported to have objected on a school visit to infants being taught 'Baa baa, black sheep': although this was later alleged to be an urban myth and in her later incarnation Constance denied it, it did actually happen. In the mid-1980s, as leader of a council that was now flying the Red Flag over its headquarters, she easily won the nomination to stand in the by-election after the local MP died suddenly.

Constance's metamorphosis into the archetypal power-dressed, obedient, New Labour woman was swift. She would become one of Tony Blair's most trusted acolytes, prepared to defend everything she had opposed in her youth: educational selection, private investment in hospitals, the authoritarian assault on civil liberties in the name of security, and the invasion of Iraq were justified by her in that prissy, reasonable tone that drove so many crazy.

It was a bitter disappointment to her when she lost her seat in the 2004 general election. She had been promised the Cabinet portfolio of Culture (a natural choice, since she despised opera, classical music, and anything else remotely elitist), but now she had to make do with becoming a peer and a Lords spokesman on constitutional reform. Even that junior ministry was taken from her when the Cabinet minister to whom she reported and whom she had hitherto outranked, decided that she was a patronising bitch and insisted she be sacked.

Constance being Constance, in telling the audience of herself she spoke in impenetrable New Labourese about a life-long commitment to radicalism, by which she explained she meant modernisation, which meant helping the young welcome challenge, seize opportunities, and feel a connection with their government. In these difficult times, what mattered most was 'the fostering of a culture of respect in a diverse society.'

She was extremely dull. Even though she spoke for under five minutes, the audience had stopped listening and the baroness, slightly regretting the third glass of wine at lunchtime, was fighting off sleep. The applause was polite.

Rowland Cunningham wasn't much better. An indifferent academic historian based in a university in the Midlands, in the early 1980s he had spotted a niche in the field of peace and conflict studies. Noting that owing to competition from ferociously learned and often belligerent military historians, studying conflict was much tougher than studying peace, he had elected to work on burgeoning peace processes. Being both timid and lazy, he had selected Northern Ireland as his specialism, for everyone there spoke English, it was less than an hour by plane from London, it was possible to stay well away from the danger areas, and as long as he was unremittingly pious, talked a lot about inclusivity, and always ended on a positive note, there were innumerable invitations forthcoming to make speeches, give lectures, and attend conferences in the United States, Canada, and Australia.

In recent years Cunningham had branched out into comparing the Northern Ireland peace process with its South African equivalent, which provided the opportunity for several lucrative trips to the sun; he kept well away from violent Johannesburg because of his terror of getting hurt. He made contacts rather than friends, but as he tried hard to avoid being controversial, he made few important enemies, yet many unimportant people hated him because he had an extremely bad temper which he took out on them. He had been given a rich reward for having written a few articles in glowing support of government initiatives on Northern Ireland by being given a peerage for services to peace.

What he told the Freeman audience in his sententious way made it seem as if he'd been anti-war and internationalist from the cradle. His platitudes were different from Constance Darlington's, but they were just as platitudinous. The baroness's chin dropped to her chest and she slept. Cunningham finished by saying that a lifetime dedicated to helping bring peace to the world had taught him how right Winston Churchill was to say 'Jaw-jaw is always better than war-war.' The mention of Churchill's name jerked the baroness awake. She noticed Betsy was looking puzzled and hoped it didn't mean she'd never heard of Churchill.

The applause was perfunctory, but Jimmy Rawlings soon woke everyone up. 'I don't want to be called Jimmy Rawlings, brothers and sisters,' he announced. 'I want to be called Mujaahid, which means a fighter for Allah, not a fighter exploited by boxing promoters. Just like the great Muhammad Ali, brothers and sisters, I saw the light and gave myself to Allah.' There was a wild cheer from the back.

A retired boxer who had discovered that rabble-rousing was more lucrative than commenting on his old sport, Rawlings told a compelling if somewhat exaggerated story of a poverty-stricken upbringing in Bristol as the child of a white mother and a Nigerian father who had disappeared as soon as he was told of the pregnancy—never to return. Rawlings looked back on this time and realised it was the pain of living in a racist society that had driven his father away. He spoke eloquently of discrimination and bullying and the hurt of knowing his home town had been central to the slave trade. He talked of how he learned to stand up for himself with his fists, and how he got into trouble with teachers. And then he told of the man who had seen him fighting another boy in the street and who had offered to teach them both to box.

Rawlings had become a British champion, and had come close to winning a world title, but he put down his failure to go all the way to a lack of spiritual depth, which made him seek refuge in drink and drugs and promiscuity. But then he had discovered Islam, the radical answer to war and discrimination and all manner of bad things.

For a long time, he explained, he had continued to be Jimmy Rawlings, but recently, seeing the suffering and exclusion in Britain of his co-religionists, for no reason except that they had a faith about which they cared, he had decided to change his name to show where his loyalties lay. 'I am no longer British. I am a Muslim. I am not Jimmy. I am Mujaahid. My loyalties are with my brothers fighting in the resistance against imperialist bullying. The West must pay for its past sins.'

The audience was split. The faculty applauded enthusiastically and at length, as did a minority of the white students and a majority of the black. There were no Asians in the audience: Marjorie had explained that they dominated the faculties of science, engineering, and computing and left those in the humanities to get on with it.

'Thank you, thank you, Mujaahid,' said a tremulous Diane Pappas-Lott. 'We are very moved. Now, will you share your narrative with us, Lady Troutbeck?'

'I'm the odd one out,' grunted the baroness. 'I'm neither a victim nor an idealist. I run a college where people are expected to read and to think, and in politics I try to stop the barbarians taking over and destroying the traditions that made my country a force for good all over the world. Unlike Mr. Rawlings, who appears to have elected to become a traitor, I am a patriot.

'I accept the label of radical, but I'm a conservative radical. The roots I am grasping with intent to destroy them are the shallow, poisonous roots that produce the shoots of self-pity, moral relativism, and intellectual dishonesty. I believe in intellectual rigour and robust debate, with no quarter given and no offence taken. I am in favour of diversity, but by that I mean diversity of thought, not of lobby-groups competing to win the victim-stakes.' She folded her arms and glared at the audience. As Dean Pappas-Lott looked at her in horror, about half the student body began to cheer.

Chapter Eight

'So how did it go?' asked Mary Lou. 'Are they going to run you out of town?'

'It was odd.'

'In what sense odd?'

'Just odd.'

'Jack, if you don't give me a coherent account, I'm going to ring off this very minute. I have enough interviewing to do professionally without having to drag information out of you.'

'Whoo! Whoo! Whoo! Whoo! Whoo! Whoo!' contributed Horace.

'Whoo! Whoo! Wah! Wah! Whoo! Whoo! Wah! Wah!' shouted the baroness. 'Horace is getting very absent-minded, Mary Lou. He's consistently forgetting half his lines.'

'Wah! Wah! Wah! Wah!'

'No, Horace. Whoo! Whoo! Wah! Wah! Whoo! Whoo! Wah! Wah!'

'Jack! I really don't have time to listen to parrot remedial class. Get on with it.'

'All right. All right. I'll cover him up.'

'OK,' she said, when she returned. 'We had to introduce ourselves. Constance Darlington produced a lot of balls-aching New Labour guff, Rowley Cunningham was dreary about peace, Jimmy Rawlings projected himself as a victim who had embraced Islam because it can solve the world's problems without conflict although since the world won't come quietly he and his oppressed brothers have no option but to use violence. Oh, and now he's calling himself Mujaahid, which means he kills for Allah or something similar. For the very best of reasons, of course.'

'Including our safety and convenience, no doubt. And you?'

'What you might expect. I called for intellectual rigour and criticised their idea of diversity.'

'What was the reaction?'

'Odd.'

'How do you mean "odd"?'

'Just odd.'

'Jack!'

'I don't think anyone gave a damn about Constance or Rowley. No one asked them any questions, except for an enterprising lad who asked Rowley—a propos his quoting Churchill approvingly about jaw-jaw and war-war—if that meant Churchill had been wrong to fight Hitler. Rowley yammered about how if they'd got the jaw-jaw right at the Treaty of Versailles there wouldn't have been a second world war to fight, but since most of them hadn't a clue what he was talking about, he lost them. The lad attempted a follow-up question, but the dean told him he mustn't hog the floor.

'There were plenty wanting to ask me and the benighted Rawlings questions. I'd expected him to be popular, but I was surprised I'd had so much applause, though Marjorie wasn't. She'd told me the students are getting increasingly conservative but I hadn't thought it possible because of the way they dress and eat.'

'Dubya wears lumberjack shirts and eats hamburgers.'

'Yes. And look how unsound he's been on free trade and public spending.'

'Get on with the story, Jack. What did they ask?'

'Rawlings was asked what he thought about 9/11.'

'And?'

'You certainly couldn't accuse him of pussy-footing. He said he'd have been in favour of it had it been perpetrated by his Muslim brothers, but in fact it was the work of Mossad and the

CIA, which was obvious since no Jews turned up to work that day, so he was against it as he's against everything produced by the global Zionist conspiracy.'

'Reaction?'

'A few boos, otherwise muted apart from a crowd of fans at the back and some staff at the front, but then another student asked him if he agreed with someone called Ward Churchill when he described the Twin Tower victims as '"little Eichmanns." He most certainly did agree, said Rawlings, as they were undoubtedly servants of Islamophobic capitalism. There were a lot more boos than cheers this time, but Dean Pappas-Lott told them to shut up as Freeman University was a temple of free speech, and everyone could say what they liked, so Rawlings produced a few more minutes of unfettered, nutty incendiary Islamobabble.

'Hang on a minute. I'm going to pour myself another drink. You'll be pleased to hear Stefano has found a brand of unsweetened tonic so I can have gin again.'

She returned, happily smacking her lips. 'That's better. Have you ever heard of Ward Churchill?'

'A fraudulent anti-Semitic academic, isn't he?'

'Marjorie tells me he's a Professor of Ethnic Studies who went a long way by falsely claiming to be a Red Indian but is now in trouble because he's been proved to be a plagiarist as well as a raving lunatic. I didn't know that at the time but I pointed out that only barking bigots denied that several hundred Jews had died on 9/11. I had a go at Rawlings and Muslims in general for being anti-Semites and then denounced all those Islamists world-wide who spread hideous anti-Jewish propaganda, upon which a faculty member jumped up to support Rawlings on the grounds that Jews were the imperialists of the Middle East. I said some things never changed and sang them a verse from that 1960s Tom Lehrer song about the asinine National Brotherhood Week.'

'I don't know it.'

'Oh, the Protestants hate the Catholics,' sang the baroness, 'And the Catholics hate the Protestants/And the Hindus hate the Muslims/And everybody hates the Jews.'

'I hope Lehrer sang it better than that.'

The baroness ignored her. 'So I followed by asking why you could rubbish Jews but not Muslims and there was a bit of a brawl.'

'How do you mean brawl?'

'A few professors came in to denounce Israel. Turns out that like that crowd of academic Jew-haters back home, they're agitating for the boycotting of Israeli academics unless they explicitly reject Zionism. So I asked them if they'd extend that to a boycott of any Muslim academics who didn't explicitly condemn Islamic terrorism, which, I pointed out, was a rather bigger sin than the Zionist one of wanting Israel to stay in existence. They got excited.' She snorted. 'Academics! Even the ones I love, I hate.'

'I know what you mean. What happened then?'

'Rawlings got excited. A lot of people got excited. You might say the air was thick with impotent expostulation. Rawlings said all non-Muslims were infidels. I said that in many parts of the world Islam was a primitive and cruel religion which treated women and homosexuals appallingly and that if it wanted respect it was about time it caught up with the Enlightenment, endorsed the concept of freedom of speech, and stopped trying to murder people because they said boo to Mohammed. I also said that even though I was an atheist, I thought Christianity was a vastly superior religion and Western civilisation way ahead of anything Islam had to offer these days, even if it was getting far too touchy-feely-weepy-waily. "When the chips are down," I asked the audience, "do you want freedom or theocratic barbarism?"'

'Wow!'

'So Rawlings said I was a wicked, white, decadent, Islamophobe, which wasn't universally popular, judging by the boos. I must say, academic politics here certainly seems livelier than what we have at home.'

'Get on with it, Jack. What questions did the students ask you?'

'What I thought about diversity studies.'

'Which was?'

'What you might expect. I said that women's studies, black studies, queer studies and all the rest of diversity studies were bogus disciplines designed by fifth-rate academics to politicise the humanities and institutionalise a complex system of apartheid in universities. Whenever anything is called studies, I pointed out, there's very little study involved.'

'Were there boos?'

'And cheers. The Dictionary of Right-on Quotations that calls herself a Dean got very rattled at this stage and asked how I could say such a thing in Freeman, which was dedicated to diversity because it honoured everyone's otherness, or some such garbage. I suggested she should look around the audience and the campus and see apartheid in front of her eyes. What she and people like her were doing, I said, was maximising difference when her job was to minimise it.

'I brought in Tom Lehrer again. He has a line about how we all ought to love one another and adds "I know there are people in the world that do not love their fellow human beings and I hate people like that."'

'Bad choice, I'd have thought. Americans don't do irony much.'

'It puzzled them, I felt. But I tried to get across the notion that enforced tolerance leads to greater intolerance. You have to go with the grain of human nature, I said to the Dean. In my college, people make friends with people they like; they're not forcibly segregated so they hang about in black groups or white groups or Asian groups or gay groups. Unlike Freeman.

'Rawlings then decided to help by shouting that Whitey had ruined the world with his so-called civilisation because so-called "primitive" societies were happy and peace-loving, so I said, "I see, so they never ate each other," and he began to rave again about how I was a typical white imperialist and I pointed out that he was living in a fantasy land and that most primitive societies rarely took a day off from trying to rub each other out. So then he played the slavery card: no one should expect

African-Americans to talk to Whitey considering what had been done to them, so I retorted that slavery had been practised by every race in the world, that the African slaves who ended up in America were first sold by Africans to Arabs, and that slavery in the U.S. was abolished 150 years ago and that it was about time blacks got over it.'

'Was that popular?'

'Very, in some quarters, but it caused a bit of an uproar in others, especially when I added that they'd be better turning their attention to doing something about Africans who were being enslaved today by Islamic Arabs in Mauritania and the Sudan. I added that American Muslims should confront their fanatics and denounce the people who were murdering Americans. Then the dean said I was undermining everything for which Freeman University stood by making such terrible and disrespectful accusations and that she was feeling the hurt, so I said that was too bad, but what else did she expect in a temple to freedom of speech. Some of the students started arguing with each other and then Rawlings got more wind in his sails and delivered himself of an outburst about why it was all an imperialist lie that Africans had sold each other and demanded that Whitey pay for slavery. He's on the reparations bandwagon: every institution that ever had anything to do with slavery is to cough up billions forthwith.' She laughed. 'What's more, he thinks Freeman should change its name. I quite like Rawlings. He adds to the general merriment.'

'What do you mean he thinks Freeman should change its name?'

'You're very slow tonight, Mary Lou. Surely you grasp that it's hurtful to remind the descendants of slaves that they once were not freemen. I did enquire how Rawlings viewed the history of white slavery, and asked from whom whites should be seeking reparation, but before he could answer the Dean completely lost her nerve and wrapped up the session double-quick in the interests of campus harmony....Oh, hang on. My mobile's ringing.'

'Oh, Mike, good. Did you get anything? Yes…yes…I can do that….Half-an-hour?…Fine. I'll be waiting outside. Be on time. And bring Velda.'

'An assignation with the shamuses?' asked Mary Lou, when the baroness switched phones.

'Yes. We're going to a diner. I'm quite excited.'

'Just spare me your complaints about the food. However, I've enjoyed the account of your afternoon. It sounds most entertaining. I hope the poor Dean has a good supply of smell-ing-salts.'

'I certainly enjoyed myself and I think I really cut the silly cow to the quick. But I'm on a crusade now that I've seen the horrors of where diversity and affirmative action lead. You see the trouble is that when a moron like the Dean looks at a group of a hundred people, she doesn't see a hundred people who agree about some things and argue about others and who benefit from exchanging ideas. Instead she searches for a hundred different agendas by encouraging people to develop grievances so they can form tiny groups and compete with the others for attention, status, and money—demanding unequal treatment in the name of equality.' She sighed. 'Wait a minute, Mary Lou. I have to relight my cigar.'

'I'm surprised you're allowed to smoke,' said Mary Lou, when the baroness returned.

'The fascists have banned it almost everywhere. All this pas-sive-smoking bilge. But Stefano reclassified this as a smoking suite. Where was I?'

'Splitting up your hundred people into competing groups.'

The baroness sighed. 'Do you remember those simple days back when we first met and the dykes were trying to take over St. Martha's? They were only a pressure group. In this univer-sity—and, I gather, most of American academia—all the PC crap's so embedded it's beyond questioning. Diversity is bigger than General Motors and has become more embedded than a fly in amber.

'You take your hundred people. First you separate them according to race—broadly white, black, Asian, and Hispanic—then by whether they're American or foreign. Then, Marjorie tells me, if they're black, you have to distinguish between immigrant and colonised minorities.'

'Huh?'

'A Nigerian is an immigrant and obviously deserves special treatment as a black, but although he was once colonised and still is, apparently, by the oil companies, he's not to be lumped together as a recipient of special favours with Americans of African descent because they have all manner of extra grievances and hang-ups and so get extra privileges, so now you've got black against black in the grant or promotion stakes.

'Then you've got the gender complication. It used to be simple, but now you're dividing people into male, female, transsexual, and transvestite, which produces competition over such great issues as lavatories. It's a hot debate at Freeman, whether a transvestite should be in the lavatory dictated by his or her clothes or his or her genitalia. They solved the problem partly by having uni-sex lavatories, which Betsy tells me a lot of girls hate, but there's a male transvestite who's insisting on his right to use every lavatory on the campus regardless of designation. He also wants a gender-blind dormitory. A sub-committee is chewing anxiously over the matter as we speak.'

'Have they considered what to do with hermaphrodites?'

'I'll put it to them. Now you throw in sexual orientation: straight man, straight woman, homosexual, lesbian, bisexual. Then there are the extra permutations offered by religion and disability. Oh, and of course no one can say anything critical to anyone else for fear of hurting their feelings. Unless they're white males. Or Jewish. In which case they're always in the wrong.'

'You've depressed me enough, Jack. I'm signing off now. Ellis has just come in. His tales of the criminal world will come as light relief.'

◇◇◇

'Just how I pictured a diner,' said the baroness. 'It's encouraging that old traditions persist.'

'It's actually new,' said Vera. 'There weren't any diners left anywhere within reach of New Paddington, but now retro's fashionable, they're recreating the 1950s.'

'Good,' said the baroness. 'A much-maligned decade. Though not without its drawbacks, I have to admit. British restaurants were not good then.'

She looked around her benignly. 'I like the booths. And even more, I like those attractive skating waitresses. I expect the food will be terrible, but I'm resigned.'

Within five minutes, the baroness had flirted with a giggly blonde who declared herself a novice skater and struggled gamely not to fall over, she had ordered steak and chips without fuss, and she was uncomplainingly sipping an indifferent California wine. 'Now take it from the top, Mike.'

'I'm not a guy that takes any crap, Jack.'

'I can see that,' she responded solemnly. She turned her head slightly towards Vera, winked out of Robinson's line of sight, and received a conspiratorial grin. 'And was there a lot of crap being thrown at you?'

'Well, this guy—Stan Donnelly—was one tough-looking punk and I thought for a while he wasn't going to come clean.'

'How did you find him in the first place?'

Robinson looked embarrassed.

'*You* come clean, Maurice-Mike,' said Vera.

'The internet.'

The baroness laughed. 'The typewriter's just a prop, I presume.'

'Saw it on eBay and couldn't resist it.'

'OK. Your guilty secret is out. I won't hold it against you that you're technologically literate.'

'Actually Mike's a whiz on the net, Jack,' said Vera. 'Better than me. That's why I gave him a job.'

The baroness raised an eyebrow. 'You can tell me about that later. What about Donnelly. How did you locate him?'

'Easy. I tracked Gonzales and Fortier-Pritchardson to the same Ohio school ten years ago. He was a student and she was Dean of Students. My hunch was that if he's tall and really dumb he'd have got to college on a basketball scholarship, so that's what I went there to investigate.'

'I surmise from your happy grin that your hunch was right.'

'Sure was. I spun a cock-and-bull story to a secretary about a long-lost uncle I was trying to trace and she showed me photo albums and then I had Gonzales and the names of the guys on his team. Stan Donnelly was the first one I found on the net because he'd become a professional player who was a coach at a small Christian college only fifty miles down the highway. I saw him this morning.'

'Good lad.'

'Donnelly was pretending he couldn't remember Gonzales, but finally I broke him.'

'By pressing the muzzle of your gun to his right temple, no doubt?'

Robinson laughed. 'Not quite. He looked hard-up, so I told him I'd give him a hundred bills if he told me something that was worth it. He coughed for one hundred and fifty. I didn't think you'd mind.'

'My dear Mike, as I told you, what I want are results. And I'm not a cheapskate.'

'I have your results, doll.' He stopped. 'Sorry, I got carried away.'

'It takes a lot to offend me, Mike,' said the baroness. 'And you, as they say here, are not in that ballpark. Get on with the story.'

Heidi came skating over with a tray of dishes, lurched as she reached the table, cannoned into the edge of the booth and fell to the floor with an enormous crash. It took several minutes for the baroness and her guests to calm her down and for the broken crockery and salad to be swept up and the trio's main dishes delivered safely.

'You need to eat up, Mike. You've had a long day. Give us the gist in a couple of sentences and we can have the full story when you've cleared your plate.'

'Gonzales was violent and mean, he was chucked off the team because of his behaviour, he got crap grades, and he'd have been thrown out of college if Fortier-Pritchardson hadn't saved him by finding that he'd suffered from racial harrassment. Donnelly said he must have been screwing the bitch senseless. When I told him Gonzales had a Ph.D. he nearly choked from laughing.' And Robinson bent thankfully to his vast plate of corned beef.

At that precise moment, the Provost was wailing to the President. 'She's crazy. Diane says what she said was certifiably crazy. And she holds her responsible for firing up Jimmy Rawlings. Supposedly he's organising a march through the campus tomorrow morning protesting our hiring an Islamophobe who insulted Allah by saying Islam was a primitive religion. I don't know what we're going to do.'

'*You* don't know what *you're* fucking going to do,' said the President. 'It's your sorry ass that's on the line, not mine. I'm in New York and none of this is my fault. You chose Lady fucking Troutbeck. And Diane carries the can for choosing Jimmy Fucking Rawlings. And so do you for accepting her recommendation.'

'I'd had several refusals when I met Troutbeck. How was I to know she was a mad right-winger? You expect senior academics to be liberals. Why's she doing this?'

'Sounds like wilful cuntishness to me. You should have checked her out.'

'I told Marjorie to, and she passed her. Said she was a radical. But didn't say anything about her being a radical reactionary.'

'You shouldn't have trusted Marjorie. Don't you remember why we got rid of her?'

'I don't trust Marjorie, but Ethan wasn't around and I trusted her enough just to run a check,' shouted the Provost. 'I was busy and in England and I didn't think there was a problem. And Rawlings would have been OK if she hadn't been here. What am I to do now?'

'It's obvious. Get some reliable students mobilised to complain about Troutbeck. If things are made difficult for her and we offer her a good package, we can get her on a plane out of Indiana double-quick.'

'Ethan's already having her trailed to see if we can get anything on her.'

'Tell him to do a bit of intimidating if necessary.'

'I'm not sure that would work,' said the Provost.

'Don't be ridiculous.'

'You don't know her like I do.'

'Nonsense. Ethan could intimidate Donald Rumsfeld.'

'What about Rawlings?'

'We'll pander to his ego by making Troutbeck his sacrificial victim. Then we'll bribe him to shut the fuck up.'

'So what's a nice couple like you doing in a job like this?'

'My dad was a P.I.,' said Vera, 'and I joined him when I finished high school. I'd still be there in Chicago if I hadn't met Mike, who had just graduated and was moving to New Paddington to go to graduate school. He wanted me, I wanted him, and he needed work so we set up M and V.'

'What made you want to go to Freeman, Mike?' asked the baroness.

'I wanted to do film studies and my college was crap at it. Freeman had a good reputation.'

'You amaze me.'

Robinson sighed, and swallowed more coffee. 'There was a really great two-year course in noir P.I. films.'

'Was? You mean you've finished it.'

'It's more like it finished me. I loved the first year, but then our prof was pushed out and a moron took over. This past year we've being going almost still by still through great movies and the books they're based on looking for racism and sexism. Can you imagine?'

'I don't want to.'

'Philip Marlowe uses words like negro and mocks Indians, Sam Spade turns a woman in even though she'll get the electric chair, all the heroes are violent, they all see women as sex-objects and are substance abusers, Sidney Greenstreet's fatness was portrayed negatively, and Peter Lorre was always being ridiculed for being short.'

'I see. So you decided to ape Mike Hammer just to wind the moron up?'

'You got it. Do you remember the end of *I, The Jury?*'

'No.'

'"How c-could you?" she gasped. I only had a moment before talking to a corpse, but I got it in. "It was easy," I said."'

'Not a sentimentalist, Mickey Spillane.'

'When I said that showed the integrity and innate justice and moral sense of Hammer, I thought Dr. Pappas-Lott would explode.'

'Pappas-Lott? What was she doing teaching you? She's the Dean.'

'She took over the course to use it for what she called a series of master classes. There are always instructors there being shown how to teach.'

'*Can* she teach?'

'If you think grading students by how many unacceptable words or actions they can ferret out of a book or a film is teaching, then she sure can.'

Vera took his hand and patted it. 'Never mind, Maurice-Mike, what good would a master's be to you anyway?'

'Didn't you finish?' asked the baroness.

'I was disqualified for inappropriate behaviour and language and I couldn't be bothered appealing. Freeman means nothing to me: I just went to classes. And who wants to be an academic anyway? Through Vera-Velda I've found a job I love. We'll move out of New Paddington soon and go somewhere there'll be work.'

◇◇◇

Before settling into her own office the following morning, the baroness called in next door and gave Marjorie a pithy account of what she had learned from Mike Robinson.

'You mean you just walked off the street and hired these children? Are they even licensed?'

'They are. It turns out that Velda-Vera is twenty-five and had five years' experience as a gumshoe in Chicago before she met Mike, moved to New Paddington, and took him on as an employee. He's been there for more than two years and has just qualified for a license.'

'So what's with this fedora/trenchcoat rubbish?'

'It's just fun, Marjorie. He's a bit bored, and he was really just putting two fingers up at Pappas-Lott and her ilk. And he and Vera-Velda seem perfectly competent and really rather sweet. I'm enjoying them. Don't be a spoil-sport.

'What's more, we now have independent evidence that Gonzales is a thoroughly bad piece of work and that the Provost is his willing accomplice. My mind is clarified. They're obviously not fit to be in their jobs and we must see what we can do to get them out. The children will be digging for more dirt on them, and also having a look again at the death of Provost Haringey.'

'What can they do that hasn't been done?'

'I don't know, Marjorie, but I'm giving them a chance. Mike Robinson has flair, and from what I learned last night, Vera is excellent at screwing information out of unlikely sources.'

'I'd be easier if it was Mike Hammer himself going after those rattlesnakes.'

The baroness yawned. 'Stop worrying, Marjorie. Everything will be fine. Besides, they're armed. Now, may I borrow some money off you? I had my wallet stolen after yesterday's punch-up.'

'How did that happen?'

'Don't know, except that there was a crush of students when I was leaving.' She showed Marjorie her bag. 'You see, it doesn't have a zip, so you wouldn't need to be one of Fagin's finest to nick the wallet.'

'What was in it?'

'Nothing important. Just one credit card. And only fifty dollars or so. It was mainly some cards and phone numbers people have given me. That kind of thing. Stefano's reported it to the cops.'

'Do you think it was an act of vengeance?'

'Probably just petty thieving.'

In response to the sound of shouting outside, Marjorie jumped up and went to the window. 'Well, Jack, come and look at what's goin' on outside. That's vengeance.'

'It's not much of a demo,' said the baroness with a note of disappointment as she stared out of the window. Trailing through the campus after Jimmy Rawlings was a small line of young people, mostly brown or black, but a few white, many bearded and some carrying crudely made placards.

The baroness squinted. 'Can you see what's on the placards, Marjorie? I can only make out the word "insult."'

'I think it's "insults." TROUTBECK INSULTS ALLAH.'

'That's quite mild. No death threats?'

'Not that I can see. In fact the others seem to be about reparations. WE SLAVED YOU'LL PAY.'

'That's quite good.'

'And there's something about Freeman. Do you think it's about the name-change Rawlings was demanding?'

'Maybe.'

The telephone rang. 'Yes, yes, yes....How many?...That was quick....What are the details....Is that so?...Thanks.'

Marjorie put the phone down. 'That was a friend in the Provost's office, Jack. Three formal separate complaints were lodged against you just now alleging harassment—one racial, one religious, and the other sexual. You'll be getting a letter from the Provost about them any time now. She's anxious to proceed against you as soon as possible. And the Goon wants to interview you.'

'What fun! What exactly are they complaining about?'

'Your line about blacks needing to get over slavery and everything you said about Islam.'

'Oh, good. And the sexual one?'

'You touched someone inappropriately. Apparently you put your hand on a girl's arm.'

'Wow! Wait till I really make a pass. When did I do this?'

'A student tried to remonstrate with you yesterday evening and you touched her.'

'If she was the boring little creep who came up to me afterwards and went on and on about the insensitivity of what I'd said about sodding diversity, it's true that I touched her in trying to get her out of my way.'

'In this university, if they don't like you, that will count as a prima facie case of sexual harassment.'

'It's a good thing they don't like me, then. I wouldn't want to miss this.'

'It's Betsy, Lady Troutbeck. Can I see you?'

'Certainly. I'm free for the rest of the day. When? Where?'

'If it's OK with you, I'll come by soon.'

'Come to the hotel. I'll feed you. And I'll leave Horace in the office so we can have some peace. He's been alternating between 'Whoo! Whoo!' and 'Beverages!' all morning, and it's beginning to drive me mad.'

Two hours later, the baroness was back in her room jabbing her finger at the antipasti. 'Have some of that salami. And a piece of the bruschetta. Paola made it and it's very very good. Come on, Betsy. You're looking peaky. You must eat up. Are you working too hard?'

'It's a lot easier driving people around than like…sorry… cheerleading,' said Betsy, reaching for some more salami. 'Though I hate being with that awful Professor Rawlings. His limo had an accident this morning and they called on me to take him to an appointment.'

'Doesn't he demand that you call him Professor Mujaahid?'

Betsy giggled and then reverted to looking anxious. 'He hardly talks to me at all. When I picked him up at the airport that time he told me to cover myself up cos I dressed like a slut.'

'And did you cover up?'

'I couldn't that time. But after that I wore long sleeves and jeans when I had to see him. But then I was replaced and this morning I didn't have enough notice to change so I had to go as I was and this time he said I looked like a ho.'

'You should tell him to go to hell.'

Betsy said nothing.

'You're afraid to because you'd lose your job.'

Betsy nodded.

'Presumably a white male wouldn't get away with that?'

'A professor was disciplined last year just for saying something about skimpy clothing that a student took as an insult.'

'The double standards in this place are truly impressive. Now, finish that salami and tell me why you wanted to see me.'

Betsy put her fork down and gazed at the baroness. 'I wanted to tell you I think you're, like…sorry, I'm getting better but the likes slip in sometimes…I think you're awesome.'

'Is that good?'

'Oh, it's really really good. I've never met anyone like you.'

'Some would think you'd been fortunate heretofore.'

'I couldn't believe what you said yesterday. You're so brave standing up to all those bullies.'

'Thank you, Betsy. I'm glad you approve.'

'You're a real inspiration. And not just to me.'

'Are we talking VRC?'

Betsy nodded.

The baroness's phone rang. 'Yes...yes...no, I'm busy....If you want to see me, ring me at the office later and I'll arrange a time when you can come and see me....Impertinence will get you nowhere, young man.' She rang off. 'Ridiculous.'

Betsy looked enquiring.

'That was that frightful Gonzales person, demanding I come and see him.'

Betsy dropped her fork. 'You talked like that to him?'

'Why not?'

'Because...because...because....'

'Come on, Betsy, spit it out.'

'We think he does bad things.'

'How bad?'

Betsy instinctively looked over her shoulder and then back at the baroness and grabbed her hand. 'Some people had accidents.'

'Who? When? How?'

'The VRC know about them.'

'Were the VRC there last night, Betsy?'

She nodded. 'Some of them anyway.'

'You are one of them, aren't you?'

Betsy looked petrified. 'Sort of. But I only like help them a bit. I'm not like at the centre.'

'What does VRC stand for?'

'I don't know.'

'Honestly.'

'Honestly.'

'And the sword?'

'Oh, I know about that, but don't tell anyone I told you. You could pretend to have guessed. It's the Sword of Truth, from a sci-fi series by Terry Goodkind.'

'Tell me about the books.'

'I haven't read them. I just haven't had time.'

'Did you really come here to tell me I was awesome? Or has someone sent you?'

'Both. Someone asked me to ask you if you'll help.'

'How?'

'I don't know. They'll have to tell you that.'

'This gets more Enid Blyton by the minute.' She saw Betsy's expression. 'You've never heard of Enid Blyton, of course. I don't suppose there's any reason why you should have, but for future reference, she's a dead, white, politically incorrect English writer for children. When do they want to see me?'

'If you agree to a meeting, someone will call you.'

'Tell them they need not hesitate to consult the Oracle. I may not be in Delphi, but I'm still the Oracle.'

Betsy gazed at her in incomprehension.

'I'll explain that another time, Betsy. Just tell them I agree.'

'I'll tell them. But I wanted to tell you how I felt even before I was asked to carry a message.' Betsy's eyes widened and she put her hand on the baroness's arm. 'Oh, Lady Troutbeck, I've got such feelings for you.'

Chapter Nine

'Do you want the cage and case in the trunk, ma'am?'

'I certainly do,' said the baroness, sinking thankfully into the taxi and placing Horace's crate beside her. Although she had been waiting only a couple of minutes, she had to mop the perspiration off her face.

'So what goes on here?' she asked, as they drove through Jackson.

He shrugged. 'Not a lot. Moistly moider.'

'Moider?'

'Yeh, lady. Moider. You know, guns and knives and dat. We got way more moiders here dan where I come from.'

'Your accent is familiar. You can't be from Mississippi. Where are you from?'

'The Bronx, lady. You bin there?'

'No. I just recently met someone from there. My parrot does an impression of her. What brings you to Jackson?'

'My wife thought it would be safer than the Bronx. What a ditz.'

◇◇◇

'Welcome to the Magnolia State, Jack,' said Edgar Brooks. He wrapped her in his enormous arms and kissed her. She responded enthusiastically. Then he stood back and looked at her critically. 'That's a real elegant suit you're wearing. You look good in white. I've always liked linen.'

'Indeed it is. I call it my Wimbledon suit, because I bring it out only for special occasions. This yellow blouse is its constant companion. I'm amazed they've survived this long without acquiring a single red-wine stain.'

They moved from the hotel lobby into the bar and he took her to a table by the window. A barman arrived immediately carrying a tray with two martini glasses and a jug. 'I had them make up a jug of martinis the way you like them. I hope that's all right with you.'

'That's most thoughtful of you, Edgar.'

'Bless your heart, you're the one who's put herself out, travelling all the way here.'

They toasted each other. 'Can your little bird still say "Beverages"?'

'There are days he says little else. I hope he'll remember it when he meets you again.'

'It'll be good to get properly acquainted with him. Now, I've been thinking about how we'll spend this weekend. You don't know much about the South, do you?'

'Except that I've always wanted a plantation, with a great, airy eighteenth-century house, a drive lined with white oaks, and a softly spoken negro butler.'

'When did you set your heart on that?'

'I saw *Gone with the Wind* several times and was in love with Clark Gable.'

'I sure regret that I'm no Clark Gable.'

'That's OK, Edgar. I'm certainly no Vivien Leigh.'

By Sunday morning, the baroness had learned a great deal. She knew that the Civil War had nothing civil about it and was properly called the War of Northern Aggression and that Jackson had been given the nickname 'Chimneyville' because when the damn Yankees burned it out in 1863, only the chimneys were left standing. She had discovered that she hated most Southern food, particularly hominy grits in red-eye gravy, which she had tried at breakfast. Having bought a cookbook to investigate Mississippi cuisine, she had been appalled to find not only that the locals were crazy about pies, but that apparently they made them by adding a few dubious ingredients to cake mixes. Even more horrifying was the revelation that canned soup was allegedly a staple ingredient of local casseroles. After listening to a litany of complaints, Brooks took the book from her and threw it away. 'Tonight,' he said, 'you'll have seafood that even you won't be able to fault.' He paused. 'I think.'

The trip to Natchez to see the glories of antebellum architecture and have a first view of the mighty Mississippi river had been a great success, as had the time they spent in the late afternoon in her bedroom back in Jackson. That evening, the baroness had donned a black cotton velvet dress with flowing sleeves that—although slinky—accentuated her ample curves to good effect. 'I'm being culturally sensitive,' she explained to Brooks as the limousine drew up. 'I'm wearing white and black alternately in deference to the racial mix of Mississippi.'

'I'm real glad you didn't know about the Hawaiians,' he said, as he handed her into the car.

The Natchez dinner had been such a triumph that they dispensed with Sunday breakfast apart from having fruit and a pot of coffee on the balcony of the baroness's suite. Horace sat on her shoulder chewing happily on a piece of cheese. 'It's hopeless cheese,' the baroness had said, 'but parrots don't have high standards.' In a water glass on the table was the magnolia blossom Brooks had plucked for her the night before.

'I've finally managed to dredge up from my memory some of those lines from Hilaire Belloc that I was struggling with yesterday,' she said.

'So, recite them.'

*'They feed you till you want to die
On rhubarb pie and pumpkin pie,*

And horrible huckleberry pie,
And when you summon strength to cry,
"What is there else that I can try?"
They stare at you in mild surprise
And serve you other kinds of pies.'

Brooks applauded.

'Mind you, if I remember rightly, they were written about Massachusetts. If Belloc had been introduced to pecan pie he'd have had a stroke.'

'Pies are the smallest of your problems, Jack,' said Brooks, suddenly turning serious. 'I've been thinking about what you told me about what you've gotten yourself into in Freeman. I know you'd have the stomach and brains for the fight, my little Steel Magnolia, but do you really want to bother?'

'Duty calls.'

'Duty to whom? Marjorie and Betsy?'

'Yes, but also to the students and all those unfortunate parents who have to find thirty grand a year to finance a worthless education.'

'I guess the parents would riot if they knew what their children are fed these days under the guise of humanities.'

'Something much worse than hominy grits.'

'Even with gravy.'

The baroness sighed. 'And, though this sounds pompous, I have an even greater duty to academic integrity.'

'Not to speak of the dead Provost.'

'Indeed. He deserves a posthumous break.'

'So what's your game plan?'

'Game plan? I don't have one yet. That's one of the reasons I rang you. I needed to get away and talk to a sensible outsider.'

'So are you any clearer now?'

'I'm still at a loss. Even though I'm sure Mike and Vera will turn up some stuff, there's an enormous amount I don't know, and I feel at a disadvantage. I'm seeing the VRC crowd—well, that's to say I'm seeing someone who claims to be their leader—

on Tuesday evening, and feel at a disadvantage knowing so little about them. I wish that at least I knew what VRC stood for.'

'VRC. VRC. VRC. Dammit. I can't think of anything that makes any sense. You don't get secret societies called visual resource centres.'

'Marjorie's already tried the internet and got nowhere.'

'We'll think about that by and by. One thing strikes me is they're ineffectual. Except for giving stuff to that newspaper, what have they done except leave silly messages?'

'Not much. I wondered if they wanted me involved because I might give them some ideas.'

'Well, here's an idea. From what you've picked up, it sounds as if they're terrified of confronting the authorities openly.'

'Marjorie told me the two kids who were chucked out—Brendan Something and Lindy Something—were treated really brutally. Not as in the sense of being beaten up or anything, but nasty threats. As I told you, according to Mike, Gonzales has form on the thug front and Betsy mentioned rumours about people having accidents.'

'Have you heard any more from Mike since the other night?'

'No. But he doesn't like to ring till he's got something.'

Brooks shrugged. 'For now, it sounds like there's nothing much you can do till you've met the VRC leaders. Then maybe you can coordinate some action. But it seems to me that what you need most are lawyers.'

'What a ghastly thought.'

'We're not all bad, Jack.'

'You're a lawyer? You've been hiding this dark secret from me. You alleged you were a businessman.'

'A businessman and a lawyer. I don't do much in the law department these days, but I'm still connected with the law firm my son took over from me. Edgar Junior's a good fella. He'll help out. We'll start by fighting your case. Give me the Provost's letter again and I'll get a copy for him.'

'And then?'

'Get your VRCs to turn the table on the authorities by col-
lecting evidence for a raft of complaints to hit the Provost's office
as fast as possible and simultaneously.'

'Strength in numbers.'

'Exactly. I'll give you Edgar Junior's phone number so they
can keep him informed. If they hit trouble, he'll intervene. Tell
these kids not to be picky. With that Goon in the Provost's office,
you don't want a revolver. This is an occasion for a Howitzer.'

'Or the elephant gun I've got at home. Family heirloom.'

'You've got the idea. You'll have to go after them with both bar-
rels. Mind you, I'd be happier if I had a better idea of what these
kids think they're up to. VRC. VRC. VRC. Darn it. It should be
obvious.' He scratched his head. 'You said you weren't able to get
hold of the sci-fi novels Betsy mentioned? We'll get some tomorrow before you go and you can do some homework on the plane.
Maybe you'll find it revolves around a conspiracy called VRC.'

'If it were, that would have been public knowledge by now.'

Horace finished his cheese, put his head on one side and
produced a short, sharp baroness-type bark. 'Rubbish,' he said.
'Rubbish. That's right. That's right.'

'That's right,' said Brooks slowly. 'That's right. That's right.
You could be onto something there, Horace. This is about left
and right, isn't it? These kids are fighting the left. Maybe the
"R" stands for 'Right.'

The baroness considered this. 'In which case, maybe the "C"
is for conspiracy?'

'Of course.' Brooks clapped his hand to his head. 'Right-wing
conspiracy. Very right-wing conspiracy? No, that doesn't work.
Let me think.' He drummed his fingers on the table and then
clapped his hands. 'Got it. Of course. VRC is the Vast Right-
Wing Conspiracy. Don't you remember? When the Monica
Lewinsky story first broke, Hillary Clinton said it had been
invented by the Vast Right-Wing Conspiracy.'

'By George, Edgar, I think you've got it. That is, you and Horrie
between you have got it. If you have, we've learned something
interesting about whoever's behind this.'

'Yes?'

'They're literate. They understand that "right-wing" is one word.'

'VLRC, then. The Vast Literate Right-wing Conspiracy.' He looked at his watch. 'We need to get going, Jack, or we'll be late for our river boat.'

◇◇◇

'So why exactly did you spurn Betsy's advances?' asked Mary Lou.

'She's a child. I'm not a paedophile.'

'Didn't you say she was nineteen? I wasn't much older when you had your wicked way with me.'

'She's nineteen going on eight. You were more like twenty-four going on eighty.'

'I suppose that's a compliment. Were you tempted?'

'Of course I was tempted. Very. It was a big sacrifice, lying about being exclusively hetero, but I had to save her face. I suppose it means all women on campus are now off-limits.'

'You're not a bad old thing, Jack. I'm proud of you. And clearly you got your just reward on this earth in Jackson.'

'I certainly did,' said the baroness. 'I'd lost his card—well, had it pinched—so it was like the answer to a maiden's prayer that he rang me straight after Betsy left.'

'Have you heard from him since?'

The baroness tried and failed to keep the self-congratulatory tone out of her voice. 'He's sent me a present. Got someone to deliver it by car from a shop in Indianapolis before I even got back here.'

'So we're talking a serious present then, not candy or lingerie.'

'Much more romantic than candy or lingerie. Practical as well.'

'Go on. Go on. What was it?'

'A Colt 45.'

◇◇◇

From: Mary Lou Dinsmore
To: Robert Amiss
Sent: Tue 22/05/2006 10.15
Subject: News from Hicksville

You certainly can't accuse Jack of hanging about. In the past few days she's caused uproar on the campus, has been protested against for being an Islamophobe, has refused for the most honourable of reasons to have an affair with the delicious Betsy, has acquired a brace of private eyes, and has enjoyed a passionate weekend in Jackson, Mississippi, with a sixty-something Southern gentleman. They got on so well he's given her a gun—and not just a gun, but a Colt 45, which has sent her into sentimental droolings about Humphrey Bogart as Philip Marlowe. No, I don't think there's any phallic significance in the present. He seems a mite concerned that someone will try to rub her out.

I'm ferociously busy learning how to be a presenter and interviewer. No major cock-ups yet, but it's still nerve-wracking. I haven't got time now to fill you in any more about what Jack's got herself into on campus, except that she seems to be the icon and potentially the leader of a group of reactionary revolutionaries whom she hasn't even met yet. She was extremely anxious that I report to you that New Paddington was no longer dull and things were getting really really interesting. Hope continues to spring eternal with her. I gave her none, and she muttered something about you turning into a girlie-man.

Ellis has nabbed his Albanians.

Where are you now? Where are you going next?

Love to both from us both,

ML

◇◇◇

The baroness finished unpacking and made a phone call. 'I'm back, Marjorie. Any news?'

'Where are you?'

'At the hotel. Just going to have something to eat and have an early night. I'm shattered.'

'I'll just call by if that's OK. Not to eat but for a drink.'

'Anything important?'

'Just something I want to talk over. I won't keep you up.'

She had just finished her cheese when Marjorie arrived and gave her a hug.

The baroness pushed her away and looked at her squarely. 'Something's up, isn't it?'

'I afraid it is. Your private eyes. I'm sorry, Jack, but they've had an accident.'

'How bad?'

Marjorie took her hand. 'They're dead, Jack. In a car crash.'

The baroness sat down suddenly. 'How did it happen?'

'I don't know. It was on the local news. It said they ran into a truck.'

'Seems an odd coincidence,' said the baroness, in as level a tone as she could muster.

'In their business, wouldn't it always be an odd coincidence if they died during a case?'

'Not if they were just looking for mislaid spectacles. Get me a brandy, Marjorie.' And she burst into loud sobs.

'I've sent Marjorie home, Edgar, and I'm well into a bottle of brandy and wondering if the accident had anything to do with me. Law of unexpected fucking consequences and all that.'

'Do you want me to find out what happened?'

'Please.'

'OK. Now be careful. I don't like the sound of this. Not one bit. Make sure your door is locked, and tomorrow, whatever you do, don't turn your back on Gonzales. '

◇◇◇

The baroness woke on the sofa just after 7.30 the following morning with a pungent smell of brandy enveloping her. At some juncture, she realised, she had kicked over the bottle. 'Just as well,' she muttered. 'At least it meant I didn't drink the lot.'

Within an hour, the breeze through the opened windows had dissipated the smell, she had bathed, dressed in a defiantly bright green trouser suit, and had consumed a light breakfast and several cups of coffee. When Betsy arrived the baroness was brisk. 'I had a phone call from your leader when I was on my way home yesterday, Betsy. He sounded very mysterious. Refused to give me his name. Do you know it?'

'Oh, no, Lady Troutbeck. I'm too junior for that.'

Betsy gazed at her with what was now her customary doe-eyed look. 'Did you have a nice weekend?'

'Delightful, thank you.'

'You look really cool. You've got a tan.'

'I caught the sun on the river. Now let's get back to the VRC. This person also refused to tell me where we're meeting. All he said was that you would pick me up. So where are we going?'

'I don't know where the meeting is, Lady Troutbeck. I was told to take you to the Wal-Mart that's about five miles out of town and park in the car park and wait. Then the person I know in the VRC will collect you. I'm not allowed to go with you.' She gazed at the baroness sadly.

'This is reminiscent of Watergate. Any minute Deep Throat will come out of the shadows.'

'Watergate?'

'Betsy, I've decided to take you in hand.' She saw the joy on Betsy's face. 'No, no, I mean intellectually. I want you to start reading books. Don't frown. I know you haven't much time, but I'll fix it for you. I'll have you paid for running errands for me while you're actually reading. Here you are. I've bought you a Jane Austen.'

Betsy took *Pride and Prejudice* nervously. 'Is it very intellectual?'

'No. It's very intelligent, but you won't find it difficult. In fact—and this is the secret I want to communicate—it'll be enjoyable. Reading is enjoyable.'

'Oh, Lady Troutbeck, thank you. I'll treasure it.'

'I don't want you to treasure it. I want you to read it.'

'I'll start it tonight. I promise. Now we should go.'

'Did you ever see "The Dead Poets Society," Lady Troutbeck?'

'No. What is it?'

'A film about an English teacher who inspires his pupils not just to love literature, but to find joy in living and to stand up for themselves and their beliefs.'

'Isn't that what all teachers are supposed to do?'

'Of course it is. But they don't. Well, at Freeman, they mostly don't. The faculty don't seem to want to teach—just do research to put on their resumés.'

'So is this the role you envisage for me?'

The flaxen-haired youth called Ryan looked across the table at her and smiled. 'You're there already. When we saw you last week we decided we'd found our Boadicea.'

'It's pronounced Buddica, but never mind that. I'm flattered by the comparison. I've always wanted to cut down my enemies with the blades on my chariot wheels.'

'Excuse me, Lady Troutbeck,' said the black youth called Mark. 'I've read that blades on chariot wheels are a later invention.'

'*Touché*, Mark. I must brush up my ancient history.'

'Do you want to know about us?' asked Ryan.

'Indeed I do. Other than that you draw inspiration from a not uninteresting science-fiction series, that you are attracted by the philosophy of Ayn Rand, that your sword is the Sword of Truth, that your initials stand for "Vast Right-wing Conspiracy" and that you draw many of your intellectual arguments from a book* of that name, I know nothing.'

The four students looked at her with open mouths. She looked back at them impassively.

---

*Mark W. Smith, *The Official Handbook of the Vast Right-Wing Conspiracy*.

'No shit, Sherlock,' said Mark.

'How did you work all that out?' asked the slight youth called Joshua.

'That would be telling.'

'We've got Miss Marple here,' said Sue-Ellen.

'I prefer Mark's comparison with Holmes, Sue-Ellen. I would rather play the violin than knit. And anyway, my friends, we should strive at all times for gender-blindness. Now tell me more.'

'I'm fine, Edgar. Any news?'

'Brake failure, Jack. The cops think it was an accident. What did the girl call him, the "silly son-of-a-bitch"?'

'Silly fantasising son-of-a-bitch....'

'The silly fantasising son-of-a-bitch drove too fast and on his way from their home to the office, when he should have slowed down at an intersection, instead he drove straight into the side of a truck.'

'Did they die instantly?'

'Seems so. It was a big, big truck and the car was an old one. They weren't even wearing seat belts.'

'Oh, hell,' said the baroness. 'Oh, bloody hell. Are you thinking what I'm thinking?'

'Gonzales? I am. But I'm told these are the kind of cops that don't seem to go looking for trouble so I wouldn't even know yet how to go about getting them interested. Do you want me to get someone on to it?'

'I do, Edgar. And I'll pay for it, whatever it takes. Mike might have been a silly fantasising son-of-a-bitch, but he was my silly fantasising son-of-a-bitch. If the Goon did this, and I think he probably did, he's going to pay.'

'Steady on, Jack. We have to keep our heads. Sure, Gonzales is a possibility, but wouldn't it have been a dumb move? Wouldn't he realise you'd hire replacements?'

'Maybe he didn't mean to kill them, Edgar. Just frighten them. And me. Besides, we know he's dumb.'

'True. OK. I'll get on to it. But meanwhile, be careful. And tell those kids you're associating with to be careful too. If Gonzales had Mike and Vera killed, he obviously knows more about what's going on than we might think. You—and they—need to start watching your backs.'

◇◇◇

'You look like you've been rode hard and put up wet, Jack.'

'I certainly feel that way, Marjorie. I really mind an awful lot about those two children being killed. But there it is. We have to get on with things.

'Now, the VRC agreed to let me tell you about them. They havered a bit, but the fact that you'd been the means of my coming to Freeman won them over. And then they checked you out with Warren Godber and that clinched it.'

'So is he running the VRC?'

'No. He's just facilitating it. When Joshua confided in him that some students wanted to become guerrillas for truth, he said he wasn't prepared to take an active role of any kind, owing to having lost any heart for battle, but that if they promised not to do anything violent he was prepared to let them use his house for meetings and give them advice if specifically requested so to do.'

'So what do they intend to do?'

'They're confused, disorganised, and completely lacking in any strategy. I told them that conducting occasional intellectual smash-and-grab raids was going to get them nowhere. This had to be planned like the great day of the Deltas in "Animal House."'

'Gee, Jack, I didn't think you'd know about "Animal House."'

'I like amusing and constructive anarchy, Marjorie. Along with "A Night at the Opera" and "The Producers," "Animal House" is my favourite film.'

'So what's your strategy?'

'The VRC are the troops. I'm the Chairman. And I need a Chief Executive.'

'Don't look at me, Jack. I've got a full-time job, a husband, three children, and several cats. Plus, I'm a marked woman since it came out that I'd cleared you as safe.'

'I understand all that, Marjorie. I'll be needing your help, but behind the scenes. I have a Chief Executive in mind, but...as you would put it...I have to go get him.'

'I'm hallucinating,' said Robert Amiss, gazing down the vast expanse of shabby grandeur that was the vista of the Grandhotel Praha restaurant.

Rachel continued to read the menu. 'I think I might try "Bryndzove halusky," since this is our last chance to eat what seems to be the Slovakian national dish.'

'Rachel, listen to me. Turn round and see if you can see what I see.'

She twisted round. 'Dear God, I can.'

'Well, since it's improbable she's looking for anyone else, I suppose I should greet her.' He strode down the room to where the baroness was still looking about her. 'Lady Troutbeck, I presume.'

'That's the wrong way round. I should be saying "Mr. Amiss, I presume." I'm the one who's found you, after all. Not vice versa.'

He kissed her on both cheeks.

'Why are you doing that European two kisses business? It's effeminate.'

'You've got off lightly. These days in Europe it's normally three.'

'Typical grade-inflation,' she grumbled.

'Besides, compared to you, we're all effeminate. Now shut up and come and join us. We're down the other end.'

Rachel greeted the baroness with a hug. 'This is an unexpected pleasure. Were you just passing through?'

Plumping herself down in Amiss's chair, the baroness chortled. 'Yes, indeed. I was en route from Vienna to Krakow and decided to drop by the High Tatras for a drink and something to eat.'

'In that case,' said Amiss, reaching for a nearby chair and pulling it up at the table, 'we should address some serious matters without delay. We're trying to decide if we should start with garlic soup and then risk the Slovak equivalent of beef and Yorkshire pudding, which is allegedly potato dumplings with sheep cheese topped with crumbled bacon. What do you think, Jack?' He handed her a menu.

'I think this deserves serious study,' she said solemnly. 'Now where's the sommelier?'

◇◇◇

'Stop complaining. Whatever reason you had for coming here, it wasn't for the cuisine.'

'If you think this is complaining....'

'Oh, sorry. Yes, we gathered from Mary Lou that you've been really really complaining in Indiana.'

The baroness recollected why she had come to Slovakia. 'However, all that's a thing of the past,' she said hastily. 'I've solved the food problem in New Paddington. Italian-Americans are doing me proud.' She looked at them hopefully. 'As they would do you.'

Amiss took a sip of plum brandy. 'Mmmmmn. Have some of this, Jack. You might decide to relocate here.'

The baroness took a sip, sucked on her cigar, leant back in her chair and stretched her legs out contentedly.

'Jack,' said Rachel. 'I realise this is a prurient enquiry, but now that your skirt's ridden up I notice that you're still sporting those directoire knickers. They don't seem quite to go with your new fashionable image.'

The baroness looked down at the eau-de-nil satin that was peeping from below her elegant charcoal-grey skirt. 'I bought a job-lot of them several years ago, Rachel, and I'm a frugal woman. Besides, they preserve my sexual integrity.'

'Your what?' said Amiss. 'You don't have any sexual integrity. You're a slut.'

'I may be a slut,' said the baroness stiffly. 'But I'm a selective slut.'

◇◇◇

It was an hour later, the baroness was on her second cigar and—by her standards—had told her story in considerable detail. 'Well, that's a right mess you've gotten yourself into,' remarked Amiss. 'What are you going to do for an encore? Visit Iran wearing a bikini?'

'It's too early for encores. I haven't had the final curtain. Yet.'

'Are you afraid the curtain might be more final than you'd wish?' asked Rachel. 'And if so, why are you going back?'

'The answer to the first question is yes, though in the sense of being run out of town, not knocked off. The answer to the second is noblesse oblige. I do not take kindly to my employees being murdered, if that's what happened. Besides, I like adventure.'

'And you want us because…?'

'Because I can't manage this alone. If I could, do you think I'd have travelled for the best part of twenty-four hours to try to cajole you into helping me? It's not my usual style.'

'Excuse us for a minute, Jack,' said Rachel. 'I need to talk to Robert.'

The baroness nodded and they withdrew.

'You're in luck,' said Rachel. 'And, as is often the case with luck, your good luck is at the expense of someone else's bad.'

'Very good that, Rachel,' said Amiss. 'It's so elliptical it's almost Troutbeckian.'

'My mother has had a mild stroke,' said Rachel, 'probably partly brought on by that ridiculous wedding.'

'Ridiculous? It wasn't ridiculous. I enjoyed it.'

'A tip, Jack,' said Amiss. 'Rachel had a really rough time over the wedding. This is not the time to disclose that you hadn't paid attention sufficiently to have grasped that even though you were told about it repeatedly. If I were you, I'd shut up and let her talk.'

The baroness nodded obediently.

'It's not life-threatening, but obviously she's very upset. So I have to go home and we have to postpone the rest of our European Grand Tour.'

'I suggest you commiserate, Jack,' said Amiss.

'Oh, yes, of course. Sorry. Put my insensitivity down to jet-lag.'

'That'll be a first,' said Amiss.

'I'm sorry to hear about your mother, Rachel,' said the baroness dutifully. 'And I'm sorry you have to call a halt to your travels.'

'Very good, Jack. Now carry on, Rachel.'

'I can't say I'm happy about seeing Robert going into what sounds like mayhem, especially if it turns out that he might fall victim to a psychopathic sociologist.'

As the baroness opened her mouth, she saw Amiss, behind Rachel's back, pressing a finger to his lips.

'We're driving to Bratislava tomorrow morning,' said Rachel, 'and the plan was to leave the van there and fly back to London.'

'But...?' asked the baroness hopefully.

'I didn't marry Robert to cage him and I can see his nostrils flaring with excitement. If it's only for two or three weeks, I'll lend him to you and soldier on without him. Just please try to return him only slightly shop-soiled.'

'My dear Rachel,' said the baroness, getting up and clasping her to her bosom. 'I will not forget this sacrifice.'

'I, of course,' said Amiss, 'have no say in this whatsoever.'

'Come, come, Robert,' said the baroness. 'That's a slight exaggeration. You may choose our route. Now let's go to reception and I'll organise the tickets to Indiana.'

Chapter Ten

'There's an extraordinary message from Betsy,' said the baroness, removing the phone from her ear.

They were sitting in a departure lounge at O'Hare. 'Is she not going to be able to meet us?' asked Amiss, looking up from his Goodkind novel apprehensively.

'No, no. It's not that. She'll collect us all right. But she says the Provost and the Goon are dead.'

'What?'

'To be precise, they've both been shot by a mad Muslim and Helen's been stabbed to boot.'

'Why would a mad Muslim want to murder the Provost and her minder? I can see why he might reasonably want to kill *you*, but....'

'And why I might reasonably want to kill *him*, but, at times, Islamists, to use the correct terminology, do move in mysterious ways their murders to perform. You certainly can't accuse them of not being inclusive. Atheists, agnostics, Jews, Christians, Hindus, Muslims, Schmuslims. It's all the same if you're doing it for Allah.'

'Can you ring Betsy and get some more info?'

A metallic voice cut in shouting about embarkation. 'They're calling the flight,' said the baroness. 'It'll keep.'

◇◇◇

Betsy's face lit up when she saw the baroness, who embraced her chastely. 'Right. Let's go.'

'Could you spare the time to introduce me to Betsy, Jack?'

'Can't you do it yourself? You're so prissy. Oh, all right then. This is my friend Robert Amiss, Betsy. He's come to our aid all the way from Slovakia.'

'Is that in Europe?' asked Betsy, as they shook hands.

'It is,' said Amiss. 'To the north-east of Austria.'

'Don't worry about it, Betsy,' said the baroness, noticing her blank look. 'Let's go. You can tell us about everything when we reach the car.'

◇◇◇

Betsy told her story holding tightly to the baroness's hand.

'Let me get this right, Betsy. Someone walked into the Provost's office at four yesterday afternoon, shot her and Gonzales dead, and then pinned a note to her chest with a knife.'

'Yeah, right.'

'And nobody heard this happen?'

'No. He must have used a silencer.'

'Any suspects?'

'The cops are working on it.'

'What did the note say?'

'They haven't released it, but according to the paper....' Betsy began to cry. 'I don't know how to tell you this....'

'Calm down, Betsy. Calm down. You won't be able to drive if you're in this condition. And we'd rather not spend the night in a car park.' The baroness fished out a voluminous red spotted handkerchief and passed it over. Betsy mopped her eyes, blew her nose, and gulped a few times. 'I'm OK now, Lady Troutbeck. I just got so scared about you.'

'About me? Why should you be scared about me?'

'The *Sentinel's* in my bag. You'll see.'

Amiss took the newspaper from the bag Betsy had tossed into the back seat. 'FREEMAN U PROVOST SLAIN: COPS SUSPECT

MISTAKEN IDENTITY,' he read out. 'Helen Fortier-Prichardson, Provost of Freeman University, has been slain by an unknown assailant in her office. Her assistant, Dr. Ethan Gonzales, was cut down in the same shocking attack. Police think he was going to her aid when the killer mowed him down.

'In a sickening twist, after shooting Provost Fortier-Prichardson in the head, the killer stuck a note to her chest with a knife. The police say they won't be releasing the full text yet, but it is believed it said she was executed for being an infidel who showed public disrespect to Allah.'

Amiss put down the paper. 'Sounds rather like a copy-cat murder.'

'You mean like Theo van Gogh in Amsterdam? I doubt it. I can't think who in New Paddington has even heard of Amsterdam.'

Amiss picked up the *Sentinel* again. 'President Dickinson said this morning, "The death of Provost Helen Fortier-Pritchardson along with that of our other beloved colleague, Dr. Ethan Gonzales, will be a cause of great grief to us all at Freeman U. But we will fight on to achieve their idealistic goals. I am appalled at the allegations made by the Provost's killer. Helen was a sensitive and caring woman who lived and breathed respect for diversity and believed there was no greater sin than to cause offence to another. There is something very wrong here. This must be a case of mistaken identity."'

Betsy gave a loud sniff. 'It's you he was after. You could be dead. It's so lucky….Oh, no. I like don't mean that. Well, I sort of do.'

'It's OK to be Pollyanna on this, Betsy. Not being a senti-mentalist, I won't pretend I think either of them a loss to the world. *Au contraire*. And I'm certainly glad glad glad it was them rather than me.'

'No qualms about being the cause of her death, Jack?'

'Stop talking rubbish, Robert. Mike and Vera may have been killed because they were investigating Gonzales at my request, as Helen and Gonzales may have been killed because someone confused her with me. In the first case, my guess is Gonzales is responsible. In the second, the cause of their death is lethal Islamist fruitcakery whipped up by that incendiary nut Jimmy Rawlings. There must have been someone in the audience who got over-excited.'

'But if he'd been in the audience, he'd have known the Provost wasn't you.'

'Maybe he couldn't tell whites apart. What do I know? If they really were after me, maybe the murder was delegated to an outsider.' She yawned. 'There's no point in speculating till we've got some hard facts. I've two questions, Betsy. Is dinner set up?'

'Oh, yes, Lady Troutbeck. I called Stefano from the airport to tell him the plane was on time.'

'And how are you getting on with Jane Austen?'

'Oh, she's really really cool. It was so exciting I finished it yesterday and then I went straight to the library and took out another one. It's called *Persuasion.*'

'That's my girl,' said the baroness. 'I'm proud of you. I'll have you on George Eliot soon.'

Betsy's face fell. 'Hey, Lady Troutbeck, of course I'll read whatever you tell me, but could I stick to female authors for a while?'

'There's another thing, Edgar. Marjorie's just come here to deliver Horace. She says she came back early from lunch yesterday and found someone in my office. The cage door was open and Horace was inside but the guy was cursing and mopping up blood from his hand. When he saw Marjorie he took off.'

'Did she call the cops?' asked Brooks sharply.

'Yes. The description wasn't too good—just a tall young white guy in a hoodie and sunglasses, but they got a DNA sample. You can guess what this means.'

'Gonzales had planned something like the horse's head episode in "The Godfather"?'

'Yes. That's certainly what Marjorie thought, which is why she took Horace home with her, for which I'm profoundly grateful, since someone broke into my hotel room that evening. There being no Horace, he began to embark on cutting up my clothes. Fortunately, he was interrupted early on by a chambermaid, who saw him run from the bedroom and out the sitting-room door. By the time reception raised the alarm, he had disappeared through the kitchens.'

'I'm mighty perturbed about this, Jack,' said Edgar Brooks. 'I know you're a tough woman, but you're not used to this kind of thing.'

'Not to people trying to decapitate my parrot, that's true.'

'Or to homicidal maniacs gunning for you, assuming you were the target and not the Provost.'

'Oh, I've more experience of that sort of thing than you might imagine, Edgar.'

'I'm real unhappy. I'd like to drop everything and come up to look after you....'

'But you're absolutely not going to. I know you've got to do that trip to London. I've got my friend Robert here now. I'll get the university or the cops to provide some security. And I've got my Colt to keep me warm. Oh, and I've seen a copy of your Edgar Junior's letter to the Provost in my defence and it's excellent. What a shame I missed the pleasure of seeing how she and Gonzales reacted.'

◇◇◇

'Did you sleep properly?'

'Yes, thanks,' said Amiss. 'And breakfast looks almost as good as last night's dinner, Jack. I don't know what you've been complaining about. So far, American food seems fine.'

She shot him a withering look.

'Beverages! Beverages! Beverages!'

'Oh, for God's sake, Horace, shut up or say something else for a change.' She turned back to Amiss. 'I'm pleased he's safe and sound, but I'm in a slightly querulous mood and he's adding to it. He's resolutely refused to learn his Chattanooga Choo-Choo, but he won't drop either the bloody beverages or the train from his repertoire. Neither of which I encouraged him to learn.'

Horace put his head on one side. 'VRC, VRC, VRC,' he said, in a passable imitation of Brooks.

'So Horace has joined our great revolutionary movement,' said Amiss. 'Now victory is truly within our grasp. After all, he's the first of us to have drawn blood.'

The baroness took an apple from the fruit bowl, cut a small piece, peeled it, and gave it to Horace. 'That'll keep him quiet for a while.'

'Any news about today's activities?'

'Betsy's taking us to the office first. Marjorie wants to give the three of us new mobile phones that will enable us to communicate with each other without fear of being bugged by agents of the markedly reduced Axis of Evil.'

'Or indeed, agents of an angry Allah.'

'Indeed. Rather more threatening when you come to think of it.'

'One question, Jack?'

'Yes?'

'It was Gonzales you wanted revenge on for the deaths of Mike and Vera. Now he's dead, doesn't that change things?'

She glowered. 'Gonzales was just the paramilitary wing of the Axis. The survivors are just as guilty. And if I've anything to do with it, they will pay for what he did. And pay heavily. Understood?'

'Understood.'

Her phone rang.

'Yes….yes…yes….We'll be with you shortly….Yes….Yes…. Good….Good.' She rang off. 'Marjorie says I've got meetings with the cops and with the President and the Dean and she's managed to fix up appointments for you with each of the VRC quartet at Warren Godber's. He's picking you up at my office to take you there himself.'

'What's happening to Horace?'

'He's probably out of danger now the Goon's dead, but Marjorie's going to look after him just in case.

'Now I've told you what to do. You've to suss out what the VRC leaders are like individually, what they think they're up to and what they're capable of.'

'Yes, yes. You've already given me full instructions.'

She paid no attention. 'Marjorie's told them you're my right-hand man and they can trust you implicitly. And you've got to suck up to Godber. When you've done that we'll talk strategy.'

'Is that it? No news from the front?'

'Except that the VRC have passed their first test. Under instructions to rustle up students for counter-complaints, and to communicate with Edgar's son, apparently they've done the business. A couple of dozen students have complained about being harassed by Jimmy Rawlings. I'm looking forward to seeing how that's gone down with the Axis.'

'So why did you get involved, Sue-Ellen?'

They were sitting in Godber's garden, sipping iced tea, which Amiss was trying hard to learn to like.

'I got really mad last St. Valentine's Day.' Sue-Ellen leaned back in her chair, stretched out her long brown legs and ran her fingers through her curly hair. 'Yep. Really, really mad.'

Amiss raised an enquiring eyebrow.

'Do you know about *The Vagina Monologues*?'

'Not a lot. Angry talking vaginas don't do much for me. I've read enough about it to know I don't want to see it.'

'It's a cult on campuses here. Gets performed every St. Valentine's Day to raise money for women's charities. I went to it, and I hated it.' She paused. 'No, I didn't hate it. I loathed and despised it. It was gross. It made me want to barf. And it was banal and preachy and pressed all the right feminist buttons.'

'So you're not a feminist?'

'Not the kind of feminist that's a feminist these days. I'd have been out campaigning for equality in my grandma's day, but that's all *so* over. Of course I'm all for liberating oppressed women abroad. But it's different in America. I like guys. They're my friends. They're *so* not the enemy. Sure, of course I'm against violence to women, but *The Vagina* fucking *Monologues* carries on as if men were nearly always brutes and women always victims.'

She sat up and poured them some more iced tea. 'It was boo to heterosexuality and hurrah for lesbians. There's a monologue in it called "The Little Coochie Snorter That Could."…'

'Sorry? I don't recognise the term.'

Sue-Ellen looked slightly embarrassed. 'If I tell you it begins with the woman describing how as a kid she impaled her 'coochie snorter' on the bedpost…?'

'Ah, I get it. How delightful.'

'Then it goes on to describe an adult dyke seducing a sixteen-year-old with the help of vodka. We're supposed to cheer. Apparently in the original version she was thirteen and the adult at one stage said "If it was rape, it was good rape." Yet they want guys arrested if they haven't got a contract to prove an adult woman said yes.'

'Modern feminists do seem a bit prone to double standards.'

'I hate double standards. I really hate them. They're an insult to our intelligence.

'Anyway, three years ago Freeman agreed like lots of other campuses that Valentine's Day was now to be known as V-Day. That's another thing I hate. I loved what Camille Paglia—she's one of my heroines—said about it. It was something like that these people were turning Valentine's Day, the one holiday celebrating heterosexual romantic harmony, into a grisly memorial to violence against women.'

'Is there a fully fledged nation-wide V-Day movement?'

'Oh, sure. And yes, it does raise useful money for charity, but it does awful harm along the way. A lot of dumb women have bought into the idea that men have stopped women talking about their vaginas and so any celebration of their genitals is one in the eye to the oppressor. They're all obsessed with raising women's self-esteem.'

She shook her head violently. 'I'm so sick of hearing that. Where I come from, you don't esteem yourself until you've done something worth esteeming. Like behaving decently or doing some hard work. This campus is full of people who think self-esteem is a human right.'

'So what happened on V-Day?'

'A lot of really disgusting stuff that made me ashamed to be a woman. Flyers were left all over the campus saying things like 'My vagina is flirty,' some of the kids dished out vagina-shaped lollipops, sold "vulva cookies" and "Vagina Warrior" T-shirts and some ran around nearly naked carrying a red plastic vagina nearly fifty feet high labelled "Cunt-fest." Oh and the Dean chaired a workshop called "Down with Paternalism: A Vagina's Right to a Dick-free Orgasm."'

'Anyone think of responding with a performance called *Penis Patter?*'

'Not at Freeman. The guys are too cowed. But at a Rhode Island university conservatives satirised V-Day with a Penis Day, a performance of *The Penis Monologues*, flyers saying things like "My penis is hilarious"—and they had a mascot called Testaclese.'

Amiss saw her grim expression. 'Am I right in guessing there wasn't a happy ending to this, Sue-Ellen?'

'No. The flyers and mascot were banned and the organisers reprimanded. They argued that women were trying to stop them talking about their dicks, but that didn't wash. They'd been offensive. I guess they were lucky. Here the Student Court would have expelled them.'

'Didn't anyone at Freeman complain about being offended by the V-Day celebrations?'

'If they did, the Provost threw their complaints out. Look, I know she's dead and I shouldn't say bad things about her, but she was a tyrant. The campus courts are rigged against the guys. It was like what you read about some Islamic countries where a man's word counts for more than a woman's, except at Freeman it's the other way round. Gonzales was the judge and everyone was terrified of him. There was a guy called Brendan Martial who was thrown out on a charge of date rape and a lot of us think the girl who complained was lying because the Provost wanted her to or Gonzales blackmailed her into it.'

'Why did she want Brendan out?'

'He was a really cool guy who was editor of the campus newspaper and he'd written something really critical about standards. Then the same thing happened to Lindy Dubois, who wrote an article describing herself as an African-American because she was born in Africa. Because she was white, an African-American said she'd been offended and out Lindy went. Then the paper was closed down and everyone was too scared to protest.'

'Was there no appeals procedure?'

'In theory you could appeal to President Dickinson, but everyone knows he rubber-stamped all the Provost's decisions. And some people who appealed got beaten up by people they couldn't identify.'

'So that was the climate around the time of V-Day, was it?'

'Yeah. And I was really furious. That sort of anti-men propaganda does awful things to our relationships with guys because they get really resentful. We complain about being victims, we act like hookers, and yet we treat men like rapists. And the faculty approves of it. As someone put it, we're supposed to believe that women are from Venus and men are from hell.'

'So you didn't make any protest to anyone?'

'No, not even when I was given a questionnaire asking what my vagina smelled like.'

'What?'

'Really. They handed those out to every woman who passed. But I was scared to say anything. You don't have to go as far as Brendan and Lindy did to get in trouble at Freeman. There's no freedom of speech of any kind if you challenge a dogma. A student was nearly expelled just for handing out leaflets for the Network of Enlightened Women.'

'A conservative group?'

She nodded. 'And I was shot down out of hand when I questioned something in one of my Women's Studies courses....'

'I'm surprised you do Women's Studies.'

'When I had my first interview with the Dean she asked me if I thought gender was a social construct.'

'Sorry?'

'Some people think there's no difference between males and females at birth.'

'Oh, got you. The differences develop because of the cultural influences they're exposed to. Is that it?'

'Yeah. So I said I thought there were big differences and she said I didn't know what I was talking about and I said I did, because I had a little brother and sister, and he was obsessed from the beginning with cars and trucks and ball games and she was all into pink and dolls. So the Dean said that was because they had been conditioned at home and at school and I said they hadn't been because my mom tried treating them just the same but she couldn't fight nature. Then the Dean stopped arguing and asked if I was a feminist, and when I said I was in favour of equal opportunities but I wouldn't call myself a feminist, she asked me if I was a womanist and I said that didn't mean anything and she told me I had to take Women's Studies if I wanted to stay at Freeman; anyway, it's compulsory if you want to get to Honours College.'

'How extraordinary.'

'For all I knew that happens on all campuses everywhere.'

'And what was Women's Studies like?'

'Full of shit. They use history and literature like a trash can that you rummage around in looking for examples of women being badly treated. I just play the game and get the credits. You can see why I didn't protest about V-Day. It's been tough for my parents to find the money to send me here. They'd be devastated if I got into trouble.'

'Have you told them anything about what it's like?'

'I haven't the heart to. I went to a good high school and my parents encouraged me to study and wanted me to have a really decent education, but what's the point of telling them the truth about Freeman? As far as I can tell most universities are as bad as each other and at least I can often get home for the weekend from here. But I complained to Ryan that this wasn't what I came to university for and we had a long talk about what was wrong and we found we agreed. And then he brought me into the VRC.'

'And what do you want the VRC to do?'

She laughed. 'Ideally turn Freeman U into what it's supposed to be. Though I can't guess how. We've been yapping a lot but we don't know how to go about things. The piece in the *Sentinel* was our first outing, but there's such a witch-hunt going on we've been lying low. I don't really want to be sacrificed. And certainly not if it achieves nothing.'

'Didn't the *Sentinel* pursue you for more?'

'No. The editor's had a lot of hassle. He's had a threatening letter from President Dickinson's lawyer and has been under huge pressure to identify whoever gave him the story.'

'And who was it?'

'Ryan. He knew someone who knew the editor. But we didn't know what to do next until we saw Lady Troutbeck. We all thought she was great and we thought she might really get the VRC to take off. But I guess now she might not be too keen to be involved. Anyone would be scared in her shoes. Even if Gonzales was responsible for having the private eyes killed, the murderer of him and the Provost is still around.'

'I wouldn't worry about that, Sue-Ellen. I've been in many sticky situations with Jack and I've never yet seen her scared. I think that gene's been left out of her DNA. Along with tact and sensitivity.'

'How are you getting on, Robert?'

'OK. Just finished with Sue-Ellen. Bright girl. I learned a lot. Now I'm waiting for Mark. How did it go with the cops?'

'At first I think they thought I might have done it.'

'Really? Why?'

'The Dean—who is now the Acting Provost, would you believe?—seems to have got hysterical about me as an enemy who was trying to destroy the Provost's achievements and told the cops I might have done her and the Goon in just to be thorough. However, when I pointed out that I could prove I had landed in Vienna that afternoon, they relaxed. Their geography is better than Betsy's. They know Europe's a long way away.'

'Did they tell you anything?'

'They said there was some violence in Indiana after 9/11 that helped radicalise some Muslim youths who weren't radical already: threats to mosques, attacks on people thought to be Muslim, that sort of thing. They described them as "hate crimes." I asked them what that meant and they said it was worse to commit a crime because you were prejudiced against the victim because of his race, colour, sexual orientation, and all the rest of the litany.'

She snorted. 'I don't follow this at all. Why is it worse to kill the Provost because she's white or the Goon because he's black rather than because she's a pill and he's a thug? You're just as dead whether your murderer is PC or not.'

'We have this at home too, Jack, as you perfectly well know. The logic is that it's worse to hate you because of your skin colour—which you can't change—than because you're a pill or a thug which you could.'

'Rubbish. Helen was a complete pill and Gonzales a complete thug through and through. With money they could have changed their skin colour or their gender, but to alter their characters would have required a couple of head transplants.'

'There's a car drawing up outside. Finish the story.'

'They're looking for a local Islamist who fits the description of a dark bearded youth who was seen running from the admin building. And apparently a woman in full burqa was seen hanging round the Provost's offices earlier.'

'But why would an Islamist kill the Provost?'

'They've no idea. While they've reluctantly decided I can't be the murderer, they're tempted by the *Sentinel* suggestion of mistaken identity. In the course of the Dean's ravings to them she also said I was Islamophobic, so they think I might have been the target. Though why anyone should come looking for me in the Provost's office is somewhat perplexing.'

'I look forward to meeting the Acting Provost. Someone with such intellectual flexibility that she can accuse you simultaneously of being both murderer and intended victim gets my vote.'

'It was being patronised that made me mad,' said Mark. 'I'm smart, and if I don't do well it's because I'm a lazy fucker, but because I'm black I'm treated like I'm a retard. What do these pricks think it does to our confidence when they lower standards for us? They don't get it that affirmative action makes people look on blacks and Hispanics as inferior however good they are.'

'I don't really know how it works in practice, Mark. Can you give me a quick idiot's guide?'

'Have you heard of SATs?'

'No.'

'SAT used to be short for Scholastic Aptitude Test, but now apparently it's not short for anything, but SATs are tests that qualify you for college. Obviously, the better you do, the better the university you can aim at.

'Affirmative action means the scores are rigged. Essentially, you juggle grades. If you got a score of, say, 1,000 on your tests, if you were black you'd be put on the same level as a white who got 1,200 plus. Latinos aren't thought to be as thick as us, so they'll only be equal to say a white with 1,150. If you're Asian, you're penalised by being put on the same level as a white with 950, as a punishment for being too fucking hard-working and good at exams.'

'In England, all things being equal, if there were two people up for a university place, the more underprivileged one would probably get it. But all things would have to be equal.'

Mark laughed. 'This has zero to do with privilege. It's race. Or gender. Or athletics, of course. They're desperate to get women into science and math so they give them extra scores in those subjects. And athletes get the same treatment as blacks. But the poor don't unless they fit the right category. Poor white guys have it rough.'

'Sounds very complicated. And unfair.'

'It's certainly unfair. My parents are well-off, I had a great education and I read a lot, but I blew the SATs because at the time I was off the rails and having too good a time to study. I shouldn't have gotten into even a mediocre school like Freeman, but affirmative action swung it for me. Which is wrong. I get given the same privileges as poor blacks. And poor whites get none at all. The whole system stinks and I'm ashamed to have benefited from it.' He took another swig from his water bottle. 'And it's not even just in exams. A lot of teachers are exaggeratedly kind to blacks. They never try to stretch or criticise us. That's why I liked Professor Godber's classes. He treats us all the same and makes us work hard. Anyone doesn't like it, he tells them to go off and find something more to their liking.'

'And he's unusual?'

'I haven't come across anyone else like him. Most professors have the minimum contact with students, their classes are pointless, and I only go to them to get the credits. And I've hit real trouble in Black Studies, which I got pressured into taking. It used to be voluntary but that bitch of a Dean made it compulsory for Blacks. I got really mad that *Othello* was reduced to a search for examples of racial prejudice instead of being a study of a great and flawed man. But when I said the approach was blinkered and self-pitying and had nothing to do with appreciating great literature, I was threatened with being flunked.'

'Do many black students agree with you?'

'About Black Studies, there are a few but only a few. Why should they? It's easy, they get the credits, so they're free to get drunk and laid. We're told there's a positive pass policy, which means they'll do nearly anything to avoid failing you, so we don't have to worry. If anyone ever gets a poor grade, the prof will raise it if they make enough fuss.'

'You're depressing me.'

'It's depressing. You see, if you've never been taught to think you don't know what you're missing. On a campus where people actually brag about buying their term papers off the net, there's no shame about being lazy or a cheat. Plus a lot of these guys really run with the victim stuff. It's an excuse for never getting off your fat ass.'

'Would most be in favour of affirmative action, then?'

'Some aren't because they see where it leads, but they don't say much about it publicly, because so many of the pro-affirmative action students are militants. You just get called Uncle Tom or Oreo. Or even beaten up.'

'Oreo?'

'It's a black cookie that's white on the inside.'

'Got you. I've a black friend in the UK who gets called a coconut.'

'I've been called that too.' Mark stood up and began to pace up and down. 'I'm an American. Period. Massa ain't going to tell me what to think just because of the colour of my skin. Being black makes me no better or worse than if I was white and I'm humiliated by the fact that lots of people will think that anything I achieve, any job I get, is because of positive discrimination. What do these fucking PC crap-merchants think they're doing? All their stupid rules and quotas and programmes do far more damage to the people they're supposed to help than they do to the people they're supposed to harm. I want them abolished in education and in the job market. I want people to think blacks are as good as whites so should be treated equally. And now I'm prepared to get thrown out of college if I can help that struggle. Me and Ryan and Sue-Ellen and Joshua, we're fed up with being pushed around.'

'The Axis survivors are very cross,' said the baroness. 'The Dean—or Acting Provost as I must learn to think of her—was almost incoherent with rage just at the sight of me. She started on about the harassment charges against me and when I said I'd fight them to the bitter end, she nearly exploded. Screamed at me that I needed gender, ethnic, and sensitivity training. She seems to have got very upset about a compliment I paid someone.'

'Explain.'

'That girl who said I'd put an inappropriate hand on her arm or whatever rubbish it was took exception to my saying I'd be grateful if she'd move her hottentottybotty out of the way.'

'Her what?'

'She had one of those attractive big African bottoms which scientists, I pointed out to Acting Provost Half-wit, had first observed on Hottentots in the early nineteenth century. She couldn't seem to grasp it, just yelled a lot. The President then tried to be mollifying and asked if in view of the Provost and the Goon's tragic deaths wouldn't I be prepared to help restore calm to the campus by considering my position?'

'Which means what?'

'Agree to go home. They seem to have decided they'd be better off this term without the DVPs, and Constance Darlington and Rowley Cunningham are packing their bags, though Rawlings is hanging in there. I've been offered a big bribe just to bugger off. Something in the region of fifty thousand bucks to compensate me for the inconvenience. Naturally, if they really really want me to go that much, I'll stay. I explained that I was an old-fashioned woman who believed in honouring contracts and that Helen's sad death made me even more determined to see it through. I could hardly be expected, I said, to feel bereaved at the death of the thug Gonzales, whom I had reason to believe was trying to have my parrot knocked off, which is when the Acting Provost opened her mouth again. "How can you speak like that of a sociologist with a doctorate?" she bellowed. I said the discovery that he was a sociologist explained everything.' The baroness paused. 'I don't think she gets jokes.'

'Cut the crap, Jack. Are you saying you have a proper contract?'

'I'm not an idiot, Robert. And I'd never trust an academic, knowing them as I do for the spineless and treacherous crew they

are. The contract Helen and I signed before I left Cambridge
was extremely detailed. That's why Freeman is stuck with paying
your fares and accommodation and even giving you a salary.'

'For what?'

'To teach the creative writing course Helen and I had agreed
on, though you won't actually have to teach. The Acting Provost
had a fit when she heard you'd arrived: for some strange reason
she believes that any friend of mine is automatically an enemy
of diversity. So she said there was no room on the time-table and
I said that was too bad and they'd have to pay you anyway.'

'I like the idea of the administration paying me to work full-
time on trying to overthrow it.'

'Why not? The British government paid unemployment benefit to all those IRA terrorists, even though they actually knew
they were trying to murder them. Now they finance raving-mad
Islamists intent on bombing the UK back into the seventh century.'

'Calm yourself, Jack. Did you meet any resistance from the
Axis, or did they cave in straightaway?'

'Not straightaway. The Acting Provost protested loudly
until shut up by the President, who made the mistake of trying
to play hardball—I could be dismissed out of hand and that
sort of threat. So I suggested sweetly he had a chat with Edgar
Junior....'

'Who?'

'I told you. Edgar Brooks' son.'

'Sorry. Blame jet-lag. I'd forgotten your squeeze provided
more than Colt 45s.'

'He certainly does. Edgar Junior is industrial strength. The
letter he wrote the Provost rejecting the harassment accusations
was a scorcher. I'd had Marjorie send him a copy of the contract
before I left for Slovakia and last night Edgar said Edgar Junior
was primed and ready to fire any time I needed him.'

'So what happened then?'

'They weren't pleased.'

'And then?' said Amiss. 'Get on with it, Jack.'

'The President asked if it was really necessary to get lawyers involved. So I said I hadn't started the legal squabbles. They'd done that by taking those stupid complaints seriously so I said I wasn't going to discuss it any more. I was a busy woman. If they wanted to talk, they could talk to Edgar Junior.' She sniggered. 'At which moment Pappas-Lott had another hissy fit and said it was typical of me to have a Mississippi lawyer and that what was more she wouldn't be surprised if I was involved in setting up people to complain about Rawlings—or Mujaahid, as of course she called him. I responded by saying that I'd be grateful if she'd add my name to the list of complainants, since although I am a tolerant woman, I objected to Rawlings inciting excitable Islamists to commit hate crimes against me. Could I, I enquired, also make a posthumous complaint against Gonzales for master-minding the attempted murder of my parrot and malicious damage to my expensive clothing?'

'Oh, very good, Jack.'

'And I added that, if they didn't ring Edgar Junior, he'd be ringing them to find out what security arrangements they were putting in place for me.'

'And then?'

'She said that the words Islam and murder didn't belong in the same sentence, and I referred her to 9/11 and recommended she study the later part of Mohammed's career closely and some of the Koran's more blood-thirsty injunctions, so she got mad again and then I got bored and said I had to fly. So I flew. How are you getting on?'

'Fine. Mark's gone now, Joshua will be here in an hour or so and in the meantime, Warren Godber is giving me lunch.'

'Tell him to stop horsing round and come on board. This is no time for fence-sitting. There's men's work to be done.'

Chapter Eleven

'Obviously I've given the catastrophic decline of Freeman a lot of thought,' said Warren Godber. 'Since I was ousted as Dean, I've had plenty of time to read and reflect. And my conclusion is that's there's no hope. Not just for Freeman, but for university education in America. Which of course has appalling implications for society as a whole.'

'Aren't you being rather apocalyptic?' asked Amiss, smearing mustard on his pastrami.

'How could anyone have any hope after what happened to Larry Summers at Harvard? He was a star, brought in to take the tough decisions. His credentials were alpha plus plus. He was a brilliant academic—had become a tenured professor at Harvard at 28. As Chief Economist of the World Bank he made it his priority to invest in the education of women in developing countries. Oh, yes, and at the U.S. Treasury, he was known *inter alia* for pushing an aid package that rescued Mexico from economic collapse. He was Clinton's Secretary of the Treasury, for God's sake, so it's not as if he could have been viewed as some kind of Republican redneck. Admittedly, he's Jewish, and anti-Semitism—more properly called Judophobia—is rife in academia....'

'Because?'

'Israel, of course. But envy, mainly. Jews are too damn smart and what is more, they seem culturally programmed to revere education and work hard and they throw up intellectual trouble-makers like Marx and Trotsky and Freud and Noam Chomsky. Historically, they're always easy to blame. Mind you, more and more resentment is geared towards Indians and Chinese and Vietnamese, who are dominating science and engineering and many of the other tough subjects that the diversity wrecking crew haven't yet had time to destroy. But they will. They are already talking up the need to teach the sciences from the points of view of various minorities. And fuzzy math, where guesswork is more important than knowledge, already ensures that at many schools you can get the grades without knowing how to solve an equation.

'But back to Summers. Of course they try to pretend they're not anti-Semitic, so no one said anything about Summers being Jewish, but you can bet it counted against him.'

'What was he trying to do that made him so many enemies? Close down Black and Women's and Queer Studies?'

'No, though he must know that they're intellectually con-temptible. All he was trying to do—initially anyway—was to raise standards and indulge in honest debate. He had many friends in high places and plenty of students were on his side, but he was driven out anyway by an hysterical intellectual lynch mob. He was already weakened by the fuss kicked up when he tried to get some academic rigour into Black Studies, thus alienating all those who think academic research is about quantity rather than quality. Not that you can blame them. The way you get tenure these days isn't to write anything that's any good, but to publish more worthless, incomprehensible but modish articles in unread journals than your competitors. Or in the case of Cornel West, the Black Studies super-star with whom he fell out, you get showered with money and prestige by hamming up your blackness and playing the violin of victimhood.

'However, it was the feminists who were Summers' downfall. They completely lost it when he suggested—just suggested—that it might be—just might be—that genetically men were more programmed towards the sciences. To suggest any genetic differences between men and women or one race and another is, of course, a hanging offence in most academic circles. So the lynch mob got going.'

'Didn't he fight?'

'Not for long. He was obviously stunned when he realised the faculty was largely against him and I guess thought that fighting would make things worse. He tried apologies. He then tried grovelling. Then he threw another fifty million dollars at the already bloated diversity budget. But none of that saved him. He had to resign. I feel for him. I thought I was a lot smarter than the people who wanted to get rid of me. But they won.'

'I once saw Jack Troutbeck decisively triumph over a PC conspiracy at St. Martha's.'

'I guess she's tougher than us yellow-bellied Yanks.'

'Any news, officer?'

'Nothing yet, ma'am.'

'Haven't you been rounding up the obvious suspects?'

'How do you mean "obvious," ma'am?'

'Dusky, bearded, Islamist youths, of course. And burqa'd ladies.'

'This takes time, ma'am. We've a policy against racial profiling....'

'What's racial profiling?'

'Singling out a particular race as suspects.'

'While I understand that you don't want anyone's feelings hurt, officer, you said two witnesses saw a dark, bearded youth running away from the building and several others saw a lurking person in a burqa. Two of them thought she was pregnant. And the message on the corpse was all about Allah.'

'Yes, ma'am. But maybe they had nothing to do with the murder. We've appealed for them to come forward. The burqa could have been covering anyone and the young man could just have been in a hurry.'

'Oh, fine. So you think the murderer might be an old white Islamist? Or even an Islamophobe trying to get Islamists into trouble?'

'Could be, ma'am.'

The baroness breathed heavily. 'I don't want to be unreasonable, officer, but I would really rather not end up sharing a mortuary slab with Helen Fortier-Pritchardson and—even worse—Ethan Gonzales. We didn't get on in life so I don't think we would in death. How long before you decide that in the absence of a young dusky bearded person coming forward to prove he was innocently on the scene you might get around to looking for him? And since I can't imagine that New Paddington is exactly heaving with burqa'd ladies, what is stopping you from having a chat with them?'

'Even if we did the first we wouldn't do the second, ma'am. We have an understanding with the Muslim community that we don't talk to their womenfolk.'

'You cannot be serious, officer.'

'I don't make the decisions, ma'am.'

'Well, put me through to whoever makes the decisions round here. And don't hang about.'

'What I don't understand,' said Amiss to Godber, 'is how what you might call the anti-intellectuals have become so powerful.'

'Through political correctness, which has become institutionalised in education—and indeed in public life in general—and over-rides all principles and common sense. You've seen here how it works in practice. Individuality is discouraged at every turn and people are pigeon-holed according to their race, gender, and so on. In the name of diversity the number of pigeon-holes is ever-increasing and each pigeon-hole is policed by commissars who persuade and intimidate the pigeons in the hole they police into seeing a closed mind as a good mind and acting in a bloc to assert their rights vis-à-vis all the pigeons in the other holes in the cote.'

'So when a Sue-Ellen or a Mark dissents from the received wisdom of the other pigeons in their holes....'

'They get pecked. And if they keep dissenting, they could end up pecked to death. Or dragged from their hole and stamped on.'

Amiss's phone rang. 'Excuse me, Warren. Hello. Yes, Jack... yes...yes...I'm having lunch with Warren Godber...pastrami on rye...very nice, in fact, however I suspect that wasn't what you rang about....Good Lord. Are there many there?...And what's the theme?...Really. Yes, I see....OK, then. Keep me posted.'

He put the phone back in his pocket. 'That was Jack Troutbeck, Warren. Interesting developments. She rang the cops to ask what progress they'd made in looking for someone meeting the description of the bearded running man and the burqa'd lady, and eventually learned that Rawlings had organised a demo in the Muslim residential area this morning and there were a few hundred still on the streets protesting noisily.'

'About what?'

'About the warning he gave them that the armed forces of oppression were about to storm their houses and drag innocent people off to be beaten up in cells and taken to Guantanamo Bay until they confessed to a murder they hadn't committed. Or something like that. He claimed the police chief is a Muslim-hating Jew.'

'Why's Rawlings doing this?'

'Force of habit, I suppose. Once an agitator, always an agitator. He's an attention-seeker who I think has political ambitions back home. He's like that black loonie in New York. What's his name? The one who inspired *Bonfire of the Vanities*?'

'You mean Al Sharpton, I guess. He's not Muslim, but the rhetoric's the same. I seem to remember him succeeding in having a Jewish shop-keeper burned out.'

'Jack says the demo seems to have paralysed the cops both in HQ and on the streets, from what she can see. She's watching it covertly from a car at the moment.'

'It could be more the District Attorney that's paralysed. He's coming up for election soon and he won't want trouble. Though

I can't see how he can avoid it.' Godber shrugged. 'People have no balls. They let themselves get walked over. I've done the same. You fight and fight and finally one day you wake up and find you don't care any more.' He took a bite of a gherkin. 'Multiculturalism is destroying our educational system and in my view the intellectual and bureaucratic establishment that has brainwashed generations into accepting it as an unchallengeable good won't rest until they've destroyed the United States. And then the whole of the West.'

He smiled benignly. 'I used to get very agitated about all this, but now I understand what's going on, I don't get mad any more. There's no point in getting worked up about the inevitable. All nations and civilisations die.'

Amiss finished his sandwich and took a quick gulp of coffee. 'You may have accepted the inevitable, but give me time before I succumb. Why would Americans want to destroy the United States? I thought all the flag-flying and pledging allegiance and singing the "Star-Spangled Banner" begins at primary school and produces patriots.'

Godber put his hands behind his head and leaned back in the kitchen chair. 'In any society there's an enemy within. During the Cold War it was communists, but there were very few of them and society watched out for them suspiciously. Now, it's different. You see, those who want to bring down this country are like Mao's guerrillas—fish swimming in a friendly sea.'

'You're saying the great American public want revolution, so they'll give succour to those who foment it?'

'No, no. The average American wants nothing of the sort, but he spends his time making his living and worrying about his family and watching baseball and eating hamburgers and doesn't think much about society, so he doesn't realise what's going on. I often think that if parents really knew the truth about universities—the sneering at patriotism, religion, and core American values—they'd march on the campuses and rescue their children. But they don't know what's going on because the media—like education—is dominated by the liberal PC left, so the average

American is constantly told that university professors are fine people and American education is the best in the world. All he wants is for his kid to come out of university with the right piece of paper and get a good job. He's certainly not going to complain that the kid's not being pushed hard enough.'

'Is it a left-right thing?'

'Not entirely. Many of the liberal left will be appalled if we end up the way we seem to be heading, but most of them have so bought into the PC view of the universe that they don't think about anything but the importance of achieving equality through increasingly frantic and unsuccessful social engineering. Not to speak of the idea that there is no greater sin than to hurt the feelings of anyone in any of those pigeon-holes—except of course those not perceived as victims....'

'...the white males in the huge hole....'

'...or the Jews in one of the small ones.'

'I'm finding all this very difficult,' said Amiss. 'The idea of political correctness as a threat to the state is rather a lot for me to take on. Take me through this gently. What do you think has happened?'

'The opinion formers in the Western world—and particularly the U.S.—are being gradually intellectually coerced into first being ashamed of and then hating Western culture. Samuel Huntingdon defined multiculturalism as "a form of mono-cultural animus directed against the dominant culture"—and that's what it is. In the U.S., what's under attack by the massed armies of commissars is the ethos of the state bequeathed to us by our founding fathers.'

'Which you define as...?'

'English-speaking, infused with the spirit of the Enlightenment and with such Judeo-Christian values as the work ethic and respect for the rule of law. That's what we've rubbed along with for more than two centuries, with our immigrants accepting these values, embracing the idea of the melting-pot and adding aspects of their own cultures and values to enhance the flavour of the whole dish. Now they're being actively encouraged by our intellectual elite to reject our core values and think of themselves as aggrieved sub-groups. The introduction of the hyphen was an act of anti-American aggression. Once Hispanics aspired to being Americans. Now they're instructed to think of themselves as Hispanic-Americans and demand the right to speak Spanish. Thus do the pigeon-holes metamorphose into ghettoes in the name of multifuckingculturalism.' He paused. 'I apologise for my language. I can still occasionally get cross. More coffee?'

'Yes, please.'

Godber re-filled Amiss's mug and emptied the last of the coffee into his own. 'You see, one of the attractions of multi-culturalism and political correctness on campuses is that it's a great leveller. An ignorant fool like my successor as Dean would be incapable of grasping or discussing real ideas, so she opts for a course of study that requires no brains and an ideology that saves her from ever having to think.'

'Which is the attraction of all kinds of fundamentalism.'

'Exactly. The Dean might have difficulty in defending in argument the moral relativism that underpins multiculturalism and political correctness, but fundamentalists don't have to argue. They just obey. Her creed requires her truly to believe that there is no such thing as truth and that each culture is as valid as any other, so because she has the heart of a fanatic, it follows that she must extol all minority cultures regardless of their worth and use them to attack and undermine the dominant culture, which she believes not only has no more right to be dominant than does any other culture, but because of its past sins, has much less.

'Oh, by the way, did you know she's introducing something called "sensitivity review guidelines"? The idea is to ensure that nowhere in any handouts or recommended reading will there be anything that might offend anyone.'

'You're talking twenty-first century bowdlerisation.'

'Oh, it'll be much more thorough than the Victorians, I assure you.'

Amiss's phone rang. 'Hello, Jack....Really?...Was that wise?...Oh, that sounds unpleasant....What? You mean they did nothing?…What! My God, you are living dangerously…. Well, yes, but isn't it illegal?…I see. Do you need me?…Are you sure?…Oh, is she?…Good….What's he got to do with it?…OK, OK….Good luck…Yes, probably sixish. 'Bye.' He turned back to Godber. 'Sorry for the interruptions, Warren, but things are escalating. Jack got curious about what was on the banners, left Betsy and the car and followed the demo on foot and Rawlings spotted her and denounced her as a disrespecter of Allah.'

'Does he want her lynched?'

'Seems so. Apparently as he was pointing at her several young men rushed towards her, and though there were some cops nearby they did nothing. Jack got a bit concerned when they started shouting about death to the infidel and when the first one arrived and hit her with his banner and threatened to behead her, she decided to take action. The last time I remember that happening to her, it was in London and she used a horse-whip. This time it was a Colt 45.'

'As used by Philip Marlow?'

'Indeed. Though I gather it's a bit lighter and more up-to-date.'

Godber shrugged. 'When in Rome…?'

'Precisely.'

'No fatalities, I hope.'

'She shot over their heads a few times and they ran away, but the cops then arrested her for not having a permit to carry a gun in public. She's down at the station, but she says they don't seem to know what to do with her, being cowed by her title, the fact that they hadn't given her any protection, her having a lawyer on the case, and her invoking Martin Freeman as a character referee.'

'I didn't know she knew him.'

'She's met him twice, she says, and they're on their way to being allies. Marjorie's trying to get hold of him now.'

'Martin pretty well owns the town, so he'll have a lot of clout. But what she's done is serious. She'll be lucky not to be deported.'

'Maybe she'd be much more lucky if she were deported.'

◇◇◇

'I'm like Sue-Ellen and Mark,' said Joshua. 'I can't stand being condescended to and I hate being told that being gay defines me. I said I wanted to major in History and English but the admission people said instead I should take Queer Studies.'

'How did they know you were gay?'

'You have to tick a box on your application form.'

'Isn't that very intrusive?'

'It sure is intrusive. Especially if, like me, you're not entirely sure what your sexuality is. And you're inexperienced. Actually, I'm trying to stay celibate for the moment. I was attracted by a couple of guys at boarding school so I thought I was gay but last summer I held hands with a girl and danced with her. So maybe I'm bi.'

'Or even straight?'

'Anything's possible. But Freeman wanted me to opt for something. And I couldn't complain that the form didn't offer plenty of choice. In the end I opted for gay because I'd heard Freeman doesn't like mainstream and I was already white and Jewish. But then they started on me to do Queer Studies.'

'You'd have been safer ticking "bi."'

Joshua looked puzzled. 'But then I'd have had to do Bi Studies. That's worse.'

'Bi Studies exists?'

'Part of the GLBT department.'

'Sorry?'

'Gay, Lesbian, Bi, and Transexual. Didn't you know?'

Amiss sighed heavily. 'No, I didn't.'

'I didn't either at the time. I asked what was the point of Queer Studies and the admissions tutor said something about how you learned about identity and desire. I said I'd work out my identity and desires myself, but I wanted to learn about the world and its past. That didn't go down well. He said I was running away from myself. I said I didn't even know if I was gay, so he asked if I'd feel more confident in Bi Studies. I said at this stage that I had a very sore toe and wondered if they had Ingrown-Toenail Studies. He offered Disability Studies....'

'What!'

'Oh, sure. It's a real subject here. So I said I'd been joking and he said jokes were inappropriate and I was lucky not to be reported. Then he looked at my form again, saw I had ticked Jewish and suggested my religion was coming between me and the examination of my sexual identity.'

'He sounds crazy.'

'Freeman is crazy. These assholes seem to think we're all narcissists who just want to see life from our own narrow perspective. Maybe I'm gay, but whatever I am, that's not the most important thing about me. The most important thing about me is that I want to learn, I want to broaden my mind, I want to know stuff. But what I'm getting in terms of an education is jack shit. And I'm really really mad.'

'Don't you have any decent teachers?'

'Even in Honour College they just pander to the dumbest. I thought we'd be having intellectual arguments, but I think even if they wanted to, the faculty would be afraid to encourage debate. Someone might say something that resulted in a minority student complaining about hurt feelings and then the professor's caught up in the complaints procedure. In one class, when a black student sneered that I came from Hymietown, no one blinked an eye, but when I said that was a bigoted remark, I was warned I was being racially offensive. I don't know if there are decent teachers, but I don't see any who are brave. They're all wieners.'

'There seems to be a reign of terror going on,' said Amiss to Godber. 'I'd thought of political correctness as something irritating and shallow. What's happening at Freeman seems more like Stalinism.'

'That's a good comparison,' said Godber. 'Political correctness is as rigid and comprehensive a belief system as was economic

Marxism. Indeed a commentator called Bill Lind has recently rightly defined it as cultural Marxism. Where economic Marxism said that all history was determined by ownership of the means of production, cultural Marxism substitutes the ownership of power. So the job of the intellectual vandals of cultural Marxism is to insist that history, literature, and the rest of the humanities be examined in the most partisan and negative possible light to see—when it came to power—who were the haves and who were the have-nots. Instead of the class war, we've got the gender and race wars.'

'And by keeping the pigeons in separate intellectual holes.... You know, Warren, I think this metaphor is becoming rather laboured. What I mean is that by ghettoising disciplines like history and literature, you guarantee that your students develop only the most narrow and partisan view of what they're studying.'

'Exactly. But there's more to it than that. Haves by definition are bad: have-nots are good. In economic Marxism, the bourgeoisie and owners of capital were the haves, who were expropriated in favour of workers and peasants. In cultural Marxism, the white straight male must yield to women, blacks, Hispanics, homosexuals, and so on—anyone who can be represented as an outsider and who plays the game by claiming victimisation.'

'Hence affirmative action.'

'Exactly. The descendants of the good are now entitled through affirmative action to be privileged at the expense of the descendants of the bad; and the humanities are to be studied purely for the purpose of reinforcing this ideology. So not only will the likes of Dean Pappas-Lott never have to think, but she's programmed to try to abolish thought, for, if anyone did think, they might point out that just as the workers and peasants didn't benefit from economic Marxism, the minority groups are doing worse rather than better as a result of cultural Marxism.'

'Tolerance of difference is a good by-product of all this, though, isn't it?'

'Tolerance comes from good manners and mutual respect—not from dogma.' Godber drained his coffee. 'PC ideology claims to be about tolerance, but it's tolerance exclusively for those who accept the dogma, who are the left. The dissenters of the right are by definition not to be tolerated.'

'Don't the right fight it on campuses?'

'Left-liberals outnumber conservatives by around ten to one, so it's not difficult to silence them.'

'So free speech is dying.'

'At Freeman it's already dead.'

'Which is why Sue-Ellen and Mark and Joshua are told they're traitors to their sex, race, or sexual orientation.'

'And to the other pigeons in their respective holes.'

'Is Freeman typical?'

'Probably worse than the norm. We were resisting the barbarians until poor old Jim Haringey died and was replaced by a PC fanatic. Say what you like about Helen Fortier-Pritchardson, she was a most industrious zealot who succeeded in a very short time in destroying everything fine for which Freeman stood. I'm sure she'd be very proud to know that.' There was the sound of a car outside. 'Ah, that'll be Ryan.'

◇◇◇

'You're certainly a diverse group of conspirators so far,' said Amiss. 'Joshua's even partially disabled by a bad toe. Dean Pappas-Lott would be proud of you.'

'I spoil it all,' laughed Ryan. 'I'm the enemy. White, male, and straight.'

'So what drives you?'

'What I've just said. I resent being the enemy. And I specially resent being classed as the oppressor when in fact I'm the oppressed. I didn't want to go to Freeman. I wanted to go to Princeton, but because of affirmative action I lost out.'

'Couldn't you have done better than Freeman?'

'When I didn't make Ivy League I didn't care much where I went. And my folks live in Chicago, so Freeman's handy.'

'What gave you the inspiration for VRC?'

'Seeing so many people really pissed about what's going on here. I couldn't believe how bad it was when I came here first, and it kept getting worse. Last year, a few guys tried holding an affirmative action bake sale to show how dumb it all is. That's where you have different charges for cookies: a dollar to a white or Asian male, seventy-five cents to a white or Asian female, fifty cents to a black male and forty to a black female and so on. First they were beaten up by a crowd of students urged on by Gonzales and then they were hauled in front of the campus tribunal and given a final warning: one more transgression from any of them and they'd be out without an appeal. Three of them were kicked out since.'

'And it's not just Gonzales. One day, just to wind up some of the left, I wore a Republican T-shirt to the canteen and an instructor kicked me.'

'Are you serious?'

'Sure. She gave me a vicious kick in the leg and then said she should have kicked me harder and higher.'

'What happened?'

'I asked her to apologise and she wouldn't. She said I'd been provocative in wearing the T-shirt and the campus was pacifist. So I made a formal charge.'

'And the Provost threw it out?'

'She sure did. She said my clothing had been inappropriate and provocative and that she believed the instructor that she'd only accidentally touched me with her shoe, because it was men that were violent, not women.'

'Had you no witnesses?'

'Too scared. You can't imagine how scared people are. Provost Fortier-Pritchardson had a reputation for organising trumped-up charges when it suited her. And Gonzales knew how to get the results she wanted.'

'So you decided to fight back.'

'Not then. But I got mad a few months later when Brendan and Lindy got thrown out. Lindy's a cool chick and she and I dated for a while as freshmen so I took it kinda personally. Then later on, I was told I'd have to take 'Whiteness Studies.' It's a new course that's being made compulsory for all whites in all departments.'

'I've got jet-lag, Ryan, and have had a very intellectually taxing day, but I know enough to presume that unlike Black or Queer or even Bi studies....'

'Don't forget Chicano.'

'What!'

'There was a big debate, Professor Godber told us, about the movement to set up something for Mexicans. The problem was that there are differences between U.S.-based Mexicans who think they're American, those who think they're Mexican-American, those who don't like their Mexican heritage but feel Spanish and want to be called Hispanos or Latinos and those who don't feel American however long they've lived here and have chosen to be known as Chicanos. It's a rude word like "Nigger," but it's OK if they say it. So the final decision was to set up Chicano Studies, though non-Mexicans have to be careful not to offend by using the term.'

'I'm feeling very very tired, Ryan, and soon I'm going to have to get back to my hotel, but please try to explain to me first about Whiteness Studies. All the other studies I've heard about are about making sub-groups feel better about themselves. I'd be astounded to hear that's what Whiteness Studies is about.'

'Of course Whiteness Studies sucks. It's about making white people feel evil because they're supposed to have invented racial difference so they could justify discrimination. And about making non-whites feel even more exploited than they thought they were. I took the first class and did the privilege walk. That's when you all line up beside each other in a big room and the instructor calls out maybe thirty loaded questions about stuff like was your mother single, were your ancestors slaves and have you ever had your feelings hurt by an ethnic or gender slur. Any yes takes you one step back and no is one step forward. So in the end the white males were all way ahead of everyone else and the instructor gave us T-shirts that said "Sorry" and told us to wear them.'

'You're making that up.'

'I'm *so* not. Our instructor was very proud of the T-shirts. Like she was proud of being female and African-American. I gave mine back and told her I was resigning from the course because I felt insulted. I tried complaining about racial harassment, but of course I was told my behaviour was inappropriate. So I said I had an issue with the instructor and that I'd pull out of college if they made me stay in the course, so they tried to make me take Masculinity Studies instead.'

'Which is about inducing guilt and lowering male self-esteem, I presume.'

'You got it. I'm taking it, because I want to stay in school for now, but it's all about the need for men to be more like women and share their feelings and be consensual. Only good thing is it's such a dumb course that as long as you play their game you can get straight A's without doing any work.' He snorted. 'Not that most of their dumb-shit courses aren't the same.'

'So how did you come to start the VRC group?'

'From reading Terry Goodkind and then through him getting interested in Ayn Rand, who was inspired by her belief in man as a rational being.'

'I've just read a Goodkind.'

'Did you like it?'

'I'm reserving judgement,' said Amiss cautiously, 'but it certainly went with a swing.'

'I liked him having heroes who confront and triumph over evil. But the real inspiration was Rand. Have you read her?'

'No.'

'She said that any alleged right of one man that necessitated the violation of the rights of another was not and couldn't be a right. Well, my rights were being violated and I wasn't prepared to put up with it any more. So I started talking to people about how they felt about what was going on and ended up with some people I could trust. Borrowing the idea of the Sword of Truth from Goodkind was maybe a bit kid-stuff, but it was fun. And having a secret name that no one could figure out was too. And passwords and all that. And then Lindy called me just to say "hi" and I told her a bit about how things were going on campus and she said why not talk to the *Sentinel*. Turned out her brother was at college with the editor. So that's why I talked to them.' He shrugged. 'But when I'd done that, we didn't really know what to do.'

'So I gathered from Jack. But Warren Godber said there's a nation-wide organisation that helps people like you fight injustice and censorship on campuses.'

'Sure. FIRE. The Foundation for Individual Rights in Education. But we couldn't agree on the right issue to go to them with. Especially because so many people had lost their nerve when Brendan and Lindy were thrown out. But we're a bit braver since we met Lady Troutbeck. And of course things are different now the Provost and Gonzales are dead.'

'They're hardly better with Dean Pappas-Lott in charge.'

'She's so dumb she'll be easier to deal with, I guess. We despise Dean Pappas-Lott, but we were afraid of Provost Fortier-Pritchardson. And totally petrified of Dr. Gonzales.'

Chapter Twelve

'Did you see what happened with Jack and the protestors, Betsy?' asked Amiss, as he buckled his seat belt.

'Oh, I did, Robert. I did. It was so scary. I wanted to run and help her but she'd ordered me to stick to the car. She's so brave. She totally wanted to protect me.'

'She'd have protected you better by not getting you to drive her there in the first place, wouldn't she?'

'Hey, it's my job to drive her. And really, like, totally, to look after her.'

'I don't think your duties extend to protecting her from the righteous anger of Islamists.'

Betsy looked worried. 'They're not righteous, are they? I know we're supposed, like, to respect their culture…oh, dear…I've promised Lady Troutbeck I'd stop saying "like"…but do you still have to do that when they don't respect yours?'

'No, Betsy. I wasn't being serious. Anyone who wants to beat you up or kill you for disagreeing with them has a culture you can safely disrespect. So don't panic. Islam OK. Islamism not OK.'

She nodded. 'That's what I think, though you have to be totally careful where you say it.'

'Have you seen Jack since she was taken off by the cops?'

'Oh, sure. I drove after them and waited outside and then took her back to the hotel.'

'How did she get out so fast?'

'All she said was she was cross they'd confiscated her gun but she hadn't been charged yet. She seemed quite cheerful.'

Amiss yawned. 'Good. Now can we head off to the hotel? I'm feeling shattered.'

'What took you so long?' asked the baroness, as she opened her door to Amiss.

'Shower, phone call to Rachel, checking emails, that kind of thing,' he shouted, over some piercing train noises from Horace, who had just been delivered by Marjorie and was excited.

'You're developing American habits,' she grumbled. 'I don't know why anyone needs two showers a day. And I hate emails.'

'Can you suspend the Luddite Monologues just for now and explain why you're not manacled in a prison cell?'

'Have a martini. I've made a jugful and it's very very good.'

'I'll have a martini and an answer,' said Amiss, throwing himself on the sofa and putting his feet on the coffee table. 'Oh, please shut up, Horace. You're making my head hurt.'

'VRC, VRC, VRC,' carolled Horace happily. 'VRC, VRC, VRC.'

'Oh, God,' said Amiss, as he took the glass from the baroness. 'Why has he that on the brain?'

'I suppose he heard me mentioning the VRC on the phone today,' she said, as she went over to put the black cloth over his cage.

'To whom?'

'Why are you always asking questions?'

'Because it annoys you to answer them. Come on, get on with it. Whom have you been conspiring with?'

'Myles rang.'

'Oh, good. Is he still in Iraq?'

'He's just popped over the border to Kuwait for a bit of R & R.'

'Has he done anything useful? Last I heard, Iraq still had its problems.'

'Not everyone is as inquisitive as you.'

'Stop being a pain, Jack.'

'He said interesting things had happened but he'll talk another time.'

'Did he have any advice?'

'Hit them fast and hard.'

'Who?'

'My enemies.'

'Directed at you, that advice is about as useful as advising Tiger Woods to take up golf. Who else was on, Jack?'

'Edgar.'

'You old two-timer, you.'

'We old-timers are adept at two-timing. What do you think Myles is likely to be doing in Kuwait?'

'I dread to think. What's Edgar's take on things?'

'There's progress on the Mike and Vera-Velda front. Vera-Velda's mother has taken on Edgar Junior as her lawyer, and after a lot of fuss the cops have agreed that the crashed car can be examined by an independent forensic expert, so they're not going to get away with sweeping murder under the carpet. I was released quickly because Edgar Junior threatened to sue the cops for trillions of dollars for dereliction of duty if they charged me and/or didn't give me back my gun, so they let me out for now after a heavy lecture about permits and violations of this and that that I didn't pay attention to.

'Now, how did you get on?'

'Towards the end, Ryan talked a lot more about Ayn Rand and the importance of individualism and how reason is all and rational self-interest is what we should be all about. Though in this case, he seems to think rational self-interest requires individuals to liberate the oppressed masses of Freeman. He had some quote from her along the lines of civilisation being the process of setting man free from man. Which could involve helping to free man from man, though then he got bogged down in some confusing stuff about the real meaning of altruism.'

'What a prat that woman was. How could anyone take seriously someone who changes her name from the perfectly OK Alissa Rosenbaum to a poncy name like Ayn Rand? And insists to boot that Ayn be rhymed with "fine."' She snorted. 'All her stuff is boring clap-trap which ends up justifying libertarianism and anarchism. Prince Kropotkin put it better.'

'Who the hell was Kropotkin?'

'I thought you were supposed to be an historian. Kropotkin was the patron saint of anarchic communism. Became very disillusioned by what happened after the Russian Revolution. I used to be very keen on him when I was a girl. I lectured my teachers about him.'

'You must have been insufferable.'

'I still am.'

'Never was a truer word spoken in jest.'

'It wasn't jest. It was a statement as obvious as most of Rand's when you strip away what I might term her intellectual directoire knickers.'

'Come again?'

'They conceal all that is valuable.'

'I'm not sure this is making much sense, Jack, except that I grasp that you're not keen on Miss Rand. Yet Ryan seemed to think you took her seriously.'

'I was being tactful.'

'That hadn't occurred to me as a possibility.'

'Despite what everyone says, I'm very tactful when I want to be and I didn't want to frighten them off. When I get the chance I'll wean them away from her rubbish Objectivist philosophy and onto the really sensible people like Aristotle and David Hume. Or even, better still, Isaiah Berlin, if they want to see how ideas affect people.'

'Don't get carried away just because you've managed to get Betsy to like Jane Austen. Though having said that, she's so heroine-worshipping at the moment she'd probably try to like Schopenhauer if you asked her to.'

'First I'll have to get out of their heads what's already in there,' said the baroness, picking up a stapled pile of paper and waving it in front of him. 'This is the stuff that Ryan gave me that he's trying to feed into the VRC. What isn't plagiaristic in what I've read that this bloody woman has produced is commonsense regurgitated pretentiously. Apparently, the basic tenets of Objectivism are: existence exists; consciousness exists; existence is identity. Kindly tell me how that differs from Descartes' *"Cogito, ergo sum"**?'

'Er....'

'Exactly.'

'Or what's new about her contradiction of Bishop Berkeley?'

'Look, Jack. I haven't read Rand and I'm rusty on philosophers. All I can remember is that Dr. Johnson thought Berkeley a bit woolly. Spell it out.'

'Berkeley thought people couldn't know if an object exists, only how they perceive it and Rand made a big thing of refuting that by saying if it's there, it's real.'

'Like those false boobs of Traci Dickinson's that you told me about?'

'In that case, false is false but is also real, since Traci's boobs are undoubtedly false but also undoubtedly exist. Look, Sam Johnson refuted Berkeley two centuries before Rand just by kicking a stone. He didn't need to deck his argument with a load of intellectual twaddle. All these clever-silly people drive me mad.'

'But how do you know they exist?'

'By kicking them. Hard. And that's what we have to begin planning to do. Have you got Godber on board?'

'I'm getting there, I think. He seemed to be sloughing off some of the defeatism and getting a bit angry again. He eventually said if we tell him what we're doing and we're not planning anything criminal, he'll help. Not that he hasn't already. I really feel I understand what's going on now.'

---

*'I think, therefore I am.'

'He's hooked. Good, now what's our strategy?'

From: Robert Amiss
To: Rachel Simon; Mary Lou Dinsmore; Ellis Pooley; Jim Milton; Myles Cavendish
Date: Tue 13/06/2006 10.30
Subject: The New Paddington Revolution

Since New Paddington is, as you know, the hub of the universe (not least because it is the present residence of one Jack Troutbeck) I thought I should issue a comprehensive news bulletin to those of you not fully up-to-date. The position is roughly that Rachel's mother is getting back to normal, that Mary Lou's had several flattering reviews, that Ellis has become increasingly multicultural and with Jim is now chasing Latvian forgers, that Myles is resting up in whatever is the Kuwaiti equivalent of a spa, that Plutarch disgraced herself by eating five substantial St. Martha's goldfish and leaving the spines at the Porter's Lodge and has been saved from eviction only by special pleading from Mary Lou and the prompt provision of a temporary net over the pond, that my marriage being in its infancy, I haven't had the nerve to ask Rachel if she'd retrieve Plutarch from St. Martha's as soon as she leaves her parental and returns to our marital home but that I hereby ask her, that Horace's fascination with train noises is driving everyone within earshot to distraction, that I think that if all goes according to plan I'll be home in three-and-a-bit weeks (having had an extension of leave from Rachel) by which time Jack and I should have seen through the revolution we're organising. When you've read this, do whatever is the electronic equivalent of eating it, as I'm sharing with you all the broad outline of our top-secret plan for taking over Diversity Farm. And please don't now start making jokes about the pigs.

The plan is to have the President and the Acting Provost replaced respectively by Martin Freeman, the university's chief benefactor, who is a sane businessman, and by Warren Godber, who believes in all kinds of old-fashioned notions like the need for people to acquire enough knowledge to be able to think. This will not be easy to achieve.

We think the President is a crook. Now admittedly, this is based on one of Jack's rather alarming intuitive leaps, but she may well be right. She has read much into the President's cosmetically enhanced airhead wife's reference to money being now no object. The implication was that the riches were comparatively recent, which sits rather oddly with the Pres having moved from Wall Street five years ago to a relative backwater like New Paddington where he isn't paid that much.

From what Jack observed, the quarter-of-a-million-or-so annual salary wouldn't begin to cover Traci's present running costs. This was confirmed when Traci somewhat unexpectedly rang Jack's room the other day (well, the other evening, to be precise; she was very animated), got me in Jack's absence, and asked me to invite Jack over for another fun girlie night to meet something called a parti-coloured teacup poodle which she had named Sweetie, which was the most darling doggie ever, had allegedly cost $4,000, already had the cutest wardrobe with matching jewellery and she was thinking of having dyed gold. With magnificent presence of mind I explained that while I was sure Jack would like nothing better, she was being tested for psittacosis which was a parrot disease lethal to dogs and humans, so it might be wise to postpone the meeting for a while. She screamed and rang off. On transmitting this message to Jack, I had great difficulty in preventing her from storming the presidential palace on an animal rescue mission.

186 Ruth Dudley Edwards

Of course President Dickinson may have made a lot of money in Wall Street and made good investments, but still....

Jack and one of our allies, Marjorie—secretary to that almost extinct breed, the Distinguished Visiting Professors (aka DVPs) and a prime source of institutional memory—maintain that since Dickinson looks like a crook and talks like a crook and acts like a crook, he must *be* a crook. Indeed they also believe he murdered the previous Provost so as to put in his own placewoman. We don't know where he would acquire dishonest money in his present job, but hypothesise that it may be a by-product of his very energetic fund-raising. Marjorie and a young member of the VRC who is a serious computer geek and knows how to hack, are looking into his finances and we're very grateful to Jim for offering to talk informally to his New York police contact.

Meanwhile, Jack has begun poisoning Martin Freeman's mind against the Pres. She says she's being subtle. I haven't met Freeman because he's in Europe, but he's rung her once or twice to ask what the hell's going on on campus, so I guess that's a good sign.

Meanwhile, what the hell *is* going on on campus, I hope I hear you are still interested enough to ask? Well, the Acting Provost, a woman who is to intellectual rigour what Hitler was to racial tolerance, was a rather foolish choice as stop-gap by the Pres, but he's away so much he's perhaps not aware of it. Her irrationality and bouts of hysteria are so frequent that her predecessor's secretary walked out within forty-eight hours claiming that she feared for her safety.

The best the human resources crew (who, Marjorie says, are so demented from trying to balance the rights of Korean lesbians with dyslexia against Nigerian transvestites with Attention Deficit Disorder) could do was to offer the A-P the services of Marjorie. This was done on the grounds that a) she had once been secretary to a Provost so knew where the bodies were buried—correction, so knew her way around the filing cabinets—and b) since two of the four DVPs decamped last week, and as we speak, Jimmy Rawlings aka Mujaahid (of whom more later), is on his way home and they don't want Jack to stay anyway, she can be spared. This is excellent news since Marjorie will be able to spy. Of course Jack kicked up a huge fuss as a form of disinformation and has now been awarded her driver and gopher Betsy as a part-time secretary as well. The A-P made a feeble effort to argue that Jack's contract should be invalidated by her having been arrested, but one phone call from Edgar Brooks Junior sorted her out. One of Marjorie's priorities is to find out what wickednesses the more recently murdered provost and her enforcer had been up to. She's hoping the A-P is too thick and mad to have thought to get rid of any evidence.

Meanwhile, the VRC no longer exists. While lamenting that it could not be renamed The Vast Reactionary Conspiracy, Jack—like its originators—accepted that what we need for a revolution is as broad a church as we can get, so we're now called SFU, short for Save Freeman U, which is boring but sensible. The quartet who set up the VRC accepted this manfully. Ryan admitted that trying to convert the student body to an arcane philosophy was perhaps a mission for another day: he had a sad little reprise of how students must have a philosophical revolution founded on the supremacy of reason and intelligent self-interest or something like that, but accepted that the immediate objective was to give them a university in which they can learn to read and write and talk and think without fearing being executed or sent to a gulag.

Meanwhile, the VRC crew and hangers-on have already recruited enough bodies under the new name to get an SFU website set up which will shortly be publicised in the *New Paddington Sentinel*. The site has so far mostly anonymous stories of what happened to students who challenged authority in any way and invites any student who has evidence of bullying, harassment, or coercion by the authorities, egregious dumbing-down or grade inflation, the condoning of plagiarism and other kinds of cheating and all the rest of it to make contact with SFU in order to spill the beans and start blogging. To give you an example of the kind of thing we need to hear about, Betsy has finally admitted that she dropped out of being a cheerleader not just because she hated the drunken orgies and the gross ill-treatment of new recruits, but because the coach wouldn't let up on trying to blackmail her into sex. She said the woman threatened and bullied her, and that she believed because of the way the campus operated that if she complained she'd be chucked out on a false charge because it was so un-PC to suggest a lesbian could be a predator. She had to lie to her mother—she thought Mom would have made everything worse—by pretending she'd lost her nerve, so the mother, who was living out her ambitions through Betsy, has been distraught for weeks.

Meanwhile, a few of us are working out what to do on Founders' Day, which is on the Fourth of July and is an occasion when families show up, there's a bit of a patriotic celebration and addresses from various luminaries including the Pres and Martin Freeman about the eternal values of Freeman U. We all fantasise about an Animal House kind of day, but that isn't what we're about. What we're trying to organise is a means of demonstrating how corrupt the university has become, how a large number of students are sickened by spending four years learning nothing and how political correctness has disappeared up its own asshole, as we say in the vernacular. All suggestions gratefully received. The choreography will be very complicated, but I'm hoping for great things from Ryan, who now that he's been given a sense of direction, has closed his books and settled down to serious planning.

He and Sue-Ellen and Joshua and Mark—the core of the old-VRC—have drawn up a list of trusties who are now busy recruiting malcontents. They have to be economical with the information they give these people, since it was known that Gonzales had a network of informers, so initially they're just testing people out by asking their opinions of individual teachers and that kind of thing.

I often wonder why I'm here and what the hell I'm doing, but the exposure to what's being done to the young has been so horrifying that I've really bought into the idea that we need to sling a shot at a few of the fools and knaves who are ruining education in the West, fomenting bad relations between races and religions and opening the gates to fanatical enemies who no longer have to work out how to break down the gates, since they're being invited in by cultural suicide bombers whose bombs are intended to blow up their own side.

I haven't yet mentioned what is most immediately appalling, the fate of Mike and Velda, the private eyes whose deaths have shaken Jack much much more than she'll admit. On the evenings after their funerals, she retired alone to her room, refused all company, and looked distinctly shaky the mornings after. She's absolutely certain they were murdered, in which case it really was murder most foul. Our top suspect is the late Dr. Ethan Gonzales, sociologist, and Beria to Provost Fortier-Pritchardson's Stalin, and no longer around to be interrogated. Other private eyes are now on the trail.

Which brings me to the small matters of the Islamist demos, the jihad against Jack, and her legal position vis-à-vis her episode with the gun. Oh, yes, and of course the interesting question of who killed Stalin and Beria. Obviously our Islamist chum is the favourite candidate for murderer, but Marjorie thinks Dickinson shouldn't be ruled out. She says he was around at the time, maybe there was a falling out among thieves and the burqa'd bird and running dusky person were red herrings. Too complicated for me.

The demonstrators got even more excited after Jack was taken off to the copshop and—with Rawlings' encouragement—did a lot of yelling about their lives being in danger, but it began to rain, they became hungry and they eventually went home. According to Marjorie, Rawlings was offered so much money to leave town that he forgot his principled need to outstay Jack, to secure a name-change for the university, extract reparations for the entire African-American population, destroy Whitey, impose Sharia law on the U.S., kill the apostates and the infidels and whatever other reforms he had in mind, and instead duly buggered off quickly with no word of farewell.

However, a few of his abandoned followers became extremely excited when the D.A. did eventually get around to authorising a raid of the relevant area with a view to seeing if anyone looked like the man who was seen running from the Provost's office. They got even more upset that policewomen began questioning burqa'd and veiled women whose shape resembled the woman seen outside the office before the murders.

The raid began early this morning and from the local news bulletins it appears some Muslims have taken noisy umbrage, though they're a bit quieter now that Rawlings is no longer inspiring them. I hope this means the radical Muslims have forgotten about Jack in their general vexedness against the D.A. We must all pray that the murderer will be discovered without his or her neighbours having their feelings hurt.

I'll keep you posted but I think I have persuaded Jack to confine herself to watching demonstrators on TV in future, especially since she no longer has a gun. She's influenced by the fact that she doesn't want to be deported right now so sees the point of keeping a low profile. Her legal position is unresolved, but the lawyer she has acquired seems not just to know what he's doing but to be revelling in it. And, grudgingly, the cops are providing her with twenty-four-hour cover. Just one man at a time, but he'll be highly visible.

That's it for now. I'm a busy man with a revolution to plan. If any of you would like to drop what you're doing and come straight over first class at the expense of Freeman, please don't hesitate. This invitation does not extend to Plutarch.

◇◇◇

'Change of scene, Robert,' said the baroness. 'I'll take you to my bar.'

'I didn't realise such an amenity existed.'

'Bolt-hole rather than amenity, although it has its virtues. Come on, come on. Your eyes will give out if you spend all day staring at that stupid computer.'

'And whose fault is it that...? OK, I'll be with you in a minute.'

◇◇◇

'Joe's,' said the red neon sign outside the tiny basement at the bottom of what looked like a derelict house near the railway line. There was a gingham half-curtain on the grimy window, under a sign saying 'Miller Lite.'

'Lite, lite, lite, lite, lite,' said the baroness. 'How I hate that word. It's almost as bad as lo-fat—both constitute a standing affront to both taste-buds and the English language.'

She swept into an almost empty room, nodded at the elderly man in a check shirt behind the bar, called 'Two pints of the usual,' and led Amiss into a tiny room at the back containing two small wooden tables with ashtrays and a few chairs.

'What's the usual?'

'Indiana Amber. It's drinkable, which is more than can be said for most of the gnat's piss that masquerades as American beer. And it's not kept at sub-zero temperatures.' She scrabbled in her handbag, drew out her pipe and its accessories, and commenced the elaborate ritual with pipe cleaner, tobacco, and pipe reamer. Then, with a mighty flame from her lighter, she settled back and drew deeply and happily.

'I see the attraction of this place. Can you smoke in all bars?'

'In bars only, as I understand it—though not, for some arcane reason, in the hotel bar—but since there are only two bars in town and the other one has loud music, it's an academic question. What kill-joys legislators are! Not that we aren't getting as bad back home about everything.'

When the beer arrived, Amiss thanked the barman but the baroness just gave him a slight nod. 'Don't go jabbering to this barman, Robert. We get on very well by speaking as little as possible. He's surly and taciturn—such a relief from the "Hi-great-to-see-you-have-a-nice-day" brigade. Makes me think nostalgically of Yorkshire.'

'Do you—as they say—come here often?'

'When I get a chance, which is rarely. I like to sip a contemplative pint, look at that mottled, crooked mirror up there with Marlboro Man on it and imagine for a minute I've found the real America. The one where men were men and women were women and they just got on with it. Any moment now a bow-legged cowboy will stalk in and say "Barman, get me a whisky and make it a large one."' She sighed. 'Gary Cooper, for preference.'

'Shouldn't you be dressed properly for this encounter? I know you're looking very smart these days since you conducted that raid on Oxfam—despite the sartorial depredations of Gonzales's frustrated would-be parrot executioner—but I fear a discreet red suit is not what your cowboy would be looking for. Shouldn't you affect something more like a corset and black fishnet stockings?'

'"See what the boys in the backroom will have…"' she began, in execrable imitation of Marlene Dietrich. 'What's the next line?'

'If I knew, I wouldn't tell you. Now we're here, I've a lot of things I need to talk to you about. For a start, there's the what seems like insuperable problem of money....'

Another pint each and almost an hour later, the door opened and a familiar voice said, 'Hi, I'm sorry, sir, I was looking for someone.' The door shut.

Amiss jumped up, ran out after Betsy, and caught her just before she drove off. 'Oh, Robert, am I glad to see you! I've been looking for you and Lady Troutbeck everywhere and your cell phones weren't working.'

'Probably because it's a basement and we were right at the back. Come on in.'

Betsy gave him a hunted look. 'But it was Provost Fortier-Pritchardson who gave permission for students to go into bars with Lady Troutbeck. Do you think it'll still be OK?'

'Jack will protect you, Betsy. Never fear.'

Betsy beamed at him. 'Hey, yeah. Sure she will.' She followed him obediently.

'Sit down, Betsy. Do you want some nasty pop?' asked the baroness.

'Oh, no. There isn't time for that. This is an emergency.'

'What's up?'

'Marjorie's been trying to get you. The police have arrested someone and now they're looking for you, Lady Troutbeck.'

'Me? What have I to do with it? I wasn't a witness.'

'I don't know. But it's serious. Marjorie said they broke down the door of your office.'

'They what?'

'It was all confused.'

'They'd better not have frightened Horace or we'll be adding a zero to the compensation claim.' The baroness finished her Indiana Amber with one gulp, knocked out her pipe in the ashtray, and threw a couple of ten-dollar bills on the table. 'Keep the change, bartender,' she called, as she headed to the door.

She turned to the others. 'OK, come on. We need to get out of here fast. I'll call my lawyer and then give myself up.'

Amiss noticed that the bartender looked at her with what was close to being an expression of interest.

Chapter Thirteen

'I'm back.'

The baroness put the phone down, kicked off her shoes, and flung herself down on the sofa. She was snoring loudly when, ten minutes later, Amiss knocked. Grumpily, she got up and opened the door. 'I thought you were Horace.'

'I am,' said Amiss. 'Beverages! Beverages! Whoo! Whoo!'

Her fussing over drinks was interrupted by the arrival of Marjorie and the transference of Horace from his box to the baroness's shoulder. His insistence on climbing up her hair and squatting on her head caused much expostulation. Eventually, he was coaxed to perch on the door of his cage and bribed into silence with a piece of banana, and the trio finally got to sit down with their glasses.

'I was not very impressed with New Paddington's finest,' said the baroness.

'The one you have outside looks OK,' said Amiss.

'He's been outclassed,' said the baroness. 'There's a much superior one lurking somewhere nearby who's one of the friends of a friend of Myles.'

'Your admirers have fascinating ways of showing their affection, Jack,' said Amiss.

'Guns. Bodyguards. What next? Oh, of course, the private eyes.'

She looked sad for a moment. 'Private eyes more experienced than poor Mike and Vera-Velda. They're digging up stuff about the provost and the Goon and Dickinson at a rate of knots, according to Edgar Junior.'

'Before we get further on to all that, what happened with the cops? Why had they broken down the door?'

'They knocked. They could hear Horace talking but failed to identify him as a parrot, and, of course, he wouldn't answer the door when requested to do so and because Marjorie had gone out for a few minutes, it was locked. Being in aggressive mood for reasons I will explain later, with guns at the ready, they crashed in.'

'I'm not encouraged that they can't tell the difference between a bird and a person.'

'I gather they did when they actually saw him face to face and they showed great restraint by not arresting him. So far these cops do not seem to be smart people, Robert. Indeed I have yet to find evidence that they have a brain cell or a ball among them.' She paused, had some more gin-and-tonic and then said judiciously, 'Well, perhaps it would be fairer to say that the ones with brain cells seem to have no balls and vice-versa. One often finds that in life.'

'It's not true of you, Jack,' said Marjorie. 'You've more guts than you can hang on a fence.'

The baroness simpered.

'Now can you hurry up the story. I've got to get home to my family.'

'Very well. The police had messed up on three things.'

'Yes.'

'Firstly, they missed the obvious point about the mysterious person in the burqa. Secondly, they thought I'd set up the Provost-Goon murders.' She appeared to go into a reverie.

'If I ever set you up for murder, Jack,' said Amiss, 'it'll be after having to prod you after every sentence when you're supposed to be telling a fluent story.'

'Stop being petulant. Thirdly, they've changed their tune on Mike and Vera and alleged—half-heartedly I admit—that I might have been involved in murdering them.'

'What?'

'Let's take this one by one.'

'I can't. Everything's interconnected. The cops picked up a bearded Muslim youth who vaguely fitted the description of the running man and he turned out to have a business card of Helen's with my fingerprints on it.'

'They've got your prints?'

'Yes, Robert. Prints and mugshot since I was apprehended with my Colt 45.'

'Threatening Muslims who were threatening you,' growled Marjorie.

'I told you these cops are not bright. The coincidence was enough to carry them away. Since this guy had form and so, in a way, do I, that was enough for the genius in charge. Obviously we must be in league to murder someone for being anti-Islamic.'

'Even though your reputation among Muslims is as an Islamophobe.'

'The thinking seems to have been that I was cunningly trying to cover my tracks.'

Amiss scratched his head. 'In that case, why would you have kept hounding the cops to look for this guy?'

'I pointed out that flaw in their logic, but they didn't seem to get it. However, when it emerged that they'd also found my prints on a wallet in the chap's possession, all became clear.'

'You'd notified them about that theft,' said Marjorie.

'Well, Stefano had, and eventually they found the relevant bit of paper.'

'So what's their theory now?'

'Their heads hurt. In so far as I could follow them, the options are: a) he was an opportunistic thief who was at the meeting, stole my wallet because it was easy, and is an ordinary decent criminal with nothing to do with the murders; b) he was at the meeting, stole the wallet, hadn't grasped my name, thought the card was my card, went off to murder me and didn't spot the difference between Helen and me; c) someone else gave him the wallet and inflamed him by telling him bad things about what I'd said and he thought Helen was this bad person; d) oh, hell, I can't remember. It's all too convoluted.'

'What's his story?'

'He said he found the wallet empty in the street and didn't look at the card, which was one of several—none of which has his prints on them. And though he has form as a petty criminal, he has none as an Islamist agitator. In fact he seems to enjoy drinking and gambling.'

'He doesn't sound like the murderer to me,' said Amiss, dispiritedly.

'Or me,' said Marjorie.

'Beverages! Beverages!' shouted Horace. 'Freeze!'

'He is rather smart, isn't he? He didn't have long to pick that up,' said the baroness. 'Give him another piece of banana, Robert. Now, what's more important than the rest of this is the business of the woman in the burqa. When I heard about the rucksack, everything became clear.'

'What rucksack?'

'The running man had a rucksack.'

'Yes.'

'If you're hiding a rucksack under your burqa, wouldn't the smartest way of hiding it be on your stomach, so you look pregnant? Isn't that what female suicide bombers do with their explosives?'

'Sure. But why would you want to hide the rucksack?' asked Marjorie.

'Because you wouldn't want to be associated with the man into whom you'd turn after committing the murder.'

There was a pause while Amiss and Marjorie took that in.

'OK,' said Amiss. 'Got it. Of course it was the same person.'

'But why wouldn't he keep on the burqa?' asked Marjorie.

'Ever see anyone run in a burqa?'

'You'd have to raise your skirts, wouldn't you,' said Marjorie, nodding. 'And you'd kinda stand out. OK.'

'I need another drink,' said Amiss. 'We haven't even got to Mike and Vera yet. Carry on while I do the refills.'

'When as a result of pressure from the Edgars and their agents, the fuzz had to take the failed brakes more seriously, they finger-printed the Chevy and found my prints. This they found deeply suspicious. I wasn't, after all, in Europe around the time of the crash. I pointed out that days ago I had tried vainly to interest someone in taking the crash seriously and that it was my lawyer that was now representing Vera's mother, but they were not to be dislodged from the view that all this was much too much of a coincidence, especially since I had never before mentioned that I'd been in that car.' Her voice went up a few decibels. 'Why the hell would I have?'

'How did you get out of that?'

'I lost my temper and said if they didn't let me call Edgar Junior, the consequent law suit would leave them without either shirts or trousers. Edgar Junior duly created merry hell and so frightened them with threats that he's garnered another piece of information. They seem to have swooped on known criminals among the local Muslims, not Islamists.'

'Because?'

'Why do you think? They're terrified of "alienating the Muslim community."'

'Hotdamn,' said Marjorie, and then recollected herself. 'I mean this is all so much crap. It wouldn't happen like this in Texas. If it were me, I'd send in the Marines. Which doesn't mean I still wouldn't put a few bucks on Dickinson having something to do with it. Maybe he paid the running man.'

'In fact we're no further forward, Jack,' said Amiss. 'You're still as much at risk as you were yesterday.'

'My head aches,' said Marjorie. 'I gotta go. Do you want me to pick up Horace in the morning?'

'How did he get on with Dean Pappas-Lott?'

'I thought she was going to strangle him when he shouted "PC rubbish." She took it worse than when he kept saying "VRC."'

'I'll rebuke him for tactlessness and send him to a sensitivity workshop,' said the baroness.

'I've already told Stefano I won't be here for dinner,' said Amiss.

'You have a hot date?'

'You might say as much. I'm dining with Traci. On mature reflection I decided it might be worth seeing if there was more to be got out of her, so I rang her to tell her the sad news that you still weren't quite in the clear on the psittacosis front and then told her how much I liked dogs.'

'If I were you, I'd wear my chastity belt,' said the baroness.

Amiss groaned and picked up the phone. 'Yes?'

'Would you like bacon and egg?' asked the baroness, who had taken to providing her own breakfast since the installation of a small cooker and toaster. She was still struggling to master the intricacies of the espresso machine that had arrived a couple of days previously.

'I think so.'

'Make up your mind.'

'Yes.'

'Fifteen minutes.'

Amiss showered, shaved, tended his scratches, and threw on a T-shirt and jeans before knocking on her door. 'Just in time,' she said. 'The bacon is *à point*, I think you'll find, and the egg is perfect. Having failed to train the hotel chef out of that terrible "over-easy" business that means everything's hard, I had to take up self-catering. I think I'm rather good.'

'Perhaps you have a future as a short-order cook.'

After a few minutes in which the baroness ate, and congratulated herself, she cleared her plate and buttered some toast. 'Excellent toast too. It must be dark brown, something they can't seem to grasp in America. And did you know they don't have electric kettles? I had to boil the water for tea in a saucepan.

Seems quite extraordinary in what's supposed to be a civilised country. What do you think is the reason?'

'Not a clue,' said Amiss.

'You're very monosyllabic this morning. What's happened to your usual chatter?'

'Traci.'

'So how was she?'

'Amorous.'

'Did you succumb?'

'No. How do you think I got these scratches?'

She peered at him. 'I hadn't noticed, but now you mention it....'

'How could you not notice these? There are six of them and they run all down my cheeks.'

'My mind was on other things. Like bacon and eggs.' She scrutinised him. 'Better put something on them. Her nail-varnish might be full of toxins.'

'It wasn't Traci who scratched me. It was Sweetie. She set him on me when I told her that though I respected her and she was of course a very desirable woman, I could not accept her offer owing to my marital circumstances. She took it badly.'

'I'm trying to picture that.'

'Very small dog, long fuschia claws....'

'Fuschia?'

'Yep. They're varnished to match hers. So no doubt doubly full of toxins.'

'Wow!' She laughed merrily. 'Or should I say "Bow-wow"?'

'She just jammed him into my face and he panicked. However, to take a Betsy approach, it could be argued that this was good news because Traci became contrite when she saw the blood and I was able to make my excuses and leave without further sexual or canine assault.'

'I hope you got something out of her apart from the wounds.'

'And more champagne than I wanted and a forced overdose of lobster and a very late night. Yes, enough to make me sure we're proceeding on the right lines. When she got absolutely pie-eyed it became clear that the real wealth is very very *nouveau.* She spoke piteously about how in the first year of her marriage she had to buy off-the-rack, and was peevish because—in order to have real money—it was necessary to live in a hole like New Paddington. Though Dickinson has promised that they'll be domiciled in luxury in California within a year or so.'

'Doesn't the bloody man realise her lack of discretion makes her a time-bomb?'

'Yes, but….'

'I know. Sex. I suppose she's good in bed.'

'So she told me. Indeed it was all I could do to stop her giving me a demo of her prowess at erotic stripping and a performance on the retractable pole in the master bedroom.'

'What a goody-goody you are, Robert.'

'If you feel like that, give her a call now and I'm sure she'll perform for you. She told me that though you were a rough diamond, there was something rather attractive about you.'

'Can't imagine what she means by rough. If I were a diamond, I would be superbly cut—in addition to being flawless, polished, and at least fifteen carats.' She paused and considered. 'And possibly yellow. Literally, not metaphorically, you understand. Right, now it's time to get down to work.'

'I fetched Plutarch from St. Martha's yesterday,' said Rachel. 'I don't think she was pleased, but the new Bursar was. Extremely.'

'Is she behaving?' asked Amiss nervously.

'If you mean Plutarch, by her standards, she's so far behaving impeccably—if you don't count our difference of opinion about her getting into the car. At least life is less dangerous since we got that cat guard. Nothing would have induced me to try stuffing her in a basket.

'If you mean the Bursar, she was well-mannered, but seemed rather strained. There had been an incident with the gardener yesterday morning, when he inadvertently stood on Plutarch's tail and had his trousers torn. However, no one was making much fuss because Plutarch is under Jack's protection and St. Martha's in turn is protective of Jack and too nervous about her welfare to be cross even about Plutarch and the gardener's trousers.'

'How much do they know about what's going on?'

'Just what's in the press, since, of course, from what I gather, Jack hasn't told anyone at the college anything.'

'Has she been in touch at all?'

'The Bursar said they have a business call every day or so, but that all Jack would say was that the papers were making a fuss about nothing.'

'Two—probably four—murders is hardly nothing.'

'That's what the Bursar thought, especially after Rawlings said all those rude things at that press conference when he got back about how she was responsible for inciting hate crimes.'

'Did the papers report Jack's response?'

'You mean the bit about how Rawlings should be ashamed to make political capital out of other people's tragic deaths? That was referred to. The Bursar was not the only person to think it rather uncharacteristically po-faced.'

'That's because I wrote it. Jack's first reaction was to say "He ain't seen nuttin' yet," which I thought rather impolitic—as well as, I hope, inaccurate—but I did let her add that bit about how she, at least, unlike Rawlings, hadn't fled America for fear of Islamists. Did the media run with that?'

'Not any papers I saw, but an interviewer put it to Rawlings on television and he seemed as mad as hell.'

'Good. What's the news of your mother?'

'Excellent. She's definitely going back to work tomorrow and I'm definitely the best daughter in the universe about whom she will never ever again utter a word of criticism. It was not wanting to lose the moral high ground that made me decide to stay here rather than join you in Indiana, which would be inviting her to have a relapse and even again start uttering the odd word of criticism. Dad indicated that she had privately got very worked up about the best daughter in the universe being put in mortal danger from anti-Semites in a foreign country, so I decided to choose the easy option even if it does mean being without you for another couple of weeks. Now tell me what's happening.'

'An extraordinary amount of work is mostly what's happening. Jack is focusing on three things mainly. Firstly, to augment the work being done by expensive private investigators, with the help of one lot of spies she's trying to find out exactly how President Dickinson has acquired his money. Secondly, with the help of other spies and a vast amount of material smuggled to her by Marjorie, she's trying to discover what Provost Prichardson and Dr. Gonzales were up to on a day-by-day basis. And thirdly, she is—as she put it—expertly playing her fishing-rod to land the big fish, Martin Freeman, Chairman of the Board of Trustees, and get him fully on the side of the revolution.'

'And how is the revolution going?'

'Not badly, if I say so myself. Considering the limitations of my army, I'm quite pleased so far. The website is almost ready to roll and between the coverage we've been promised from the local newspaper and the emails that will go out on Website-Day to every student in Freeman, I'm expecting a big response. You should be able to follow quite a lot of events vicariously.'

'And what happens then?'

'No decisions until Jack comes up with some results and we see what the website provokes.'

'Robert.'

'Yes.'

'Doesn't it bother you that the murderer is still out there?'

'Well, yes, of course I'd like him locked up. But if it was mistaken identity and Jack is the target, I'm not too worried because she really is being well guarded. If the targets were Pritchardson and Gonzales, I haven't a clue and I haven't got time to think about it. I'm fantastically busy.'

'Any sign of life from the police?'

'The D.A. is having talks with the local imam, we're told. Oh, and negotiations between Jack's lawyer and the cops look set to have the charges against her dropped in exchange for her agreeing not to sue.'

'And her gun?'

'Still a subject for negotiation. But she doesn't seem too exercised about it at the moment and I'd be just as pleased if they held on to it. I haven't yet developed an American insouciance about guns. I may be trying to bring about a revolution, but it's unarmed, and call me a wimp—as, come to think of it, you frequently do—I'd rather it stayed that way. Having Jack modelling herself on Annie Oakley is one complicating factor I can do without.'

'Lady Troutbeck.'

'Yes, Betsy.'

'Why does everyone hate us?'

'This is really rather good,' said the baroness, finishing her espresso. 'Hot enough, if not quite strong enough, but I think I've cracked it.' She looked over at Betsy, who was still sipping her Diet Coke. 'Who is everyone? And who is us?'

'Everyone is the world. And us is Americans.'

'And what makes you think the world hates you? Not just Rowley Cunningham and Jimmy Rawlings?'

'Oh, no, but they kinda started me thinking about it. And then since I got to know you I've given myself a programme of reading stuff on the internet about abroad. And it's not just all those Muslim countries but places like Europe and France.'

'Pay no attention to the French, Betsy. When there was some little unpleasantness about Iraq some of your countrymen rightly described them as pansy-ass, limp-wristed, knock-kneed, cheese-eating surrender monkeys. You couldn't expect them to like Americans.'

'But even the English don't like us, Lady Troutbeck. Some of your famous people say totally horrible things about us, like that we're the biggest danger to peace in the whole world.' She smiled wanly. 'And that we're the fattest and greediest too.'

'So what do you think is the explanation?'

'Is it cos we're bigger and richer and fatter than anywhere else?'

'That's a part of it. You were much more popular when there were two big boys in the playground—you and the Soviet Union. Compared to the big communist bully you seemed very attractive. Well, that is, attractive to anyone half-way sane. And then the Soviet Union fell and you were the only big boy standing.'

'And little boys think big boys are bullies.'

'Exactly. And like cheeking them.'

'Are we bullies?'

'Of course you are sometimes. You're open-hearted and well-meaning, but you can be dangerously self-centred and selfish and prone to throw your weight about. It comes of being an only child.' The baroness laughed. 'I should know.'

'Oh, gee, Lady Troutbeck. Are you an only child? So am I.'

'In that case, you're what is known as the exception that proves the rule, Betsy. Only children are usually much more like me. And America. As a young nation America has had a vast expanse of territory to itself without powerful neighbours to have to get along with, so it had things its own way and expects everyone to see things from its perspective. It's not surprising in what, in terms of development, is an adolescent nation. Europe is full of old nations who've had to fight with each other every inch of the way just to survive. At the very least, that meant we've had to take account of the neighbours.'

'So you mean we're spoiled?'

'In many ways yes. You're blessed with ample resources and your homeland has been a haven. Until 9/11, that is, which countries who were devastated in the world wars sometimes think you make too much fuss about. Though personally, I don't. But then I'm in favour of waging war on terror. I think we're seriously up against it vis-à-vis Islamist global anti-Western fanaticism.'

Betsy's forehead went into its familiar furrow. 'And being fat and greedy? Is that part of being adolescent?'

'Whoo! Whoo! Praise the Lord. Whoo! Whoo!'

'Damn! He's finished his fig. Hang on, I'll shut him up with a grape.' The baroness shook her head as she returned from bribing Horace. 'That bird is going to end up as fat as an American, the way things are going. And with less excuse.

'Oh, by the way, Betsy, I quite like adolescents, so I've been trying to look at things from America's point of view, and I've come to the conclusion that the main reason why Americans eat too much and are obsessed with material goods and choice and so on—not to speak of a preoccupation with being safe and living for ever—is because they're almost all descended from tired, poor, and huddled masses who fled pogroms and famines so terrible they were prepared to risk their lives crossing a dangerous ocean.'

'Like it says on the Statue of Liberty.'

'Exactly. When they got to America they thought they and their children would be safe and free and fed and housed for ever. All this over-consumption is a reaction to that history. As is the preoccupation with quantity rather than quality.' She laughed. 'Anyway, I like America so I'm putting the best gloss on it.'

'Why do you like us?'

'You are courteous and kind, Betsy, and unlike many people in Europe, I remember our history. I remember that Nazism would have triumphed and we would have lost the Second World War without America's help, that it provided the money to rebuild Europe and that without America standing up to the Soviet Union, freedom would be a distant memory for all of us.'

'Oh, Lady Troutbeck. You make me proud to be an American.'

'Someone has to do it, Betsy. But I have to enter a caveat. That's another word for caution. It's because of that history that you overestimate how much freedom matters to people in other parts of the world. Some people actually like servitude. Look at all the people who vote for Islamist parties.

'Now, how are you getting on with *Middlemarch*? Tell me when you're finished, and I'll give you an interesting story called *Animal Farm.*'

'The *Sentinel*'s certainly done us proud,' said Amiss, dangling the paper in front of the baroness's nose. 'Look.'

'"save freeman u" website launched: provost condemns troublemakers.

'Good. Good. I can't read it until I've finished tending to Horace. What's the story?'

'What they were given. It's enormously long and rehashes quite a lot of the stuff they produced before from the VRC, but the gist is that idealistic students with a thirst for education and backed by a generous mystery donor....'

The baroness smirked. 'I like being a mystery.'

'...have launched a website—www.savefreemanu.com—calling on fellow students and friends of Freeman U to help their campaign to abolish corruption, intellectual decadence, and censorship on campus. They say that while they deplore the murders of the Provost and her personal assistant, both were implicated in an assault on the integrity and inspiration for which Freeman U used to be a by-word. The website explains how to set up anonymous email addresses, so concerned students can safely send in their stories and get blogging.'

'What's blogging?'

'You know perfectly well, not least because you've been told several times. It's the technological equivalent of a phone-in. Considering you're now the major benefactor of a website, it's time you stopped affecting complete ignorance of anything since the abacus.'

'I like abacuses.'

'The Acting Provost is unhappy,' reported Amiss, raising his voice slightly. '"The students behind this are racist, sexist, homophobic subversives,' she said when contacted by this newspaper. 'They will be expelled when we find them. Freeman U does not tolerate any kind of intolerance and we will be taking action to have the site closed down immediately.' A spokesman for SFU said, 'We are grateful to Acting Provost Dr. Diane Pappas-Lott for so succinctly demonstrating how American values have been under attack for the past four years by the stifling of free speech on the FU campus. I couldn't resist calling it "FU." Just once.'"'

'Otherwise a most restrained comment.'

'Restraint is what I'm counselling.' Amiss's phone rang. 'Yes, Mark....Excellent...OK, I'll get going. 'Bye.' He ended the call. 'I'm going over to HQ to monitor what's going on with the website, Jack. Apparently the response is fantastic. Two thousand hits within the first hour.'

'I hope they're palpable hits.'

'Are you coming?'

'No, I'm staying here for now. All of you will become over-excited by this electronic gibberish. Someone has to think.'

Chapter Fourteen

The baroness gazed with distaste at the screen of Amiss's laptop. 'I can't read this stuff. It's all impenetrable, illiterate crap.'

'It's a goldmine, Jack.'

'It may well be, but I'm not going to be the one to put on a tin hat with an in-built lantern and go down in the lift carrying a canary. Or even a parrot. Horace and I would instantly expire from the effects of the noxious gases of ignorance.' She paused and jabbed her finger at the screen. 'Look at that.'

'Hey, baggyshorts,' read Amiss, 'I just wanna say I know your really sad but don't loose all your hopes and dreams your luck might get enlightened. I know im goofy dude but ive worn that asshole's t-shirt and I got thru and he didnt go find someone to hug and chill out with.' He sighed. 'Trust you to select an example like this, though even this has value.'

'What does it mean?'

'Give me a minute.' Amiss rapidly scrolled up a few times and then returned to the orginal place. 'It's following a thread about our late friend Dr. Gonzales. This particular blogger—who goes under the pseudonym of "coolchick" and who, I grant you, is grammatically and syntactically challenged—is sympathising with a male using the pseudonym "baggyshorts"….'

'How do you know baggyshorts is male?'

'Apart from the evidence of his own earlier blog, coolchick—who has clearly been reading all his contributions—calls him "dude," which to the best of my knowledge is used only of males. Or, of course, female-to-male transsexuals.'

She snorted. 'She should know better than to trust anyone wearing baggy shorts.'

'In any case, if you will permit me to continue this exegesis, which you did after all request, baggyshorts had testified that Gonzales had had his—baggyshorts'—scholarship taken away from him for complaining publicly that someone who never turned up had improperly passed one of the courses baggyshorts was taking, and thus he—baggyshorts that is—had had to drop out of college. Coolchick—who in confiding that she had worn the same T-shirt is using a metaphor to indicate having had a similar unfortunate experience with Gonzales, aka asshole— hopes baggyshorts will overcome this setback....'

'It's beginning to sound like the plot of an Italian opera.'

'...by finding someone to hug and relax with.'

The baroness scrutinised the screen. 'Coolchick didn't say that. She said *asshole* didn't go and find someone to hug and chill with. Not that I quite follow her reasoning. I should have thought being murdered was a bigger problem for asshole than a lack of affection and the opportunity to unwind. There's a certain finality to it.'

'She omitted the full stop after "didn't."'

The baroness reread the paragraph. 'You may well be right,' she said grudgingly. 'Now how many of these entries are there?'

'Last time I checked there were in the region of eight thousand. Probably twice as many by now.'

'I certainly don't want to read any more of this bilge. How big is your army of trained interpreters?'

'I don't need trained interpreters. Just young Americans. And I've a couple of dozen of them at work now selecting what's significant and responding to it where appropriate to try to elicit further information and/or recruit people to help with our day of action. Then there's the crack unit downloading the information that helps bolster the case you've already constructed against Dickinson, Prichardson, and Gonzales. We'll keep it coming.

Betsy's taking me back to Godber's and will be straight back to the office to feed you the stuff as it arrives on her computer.'

'Just try to make sure it's in some known language,' grumbled the baroness.

'You and your fucking parrot,' shrieked Acting Provost Pappas-Lott.

The baroness threw a cloth over Horace's cage to discourage him from continuing to shout "Rubbish."

'Come, come, Diane. I don't know what's particularly bothering you at present, but you shouldn't take it out on an innocent bird. You might hurt his feelings and then where would you be? He recently learned my lawyer's number.'

'You're behind this. I know you are. Don't deny it.'

The baroness leaned back in her chair and put her feet on the desk. 'Behind what?'

'This anti-diversity campaign. You've probably paid for the website, you motherfucker.'

'The what? Oh, that Save Freeman University business they're talking about in the local paper? What a quaint thought. I am but a humble British academic and a proud technological illiterate to boot. And incidentally, should you of all people really be using "motherfucker" as an epithet?'

'You've done nothing but sneer and mock since you got here.'

'I just make the odd joke.'

'We don't have jokes in Freeman U. How often do I have to tell you that humour is inappropriate.' She fell into a chair and began to scream. 'I don't know why you're trying to uphold the white patriarchy, but you're probably working for the CIA. You probably had Helen and Ethan murdered.'

The baroness reluctantly removed her feet from the desk, stood up and went over to her recumbent visitor. 'If you don't stop screaming, Diane, I'll slap you. I don't want Horace learning how to imitate you.'

The noise stopped abruptly.

'Now tell me why you're here,' said the baroness, in her most soothing tone.

The Acting Provost gulped. 'I panicked. There's a message from the President telling me to close down the website and I don't know where to start.'

'Well, I wouldn't start here if I were you. Haven't you asked the campus police? Or your IT people?'

'They say it isn't illegal.'

'That never stopped Dr. Gonzales.'

'I don't know what you're talking about.'

'Have you consulted the faculty deans?'

She began to cry. 'They won't take me seriously. They're all men.'

'In that case, Diane, I suppose you're stuck with the issue. Why is it a problem? I don't know anything about websites, but aren't there a lot of them out there? Why not let students give their opinions?'

'They're challenging everything we stand for.'

'Well then you need to respond to the challenge, don't you? Why don't you go back to your office, send a message to the President that you can't get the website closed down, read what's appearing on it and see if you can get stuck into the debate. Maybe you'll find some common ground. Isn't that what you're supposed to do at universities?'

'Not at this one,' sobbed the Acting Provost, as she trailed out of the room.

The baroness rang Amiss. 'To misquote the Duke of Wellington,' she said, 'I have seen the enemy, and by God she doesn't frighten me.'

It was a week later and the baroness was sitting with Martin Freeman on the terrace of his New Paddington home drinking home-made lemonade. He raised his head from the thick file she had presented him with and gazed at her in horror.

'I'm deterring the children from taking law suits for the moment,' she said. 'No point in bankrupting the university. It'd be better to hang on to the money and try to restore Freeman University to what it's supposed to be.'

'I feel sick,' said Freeman. 'Sick and shocked. I was chairman of the Board that selected Henry Dickinson.'

'What did he have that the competition didn't have?'

'The previous President had died suddenly and we needed an urgent replacement. We'd had a few disappointments by the time we interviewed Dickinson. Not that many people want to live in a backwater like New Paddington. Henry had a good reputation in Wall Street. Nothing flashy, just steady performance. And he seemed to be energetic and enthusiastic. I remember telling my wife that even if he didn't live up to expectation, he'd be a heck of an improvement on his predecessor when it came to fund-raising. And he was.'

'Had you met his wife at the time he was appointed?'

'No. He said she couldn't come with him to be interviewed because she was looking after her sick mother. If I'd known he had acquired someone like that tart, I'd have thought more than twice about his judgement. You think she drove him to it?'

'I think she fired the engine of corruption.'

Freeman leafed over a few more papers. 'But I can't believe what's here. How could I let this happen on my watch?'

'I'm afraid you fell into the trap Edmund Burke described of being a good man who did nothing and let evil prosper.'

Freeman looked distressed. 'I didn't want trouble and I took refuge in the family belief that we should never interfere with the academic side of things. But you're right. That doesn't excuse me for having let all this go on under my nose.'

'You weren't much interested in the humanities, were you?'

'No. Knew nothing about them. History and English and sociology and all that stuff were beyond me. I was always being told by the Provost and the President that Freeman U was at the cutting-edge of post-post-modernity and virtual savvy, whatever that meant. I didn't pay attention. Engineering and Science were my thing and so at social functions I'd be inclined to talk to their deans or professors.'

'And as you'll see from the file, standards were up to snuff there until recently.'

'How Dickinson could have thought he could sell places in those faculties beats me. Either the kids can do the math or they can't do the math. Bridges have to stand up.'

'It rather looks as if he'd decided to have a final grand sale before he rode into the sunset. If you look at the figures we've dug up, he seems to have acquired several million dollars in the last two years alone.'

'How the heck could he do that?'

'Rich, unscrupulous parents of thick, lazy children.'

'There's no lack of those, I guess.'

'Certainly not where Freeman is concerned. Dickinson was offering a fine service, which presumably became quickly known about through word of mouth. The key was to do what the diversity industry call "de-emphasizing SATs." Just by claiming minority status, applicants could get in through a rigged exam and interview. Best was to be black, of course....'

'So that explains why Dickinson had established Africa as a good market....'

'That's right. But even if your child couldn't plead colour, there was always sexual orientation. If no one's asking questions, just claiming to be bi-sexual is enough.'

'And they got decent grades....'

'Because standards plummeted, courses were introduced which my parrot could probably have passed assuming he'd turned up to class and claimed to be bi-sexual, and there were no penalties for plagiarism. In the case of the really rich and corrupt, you could order your essays and course-work on the internet, cheat at exams, and even pay another student to do everything for you including physically taking your classes. Hence the high turnover in staff and the demoralisation of good people like Warren Godber.'

Freeman looked even more depressed. 'Why didn't he come to me?'

'It would have looked like sour grapes. Besides, your policy of non-interference was well-known.'

'The Provost? What was going on with the Provost? Was she corrupt as well?'

'A different kind of corruption, as Dickinson realised early on. Our investigators have established that they knew each other while Haringey was alive.'

'I didn't know that.'

'Why would they tell you? Dickinson knew how he could make real money, but he needed a compliant Provost, so when he met Helen at a conference and got to know her, he realised he had what he was looking for: she was fanatical, smart and ruthless. As a natural totalitarian who hated everything for which a good university stands, particularly the curious, sceptical mind, she was desperate for power and prepared to do any deal to get it. As a mere Dean at the time, she was limited in the damage she could do.

'As far as Helen was concerned, Dickinson could do what he liked as long as she could too. She had the invaluable help of her PA and probably lover, Gonzales, a student she had saved years before in a different college from being thrown out for indolence and violence and who had later purchased himself respectability with a bogus Ph.D.

'Haringey died and Dickinson influenced the head-hunters to recommend Helen, who embarked joyfully on her great experiment in social engineering by making students follow the party line and kow-tow to authority. Standards were a matter of no importance, so she lowered them to please Dickinson. In no time at all, her files reveal, with the help of Gonzales, she was proving the point that absolute power tends to corrupt absolutely.'

'But she was so charming.'

The baroness raised an enquiring eyebrow.

'Hey, sorry, Jack. I should know better than to say something so dumb. Look at businessmen. And politicians. Why shouldn't academics be as false?'

'Quite. Indeed why shouldn't they be even more false? The people in their power are children who are easily taken in and staff terrified of missing out on tenure. Or of being framed.'

Freeman flicked back a few pages. 'But you're saying that Gonzales was that ornery? That he actually had kids beaten up.'

'Beaten up, threatened, frightened, blackmailed—whatever it took. He was a cunning chap who had excellent sources of information on campus. Paid sources. And the kangaroo-court....'

'You mean the Office of Student Judicial Affairs?'

'That's it. Helen introduced it with the backing of the President so thenceforward the troublesome and comparatively poor among the students stood no chance. Once they introduced the notion that if someone felt hurt by something you said, you had said something hurtful, and that if someone thought you had demonstrated prejudice towards them you had done so, there was ample scope to throw out Jesus Christ on trumped-up charges.'

Freeman thumbed through a few more pages. 'There is some terrible stuff here. Do you really believe that it was the raped and injured that mostly were punished by the authorities after those frat and sorority hazings?'

'The evidence is overwhelming, Martin. Think about it. If children know their parents have bought their places and that essentially they can do what they like as long as the money comes rolling in, why would they not do what they like? The same applied to the star athletes who were allowed to get away with anything—even sexual assaults on cheerleaders. We're mostly savages at that age, if not tamed by discipline and authority. So your sense of impunity is liable to show itself in ill-treating the poorer and most vulnerable students when you're all drunk together. And when you're seen to escape the consequences, you encourage others.'

'Absolute power and all that....'

'Precisely. Which takes us to Haringey.'

'Jim Haringey was a good man,' said Freeman. 'I was real sorry when he had his accident.' He looked at the baroness. 'Oh, I guess you think it wasn't an accident.'

'What do you think?'

'I suppose it would have been one heck of a coincidence.'

'You'll see an analysis of it in that file, Martin. Either Dickinson is a murderer or he's incredibly lucky. Marjorie said Haringey was thwarting him at every turn by insisting that academic standards were immutable. And he'd met his ideal replacement.'

'So that's likely one murder. You think Gonzales was responsible for the car crash.'

'The brakes were definitely tampered with. Crudely. Gonzales may well have done it himself but I'm sure that at the very least he had it done. We've established from one of his spies that he knew I'd been to see Mike, and I bet he had him followed to Ohio.'

'But who then killed Gonzales and Helen?'

'I haven't a clue, though maybe there'll be a breakthrough in the next day or so. Marjorie thinks Dickinson, though there's no evidence at all. I've heard the D.A. has finally decided to do something to locate the mysterious running man. Mind you, I think it not impossible that one of the people victimised by the Provost and/or Gonzales might have been opportunistic enough to do him in. I've got a P.I. checking out which of their victims might have been around New Paddington at the time of the murder but he's found nothing yet.'

'So what are we going to do now? Have Dickinson arrested for corruption or murder or both?'

'We've no proof that would stand up in court even on corruption as yet, Martin. I think Dickinson's lawyers would have a field-day with what's here. A lot of our evidence has been gathered illegally through hacking or through copying confidential university documents. Much of the students' evidence is still anonymous. They're going to have to take a deep breath at the right moment and stand up together knowing they won't be victimised.'

'So what's your plan?'

'Take over Founder's Day for a massive protest against the President in the presence of thousands of parents. We'll need your help.'

'You're really a pirate, aren't you, Jack,' observed Freeman. 'Very well. Tell me what I have to do to help you take over the ship.'

'I've done my job,' said the baroness, smacking her lips as she tasted her wine. 'Hmmmmmmmmm! I really like that Barolo. Stefano has done well, don't you think, Robert?'

'There's much more to be done, Jack. Getting Freeman on side was the easy bit. Now we have to get the troops on the parade ground disciplined and drilled.'

'That's a job for a sergeant-major. Not for a general. Generals sit in their armchairs sipping good wine and planning how many troops to send over the top at dawn.'

'That was World War I generals, Jack. This is the twenty-first century. Even generals have to be more egalitarian these days.'

'Heaven forfend! This campaign is supposed to be about turning the clock back, dammit.'

'Jack!'

'You're such a spoil-sport.' She reached out for the bottle with a sigh of resignation. 'Oh, very well, then. What do you want me to do?'

From: Robert Amiss
To: Rachel Simon; Mary Lou Denslow; Ellis Pooley; Jim Milton; Myles Cavendish
Date: Fri 30/06/2006 21.07
Subject: Viva la revolution!

The last few days have been so enjoyable I've been thinking I might go into the revolutionary business full-time as a mercenary. I'm already well paid here for my labours, but I need to hit the big-time, perhaps starting by taking over obscure African republics and then moving into more challenging territory in Central America. Should be pots of money in it and then I can write my memoirs.

Something's got to be more lucrative than writing crime novels.

Straight from the Department-of-You-Couldn't-Make-It-Up is the fact that Jack Troutbeck is leading a 'Save Freeman University' army of neo-Puritans acquired through the imaginative use of new technology. What's even more satisfying is that our New Model Army seems to be as diverse as even the deceased Provost could have wished: I don't know if we've any cross-dressers or trans-sexuals, who were mostly figments of the administration's imagination, but our recruits include most categories of sexual orientation, race, and religion. Quite apart from the students who were already in a state of silent desperation about the state of affairs on campus, there are innumer-able others who have been radicalised by the revelations of the website and who are dying to participate in a demo to bring about regime change. There's a large body of Muslim students who are particularly enthusiastic, since they are as keen on the work-ethic as they are revolted by debauchery and they are sick of being assumed to be Islamists.

A website innovation of which I am particularly proud is the space we've offered the FU administration to make its case. I know those of you with time to idle away on the computer will already know this, but for those of you who haven't, trust me, it has truly been priceless. True to her previous form, the Acting Provost provided a rambling defence of diversity laden with pious quotes, e.g., from Maya Angelou, 'We all should know that diversity makes for a rich tapestry, and we must understand that all the threads of the tapestry are equal in value no matter what their color.'

Since if you've the internet and brains you can find quotations in no time, I set someone on a counter-attack, starting with Martin Luther King's 'I have a dream that my four little children will one day live in a nation where they will not be judged by the color of their skin but by the content of their character.' A neat statement of one of the tenets of SFU: that we should have a colour-blind society.

We dragged the debate onto the issue of conformity of thought and speech, of which the Acting Provost's quotes were all in favour, and threw at her good liberals like JFK ('Conformity is that jailer of freedom and the enemy of growth') and the feminist lesbian Rita Mae Brown ('The reward for conformity was that everyone liked you except yourself.')

And when she was on the ropes, we upset her with an attack on moral relativism. When she produced some crap about all cultures being equal, we came back asking her if she approved of wife-beating, female circumcision, and beheading gays. And to finish off, we threw in some heretical quotes from such dead white males as Mark Twain ('It were not best that we should all think alike; it is difference of opinion that makes horse races'), Robert A. Heinlein ('One man's religion is another man's belly laugh') and finally William Henry III ('It is scarcely the same thing to put a man on the moon as to put a bone in your nose.') After that she retired. Presumably in hysterics.

The President's contribution was a colourless, blustering condemnation of lying trouble-makers and no other members of the faculty stuck their heads over the parapet. So we've won the preliminary skirmish.

What amazes me is that although the *Sentinel* is running with stories from the website daily, and students from all around the country are joining in, there's been next to nothing in the rest of the media, which gives force to allegations about the conformity of the self-consciously diverse liberal press. Or maybe it's just too confusing. Certainly, they don't have the advantage of the numerous appalling stories that have been emailed to us off-site and that have been used by Jack in her indictment.

God knows what the President is thinking, but he's continuing to absent himself as much as possible. He wanted to cancel Founder's Day on the grounds that some students might cause trouble, but Martin Freeman refused the request out-of-hand and Dickinson had no option but to cave in since Freeman essentially *is* Founder's Day. Freeman guesses he's so corrupt he's probably incapable of grasping that the campus might be in a state of moral outrage.

I summoned the officers and NCOs yesterday evening to be addressed by Jack in Henry V mode. The old bat is extremely good at inspiring confidence, so she managed to convince even the most nervous that their liberation struggle is a glorious thing and that even if their parents disapprove, there isn't anything worse than continuing in the servitude of the thought-police state. By the end, they all seemed to think—like Betsy—that if the worst came to the worst, they could hide behind her ample skirts.

What's extremely cheering is to see how the kids have taken enthusiastically to the idea that university is about thinking for yourself.

I'm off now, as I have to get back to work. Choreographing the big day is an enormous headache, and Jack's contribution is mainly to wave an airy hand and say 'Robert's in charge and it'll all be fine.'

Oh, I nearly forgot. There was no difficulty in identifying the assassin who came after Horace, because it turned out that the campus police had the DNA records of all the students. Yes, of course I thought this was an unspeakable infringement of civil liberties and contrary to the laws of the land, but apparently it was something everyone had to agree to if they wanted to be accepted on this totalitarian campus. This fellow turned out to be a dodgy IT student called Dwight who admitted he had done a deal with Gonzales that he would get through his exams despite his manifest stupidity and ignorance if he became one of Gonzales's paid part-time secret police. And once Dwight agreed to be a stool-pigeon, of course he got further enmeshed, leading him to feel he had no option but to follow orders to dispose of Horace as an 'orrible warning to Jack. He wasn't going to behead him, apparently. Too squeamish. Just knock him on the head or strangle him and leave the body on her desk.

Poor Dwight knew nothing of parrots.

Gonzales bawled him out when he reported failure, so it was some other agent of the Axis of Evil who ended up attacking Jack's wardrobe. She now has enough evidence to sue the university for replacements for her Oxfam-acquired designer clothing should she so wish.

I was pleased to learn that although Dwight's wound was deep and he will always have a scar, there are no indications that he proposes to sue Horace for using unreasonable and unnecessary force. And, of course, if he did, Horace would counter-sue for Post-Traumatic Stress Disorder.

One of the things I enjoy about America is that it encourages one to be eternally ingenious.

Now back to Founder's Day. Sue-Ellen and Mark were chosen (female and black) and bravely agreed to put their names to an e-mail to the President, copied to Martin Freeman, asking permission for the SFU to be allowed to hold a modest demonstration just before the main ceremony began. Left to himself, Dickinson would of course have given them the bum's rush and expelled them, but Freeman, who had been well-primed, told him that it was better to get it over and done with so their child-ish little protest could be answered and discredited in the presidential speech. It would be no harm to flush out the trouble-makers, he said; they could be dealt with later.

So Dickinson e-mailed back that SFU could have a five-minute silent protest at 2.55, and we doctored it so it read fifteen minutes at 3.00, took out the word 'silent' and forwarded it to all the student groups participating in the official ceremonies so they would stand idly by as we got going. They will be confused enough as their numbers deplete.

In the final words of Jack to the troops (taught her by me, I hardly need to say, since she has made not the faintest effort to learn American): 'It's time to step up to the plate and hit a home run.'

Chapter Fifteen

Betsy came out first at the head of a couple of dozen cartwheeling cheerleaders, who tumbled all round the stadium to thunderous applause from the assembled parents, staff, students, and dignitaries, who thought this the beginning of the official proceedings. Despite her worst forebodings, Betsy had managed to rehearse the cheerleading dissidents long enough to manage a few basic stunts, culminating in a three-rung pyramid, which—though slightly unsteady—held. When the pyramid dissolved, the girls ran to the sidelines, took up their positions on both sides of an enormous furled banner and a pile of crimson and blue pom poms and began their chant through the microphones on their lapels:

Hey! Hey!
Yea! Yea!
Whoo! Whoo! Whoo!
Save Freeman!
Save Freeman!
Save Freeman U!

As they chanted, the back rows began their pom pom routine and the front row unfurled the banner to reveal—in enormous red letters on a blue and white background—
SAVE FREEMAN U

Right on cue, a light plane appeared over the stadium with the same message trailed underneath on a huge banner, and red, white, and blue streamers, balloons, and leaflets began to drop onto the field and the stands. A large multi-racial group of students with SFU T-shirts ran out, picked up leaflets from the field, and ran around the stands distributing them to those parts of the audience that had missed out. When they finished they left the audience reading and ran back down the tunnel.

There had been much anguish about the content of the leaflet, but Amiss and the baroness had won the battle to keep it simple. In heavy black type against a background representation of the American flag, it read:

TO ALL PARENTS AND BENEFACTORS THIS INDEPENDENCE DAY

- You chose Freeman U for your children and your generous donations because you believed it offered a fine education in how best to contribute to making America an even better place.

- We, the students who have formed SAVE FREEMAN U, came to college full of hope and determination to succeed.

- Instead, we found corruption and intimidation and a system that allowed none of the freedoms our country holds so dear.

- Students were forbidden to debate or think or just express ourselves.

- The fine and idealistic concept of embracing diversity of beliefs and culture was perverted into the encouragement of bitter division on racial, religious, sexual orientation, and many other grounds.

- The only competition allowed was competition in victim-hood.

- Political correctness became a crushing ideology.

- Educational standards were sacrificed to greed.

- Sexual depravity was condoned for the privileged.

- Christianity was virtually outlawed.

In a climate of fear, we are standing up to be counted.

- We want Freeman U to return to the principles on which it was founded.

- We want our corrupt President and our useless Provost fired.

- We want leaders who have at heart the interests of Freeman U and its students.

- We want knowledge.

- We want education.

- We want diversity of thought.

- We want high standards.

- We want free speech.

- We want to be Americans first and foremost.

- We want integration, not segregation.

GOD BLESS AMERICA
www.savefreemanu.com

The baroness, who had positioned herself at the far end of the dignitaries' section so as to have the best possible view of the faces of President Dickinson and his Acting Provost in the adjoining faculty area, was delighted by their stunned expressions. The Acting Provost then began to cry, as did Traci Dickinson, who hugged her. Martin Freeman, who had insisted on sitting beside Jack, chuckled in her ear. 'Hey, it was sneaky, but it worked so far.'

Up through the tunnel came the marching ranks of thousands of students in Freeman University T-shirts waving American flags and chanting along with the cheerleaders—each group parading off more or less efficiently to the pre-ordained space laboriously mapped out for it by Ryan and Joshua. As they reached their halting-place, each group unfurled an enormous banner. Within minutes the audience were trying to take in dozens of negative messages ranging from BLACKS AGAINST BRAINWASHING, through CHRISTIANS AGAINST CONFORMITY and ITALIANS AGAINST INTIMIDATION to SIKHS AGAINST STALINISM.

When they had all taken up position, they ceased chanting. There was the blast of a bugle and each banner was turned to reveal such positive messages as ASIANS FOR ASPIRATION through MUSLIMS FOR MERIT and QUEERS FOR QUALITY to TURKS FOR TRUTH.

'I thought they didn't want to be divided into separate groups,' whispered Freeman. 'Isn't that what most of this was all about?'

'Be patient.'

The bugler sounded the reveille, and the groups put down their banners and began to mill about until the pitch was a mass of black, oriental, and white young people talking to each other randomly and animatedly. Higgle-piggledy, they sauntered over towards the tunnel and stood at ease, leaving a pathway for the cheerleaders.

Betsy clapped her hands, and the first banner was furled and put down and the second picked up. The cheerleaders marched in formation to the centre of the pitch until she clapped her hands again and they halted. The new banner was unfurled to reveal:

UNITED WE STAND
DIVIDED WE FALL

The bugle sounded again, and out of the tunnel emerged part of the Freeman University marching band, led by the drum major and playing a medley of patriotic tunes. 'Recruiting him was a coup,' whispered the baroness to Freeman. Among the defectors were the entire percussion section, several trombonists, and a saxophonist, so they were able to strike up "The Star-Spangled Banner" with a satisfactory amount of noise. As the students began to sing 'O say, can you see, by the dawn's early light/ What so proudly we hail'd at the twilight's last gleaming?' the spectators stood up and joined in. After a moment's hesitation, the President and the entire faculty followed suit. Unlike the students, who were armed with the words, most of the onlookers began to falter, but they hummed along and joined loudly in the conclusion: 'And the star-spangled banner in triumph shall wave/O'er the land of the free and the home of the brave!'

Slowly, the students turned towards the tunnel and began silently to file off the pitch. The vast majority of the crowd applauded rapturously.

'What happens next?' whispered Freeman.

'Your guess is as good as mine,' said the baroness. 'The ranks of official participants are sorely depleted and therefore will have great difficulty in carrying out their manoeuvres if ordered to do so. We seem to have got more than half the student body on board.

'Let's see how Dickinson copes. Look at him. You'd think he'd been beaten over the head by a brace of dead grouse.'

Dickinson got slowly to his feet. 'Ladies and gentlemen,' he said, his voice shaking. 'What has just happened is…is…is….' He stopped, looked down at his bewildered wife, grabbed her by the hand, and started pulling her towards the exit.

To general alarm, Ryan, who had been lurking below the faculty stand, ran up the steps and shouted, 'Come back, you bastard,' through the microphone to Dickinson. Dickinson stopped, shook his head, and began to run. 'You're not getting away,' shouted Ryan. 'I'm mad as hell and I'm not going to take it any more.' He reached down to the end of his baggy trousers, drew out a gun from the ankle-holster and aimed and fired at Dickinson. As Dickinson fell, Ryan fired at him twice more. He turned, and as he took aim at Acting Provost Pappas-Lott, the baroness took a small gun from her handbag and shot him in the right shoulder.

Wincing, he reached with his left hand for the gun he had dropped. She shouted, 'Don't, Ryan, or I'll kill you. It's the only rational thing to do.' He hesitated just long enough for a professor of Black Studies, who was known to be keen on the martial arts and behind whom the Acting Provost was now hiding, to shout, 'Come on, guys, let's roll' to the rest of platform. Just two of them, both junior historians desperately hoping for tenure, helped him jump on Ryan and save his life.

It was too late for Dickinson.

'What the hell was all that about?' asked Martin Freeman.

It was five hours later, and he was sitting in the baroness's sitting room. From the moment that Ryan had been disarmed, there had been an interminable sequence of frustrating events. Freeman's appeal to the crowd to be calm and stay put had dampened down the threatened hysteria, but while the police sent almost everyone home within half an hour, they required a dozen or so witnesses to stay on. So Freeman, the baroness, and several others had to wait about until Ryan had received medical attention and been taken away to be charged, Dickinson's corpse had been removed, and they had given statements to a couple of slow policemen. It was only through Freeman getting rough with the D.A. that the baroness had not been charged as well.

'Ayn bloody Rand,' said the baroness, who was in low spirits.

'What's that?' asked Freeman.

The baroness sighed. 'Tell him, Robert.'

'I'm not clear how she's responsible, but she's a philosopher of the last century who had an intellectual grip on Ryan. She believed in rational self-interest, individualism, and unfettered capitalism.'

'Why should that make him shoot Henry Dickinson?' asked a bewildered Freeman. 'If anyone ever went in for rational self-interest, individualism, and unfettered capitalism, it was Henry.'

They both looked expectantly at the baroness. 'When I bent over Ryan after the academics got off him, he said something like, "I had to do it, Buddica. Like Howard Roark did."'

'Who the hell is Howard Roark?' asked Amiss.

'A hero Rand created in a novel called *The Fountainhead* who was apparently her ideal man.' The baroness got up, went over to her desk and scrabbled around until she found a pile of paper which she took back to her armchair and riffled through. 'This is all the crap Ryan gave me ages ago,' she said. 'Listen to this: "Howard Roark takes pleasure in the act of creation, but is constantly opposed by 'the hostility of second-hand souls.'" One of the ways Roark shows his heroic mettle is by blowing up a building of which he disapproves for reasons I won't bore you with. Though he certainly doesn't go round shooting people.'

'How do you know this?' said Amiss. 'I thought you completely dismissed it.'

'I did, but I had another look at it recently, because I was concerned about Ryan.'

'In what way?'

'I'd come to the conclusion that he had murdered Helen and the Goon.'

'What!' said Amiss. 'You never said anything about that.'

'I wasn't certain. I had no evidence. And it wasn't the time to deal with it. I was waiting until we'd got through Founder's Day.'

'Explain.'

'Intuition. His desire to be a hero as evinced in all that Goodkind rubbish. He was in search of an ideology, and people like that always worry me because of the ease with which ideologies can be perverted.' She shook her head. 'And I couldn't believe in the crazed Islamist. There were a few who threatened me who might be capable of doing something unpleasant if given proper training in terrorist camp, but they looked like very small-town agitators from what I saw of them. I couldn't imagine any of them being up to planning and executing what happened in the Provost's office. Whereas Ryan thought the

Axis really was evil.' She sighed. 'And I had told him and the others that Gonzales might have had Mike and Vera murdered. I intended to warn, not provoke.'

'But the bearded brown running man?' asked Amiss.

'Theatrical make-up. False beard. Not difficult.'

There was a silence, then Amiss said, 'But you were always complaining that the cops hadn't properly gone after the Islamists.'

'That's because they weren't doing it for all the wrong reasons. And anyway, considering how they'd got away with threatening to kill me, I thought a bit of inconvenience was in order. We know what happens when people think they're invulnerable.'

'I still don't get it,' said Amiss. 'Are you saying he was murdering bad people on principle? Wasn't Rand against altruism?'

'Yes, but....' She rummaged around the pages. 'This comes from the appendix to her *Atlas Shrugged*, which is apparently a fantastically successful cult novel: "My philosophy, in essence, is the concept of man as a heroic being, with his own happiness as the moral purpose of his life, with productive achievement as his noblest activity, and reason as his only absolute."'

'So killing them was a rational act and a noble productive achievement?' said Amiss. 'Which made him happy?'

The baroness shrugged. 'There's no accounting for taste.'

'You know that Goodkind novel I read, Jack,' said Amiss. 'It had something called a Wizard's Rule, which was along the lines that the greatest harm can result from the best intentions.'

'Pity he didn't take that to heart,' she grunted.

'I told you I didn't understand the humanities,' said Freeman. 'I doubt if this philosophy he's so keen on will seem so sensible when he ends up being sentenced to death.'

'Oh, God, you've got capital punishment in Indiana, do you?' asked Amiss.

'Yep. Though if his parents have enough money and all the dirt comes out about those three scoundrels, maybe the mitigating circumstances will outweigh the aggravating and he'll get away with life. Might even get out within thirty years.'

'He was going to kill that fool Diana Pappas-Lott as well. That won't help.'

'I have a very nasty feeling he was going to kill a lot more people than that,' said the baroness.

'You mean he was planning a Freeman University massacre?'

'It's possible.'

There was another silence. 'Heck,' said Freeman. 'I can just understand why he might have thought he should knock off the Provost and Gonzales, because they were ruining the university, but Dickinson and Pappas-Lott were about to get their comeuppance from the revolution Ryan had put so much effort into.'

'Maybe he needed to be the star. He always liked to be the centre of attention.'

'*I* always like to be the centre of attention,' said the baroness, 'but I'm not prepared to risk death row to get it.'

There was a knock on the door. 'Oh, thank God, that'll be dinner. When we've regained some strength we'll talk about what's to be done next.'

Epilogue

'No, I can't say my visit to Indiana was an unmitigated success,' said the baroness as she looked around the restaurant table. 'I refuse to blame myself for hiring Mike and Vera, but the fact remains that they would be alive if I hadn't. Also, I have reservations about shooting students, and Ryan's arm was badly injured. Betsy has pointed out that I was fortunate I didn't have to shoot him in the head. Ryan of course may not think so. I don't think Indiana state prison is a pleasant place.'

'We have triumphed in academic terms,' said Amiss. 'The latest report from Marjorie suggests Martin and Warren Godber are cleaning things up fast. Nearly all the parents are on our side, as are the alumni, who'll be bankrolling the reforms.'

'Well, I'm glad you sound as if you're cheering up, Robert,' said Rachel. 'You've been beating yourself up ever since you got home.'

'Jack,' said Mary Lou, 'how did you come to have a gun?'

'Edgar had a Beretta Tomcat delivered to me after the Colt 45 was confiscated by the fuzz. Nice little light thing but effective and easily concealed in a handbag. And considering how lively Freeman campus was, I thought it sensible to carry it about.'

'Even though you'd already been done once for violating the law?'

The baroness shrugged. 'There would be a few more dead bodies if I hadn't broken the law. That was the point Edgar Junior made extremely forcefully to the D.A., which is why I'm here rather than being cooped up along with Ryan or deported with instructions never to return.'

The waiter arrived with pad poised. 'Still no sign of the gentlemen, Madam?'

'We should start without them, don't you think?' said the baroness to Mary Lou.

'Yes. They mightn't be here for an hour. Or ever. Last heard of going into what was likely to be a long interrogation. Jim said he'd try to release Ellis early, but it doesn't look promising. What about Myles? There isn't a place laid for him. Isn't he back?'

'Not for another couple of weeks.' The baroness turned to the waiter. 'You can bring our starters now.'

Mary Lou put her hand on the baroness's arm. 'You're very low, aren't you?'

'I heard today from Edgar, who got it from a police source, that Ryan had enough ammunition on him to kill an awful lot of people. His Glock packed fifteen bullets and he had three more 20-shot clips.'

'Shit,' said Amiss. 'Sounds like aggravating factors to me.'

'Certainly does,' said the baroness.

The waiter arrived with the starters, and the baroness's mood lightened. 'There's always food,' she said. 'Not to speak of drink. Do you like this wine?'

The other three grunted approval.

'What's the news of Betsy?' asked Amiss. 'Have you been in touch?'

The baroness swallowed her first bit of smoked duck breast and smiled broadly. 'I certainly have. I've just fixed up for her to come to St. Martha's next term to take up one of our remedial scholarships.'

'Remedial?' asked Rachel.

'I instituted them a couple of years ago. They're for people with brains who've been very badly educated. We reckon that within a year they're fit to join the mainstream.'

'How did she win that?'

'Martin Freeman has just endowed four in perpetuity. The stipulation was that they would be reserved for Freeman students for the first four years. After that, if Godber does his stuff, they shouldn't need them.'

'Was there a competition?'

The baroness leaned forward and jabbed her finger at Rachel's plate. 'Eat up, eat up,' she said, 'and stop asking what I know are puritanical questions. Betsy's bright enough to qualify and I'm a believer in enlightened nepotism. That's why Mark and Joshua and Sue-Ellen—who are bright too—are getting the other ones. They've had a rough time and they need cheering up.'

She speared another piece of duck. 'And so do I.'

Her phone rang. 'Yes…yes…certainly…when?…right…I'll book a ticket in the morning….'Bye.'

She beamed at her three friends. 'I'm cheered up,' she said. 'That was Edgar. We're going to meet in Las Vegas the day after tomorrow. A great blast of American vulgarity is exactly what I need. Waiter, we require champagne.'

To receive a free catalog of Poisoned Pen Press titles, please contact us in one of the following ways:

Phone: 1-800-421-3976
Facsimile: 1-480-949-1707
Email: info@poisonedpenpress.com
Website: www.poisonedpenpress.com

Poisoned Pen Press
6962 E. First Ave. Ste. 103
Scottsdale, AZ 85251